RISING WIND: LIKE FEATHERS OF A WING

BOOK FOUR

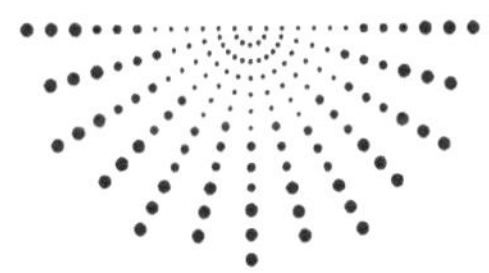

DIANE OLSEN

CONTENTS

Untitled — v
Last recorded prayer of "Black Elk Speaks" — ix
Acknowledgments and Citations — xiii
Telepathic Communication — xvii
List of Characters — xix

1. On the Rocks — 1
2. Coffee with a Farmer — 7
3. A Growing Need — 10
4. Bill's Story — 16
5. Gathering in Missoula — 19
6. The Video Taping "Ur Mazd" — 25
7. The Dean of Social Sciences — 38
8. The Unusual Suspects — 44
9. Aha — 49
10. Confrontation of Doom — 60
11. The Den — 70
12. High Resolution — 76
13. Weah Washtay — 82
14. Aryan Pre-History — 86
15. Peace — 96
16. Trouble at Work — 99
17. Joshua Bader — 104
18. "Creation Stories" — 109
19. The Climb — 134
20. "Seconds Please" — 138
21. "Age of Metal" — 146
22. Everything Changes — 159
23. The "Stans" — 165
24. Cold Desert — 171
25. The Camp — 178
26. Joy, Desert-Style — 188
27. Decisions — 192

28. Maja Turandokht   203
29. Caves and Villages   211
30. Nameless River   220
31. Rugged Terrain   228
32. Struggles   236
33. The Cave Scourge   243
34. Death of an Icon   249
35. Many Happy Returns   252
Epilogue   259

Untitled   263
About the Author   265

Rising Wind: Like Feathers of a Wing

Book four of the Rising Wind Series. Deep informative and pertinent

Man must be a lover of the Light, no matter in what lamp it may shine.

— BAHA'U'LLAH

LAST RECORDED PRAYER OF
"BLACK ELK SPEAKS"

After the conclusion of the narrative, Black Elk and our party were sitting at the north edge of Cuny Table, looking off across the Badlands ("the beauty and the strangeness of the earth," as the old man expressed it). Pointing at Harney Peak that loomed black above the far sky-rim, Black Elk said: "There, when I was young, the spirits took me in my vision to the center of the earth and showed me all the good things in the sacred hoop of the world. I wish I could stand up there in the flesh before I die, for there is something I want to say to the Six Grandfathers. So, the trip to Harney Peak was arranged, and a few days later we were there. On the way up to the summit, Black Elk remarked to his son, Ben: "Something should happen to-day. If I have any power left, the thunder beings of the west should hear me when I send a voice, and there should be at least a little thunder and a little rain." What happened is, of course, related to Wasichu readers as being merely a more or less striking coincidence. It was a bright and cloudless day, and after we had reached the summit, the sky was perfectly clear. It was a season of drouth, one of the worst in the memory of the old men. The sky remained clear until about the conclusion of the ceremony.

"Right over there," said Black Elk, *indicating a point of rock,
"is where I stood in my vision, but the hoop of the world about
me was different, for what I saw was in the spirit." Having
dressed and painted himself as he was in his great vision, he
faced the west, holding the sacred pipe before him in his right
hand.*

*Then he sent forth a voice; and a thin, pathetic voice it seemed
in that vast space around us: "Hey-a-a-hey! Hey-a-a-hey! Hey-
a-a-hey! Hey-a-a-hey! Grandfather, Great Spirit, once more
behold me on earth and lean to hear my feeble voice. You lived
first, and you are older than all need, older than all prayer. All
things belong to you—the two-leggeds, the four-leggeds, the
wings of the air and all green things that live. You have set the
powers of the four quarters to cross each other. The good road
and the road of difficulties you have made to cross; and where
they cross, the place is holy. Day in and day out, forever, you
are the life of things.*

*"Therefore, I am sending a voice, Great Spirit, my Grandfather,
forgetting nothing you have made, the stars of the universe and
the grasses of the earth. "You have said to me, when I was still
young and could hope, that in difficulty I should send a voice
four times, once for each quarter of the earth, and you would
hear me.*

*"To-day I send a voice for a people in despair. "You have given
me a sacred pipe, and through this I should make my offering.
You see it now. "From the west, you have given me the cup of
living water and the sacred bow, the power to make live and to
destroy. You have given me a sacred wind and the herb from
where the white giant lives—the cleansing power and the healing. The daybreak star and the pipe, you have given from the
east; and from the south, the nation's sacred hoop and the tree
that was to bloom. To the center of the world, you have taken
me and showed the goodness and the beauty and the strangeness of the greening earth, the only mother—and there the spirit
shapes of things, as they should be, you have shown to me and I*

have seen. At the center of this sacred hoop, you have said that I should make the tree to bloom.

"With tears running, O Great Spirit, Great Spirit, my Grandfather—with running tears I must say now that the tree has never bloomed. A pitiful old man, you see me here, and I have fallen away and have done nothing. Here at the center of the world, where you took me when I was young and taught me; here, old, I stand, and the tree is withered, Grandfather, my Grandfather!

"Again, and maybe the last time on this earth, I recall the great vision you sent me. It may be that some little root of the sacred tree still lives. Nourish it then, that it may leaf and bloom and fill with singing birds. Hear me, not for myself, but for my people; I am old. Hear me that they may once more go back into the sacred hoop and find the good red road, the shielding tree!"

We who listened now noted that thin clouds had gathered about us. A scant chill rain began to fall and there was low, muttering thunder without lightning. With tears running down his cheeks, the old man raised his voice to a thin high wail, and chanted:

"In sorrow I am sending a feeble voice, O Six Powers of the World. Hear me in my sorrow, for I may never call again. O make my people live!"

For some minutes the old man stood silent, with face uplifted, weeping in the drizzling rain. In a little while the sky was clear again.

Black Elk Prayer (used with gracious permission—University of Nebraska)

Postscript, pages 170 and 171 from "Black Elk Speaks" by John G. Neihardt

ACKNOWLEDGMENTS AND CITATIONS

I am grateful for the patience, friendship, and assistance, of friends and family. I especially would like to mention:

My sisters, **Sandra Munoz** and **Valerie Inmee** who were indispensable with editing assistance. Thank you to my husband, **Penisimani Ikavuka Toutaiolepo**, and my son **Andrew Olsen**, who put up with a lot of plotting and scheming. In fact, family members have inspired a number of characters over the years.

I have received heart felt encouragement from **Kimberly Taillon, and Mary Thompson, Barbara Krejci, and Jannette Montgomery Sasha Thompson.**

I will always be grateful **Catherine Townsend-Lyon** Author promotor extraordinaire

J. Schlenker – Author and design angel

Barbara Daniels Dena – Author, Beta reader, and copyeditor

Lake Mancos Ranch memories of half-day trail rides

Dave - JD&J Design LLC

Books and resources, I've struggled to understand:

"Ancient Ways": The Roots of Religion. Some of the religious stories come, at times verbatim. I have permission from the author, Diane Mulberger Olsen.

"The Arctic Home of the Vedas" Bal Gangadhar Tilak 1903
    (1856-1920 An amazing Indian Journalist philosopher, social reformer and he fought for Indian independence.)

"The Bundahishn," is a collection of pre-Zoroastrian beliefs, regarding "Primordial Creation."

Farvardin Yasht 13.8 as the Gar-Shah, King of the Mountains

"Gayomart Protoplast of Man" http://www.cais-soas.com/CAIS/Mythology/gayomart.htm in translation of Tabari, Bal´amî, ed. Bahâr, p. 123).

"Gems of Divine Mysteries" — writings of Baha'u'llah

"The Great Initiates" Edouard Schure 1889
    The Gods of the Egyptians 1899, Vol 1 pp 405-415, by E. A. Wallis Budge

"The History of the Prophets and Kings" Muhammad ibn Jarir al Tabari, a pure hearted 10th century Persian scholar, ascribed to Gayomart a *Collection of Apothegms*, around AD 915, 1,099 years ago along with **Commentary on the Qur'an:** together known as the **Annals or Tarikh al-Tabari.**

The Legend of Haic, a book about *Armenian Legends and Festivals,* written by Louis Boettiger in1920, which I found on the TOTR website.
    "Lucifer Sam" who posted a story about the Armenian Genocide

"Oxford Introduction to Proto-Indo-European and the Proto-Indo-European World" Mallory, James P.; Adams, Douglas Q. (2006). Oxford University Press.

"The Persian Creation story" (http://www.oocities.org/west_johnny2001/Persia/Persian_Creation.htm) ("Keyumars" http://en.wikipedia.org/wiki/Gayomart)

"The Saga of the Aryans" written by the well-known Parsi writer, Porus Homi Havewala, and first published in 1987. The Saga of the Aryan Race is a historical epic about the origins of the Aryan people. The Saga chronicles the ancient Indo-Europeans of twenty thousand years ago, who proudly called themselves the Aryans - the Noble Ones. They were the first worshippers of Ahura Mazda, the name of God in the ancient Aryan tongue of Avestan.

The first volume of the Saga describes the Great Migration of the ancient Aryans from their homeland at the North Pole following the sudden climate change.

"Tablets of Baha'u'llah" p. 137

The Upanishads: Breath of the Eternal Prabhavananda and Manchester,1948 Mentor Books, New York, and Toronto; Pp 123-127 Translated from Sanskrit by Swami Prabhavananda and Frederick Manchester

AMAZING Purity! – Perfection! This Upanishad could have been revealed today, rather than thousands of years ago.

The Upanishads: Breath of the Eternal Prabhavananda and Manchester,1948 Mentor Books, New York, and Toronto; Pp 123-127 Translated from Sanskrit by Swami Prabhavananda and Frederick Manchester

AMAZING Purity! – Perfection! This Upanishad could have been revealed today, rather than thousands of years ago.

Zoroastrian Heritage - massive web site K E. Eduljee

TELEPATHIC COMMUNICATION

Baha'u'llah told humanity to seek a universal auxiliary language to improve communication. But He didn't tell us which one. In fact, He didn't use the term "world language." Instead, He said "universal language." Black Elk's prayer gives us another suggestion.

What if *telepathy* is the auxiliary form of connection? God hears our prayers and the wishes of the animals and plants, whether they are voiced or not. Besides communion with God, some of us converse with plants, animals, aliens, or those who have passed on—or even with Bigfoot in thought language.

We might know our sister is going to call, or that a relative has died before the announcement. I have felt the assistance of Black Elk while writing these books, and I acknowledge the help of others in the "Concourse on High." Otherwise, I simply wouldn't have had much to say. We, as individuals, may not be very good at it, but telepathy is universal—a powerful connector—perhaps even connecting us with mountains, trees, and rain clouds. Hetchetu aloh.

"There is a world somewhere between reality and fiction. Although ignored by many, it is very real, and so are those living in it. This forum is about the natural world. Here, wild animals will be heard and respected... a glimpse into an unknown world."

— PETER BROEKHUIJSEN WWW.WILDFACT.COM

LIST OF CHARACTERS

Alai Santiago - A sensitive, a medium. Alas, last of her tribe due to a mudslide, Grandmother to Monta at request of her dead mother.

Aparu of Cliff City - Guero healer, married to Jane, father of their three children.

Bill Hoffmann - Grad student and cryptid photographer, son of Dan and Elena of Bonners Ferry.

Black Elk Hehaka Sapa of the Oglala band of the Sioux Nation - A holy man, heyoka, and treasured inspiration for these books.

Clive Bull Bear - Jane's friend, works for the Pine Ridge Tribal Police.

Destiny Hawkins - New Dean of Social sciences.

Dr. Iris Snowden. Cultural Archaeologist, married to Kantun, has one child. Secora's sister.

Dr. Jane Roanhorse - married to Aparu, three younger children, and mother of Kyah. Gideon's sister, PHD in anthropology and archaeology.

Dr. L.W. Dalton – Curator of South American Antiquities, wife of Sage, mother of Iris and Secora.

Dr. Sage Dalton – infamous anthropologist specializing in Human

Religion. Father of Iris and Secora – honorary Godfather of Jane Roanhorse.

Dr. Secora James – Paleontologist, teaches Paleontology and Archaeology classes at the university. Adoptive mother of **Monta**, married to Gideon.

Gideon Yellow Thunder: Lakota realtor at Treasuremont Realty. Has Thunderbird visions and some call him Heyoka.

Guillermo Santiago- Husband of Alai, Kallawaya, and father figure to Secora.

Jamal Hasan – Father of the loveable, Kamal Hasan, now deceased, and owner of the Resort property at West Glacier, neighbor to Ken and Sue who run the nearby Buckeye Dude Ranch

Jamal Landsing – Somehow related to Jake wink, wink. Formerly known as Billy Riggins the mammoth hunter.

Jeannie Rutherford –most able secretary for Treasuremont Realty, and devoted motherly friend of Gideon and Mitch.

Jimmy Lizardeye - Lakota Wichasha Wakan (holy man) Half Tewa (Pueblo). Gideon's mentor and closest friend. A war veteran who served in Iraq. Uncle and protector to an extended family.

Josh Bader - Troubled realtor. Husband of Sokhela, a gambling addict.

Kantun of Cliff City - Guero herbal healer, married to Iris, father of their child.

Ken and Sue - run the Buckeye Dude Ranch

Kheridan Kocherian – Armenian driver, guide, and brave friend of Secora and Gideon.

Kyah Roanhorse. Jane's son, Gideon's nephew. Grad student working in Peru, Duendes friend.

Maja Turandokht: Armenian historian, mechanic, and Kheridan's bride.

Manzoor Nadeem Agni of Termez - Seamus' army buddy extracting water from desert air with **Raffique, Gullah, Sher Rahm,** and their families. Kind, knowledgeable, and spiritual souls, proactive in water technology in the Afghan Karakum desert.

Mitch Stevenson – Realtor, Assistant, and close friend of Gideon, keeps him grounded always ready to help him out of trouble.

Monta James - Sensitive, Andean orphan, Secora's adopted daughter.

Owings MacLeish: Clive's relative, tiny house designer, and contractor.

Seamus McGill: Former farmer turned water technologist. Irish friend of Secora and Gideon.

Tarkio Cyr – Best darn graduate student around. Husband of **Anida** and father of **Frederick**.

Viracocha – Charismatic Prophet whose teachings spread from North America to Tierra del Fuego. Came and left by sea, perhaps from Central Asia, reportedly had light-skin, red hair, and blue eyes. Known as Viracocha in the Andes, Quetzalcoatl - the Feathered or Plumed Serpent, also: Nine Wind, Kukulcan, Gucamatz.

Wakinyan Tanka: Thunderbird, the great thunder being,

Previous Characters for Reference

Azalea Peterson - Ex-policewoman, into forensics. Assassin died from a terror bird attack.

Billy Riggins - Renowned. Field paleontologist, specializing in mammoths and mastodons.

Diego Santiago - Pure hearted Kallawaya, Secora's deceased fiancée, Guillermo and Alai's son

Dr. Donald Chastain – Former Chair of the Paleontology Department. Uptight and old school.

Duendes - short on stature – long on courage

Glen Greenbriar – Gideon's deceased partner at Treasuremont, eaten by a Thunderbird.

Guanaco and Rocio - Kallawayas and dear friends of Guillermo and Alai, L.W. and Sage.

Rocky Bernardillo - Excellent pilot of the Messerschmitt helicopter.

1

ON THE ROCKS

Secora and Gideon had escaped work for the morning, and they were passing through Bonner, then following the highway up the pass. Several miles up the road, they turned their vehicle left, crossed a bridge, and moved onto a side road. To call it a road of any kind would be an exaggeration. More likely, it was the remains of an old logging track off the Blackfoot River highway.

It had been a difficult grind for their pickup to wend up the backside of a nameless cliff. Secora corrected herself. *The cliff probably has a name, but I don't know it.* Eventually, they reached the top of a ridge and stopped when a fallen tree put an end to the track.

When he turned the key off, Gideon stayed inside for a few minutes to take an incoming call from Mitch. Reception was spotty up in the mountains, and he didn't want to miss this opportunity.

Spring perfumes filled the clear mountain air. Secora's hair lightly shifted in the wind as she perched on a large semi-flat rock, considering her life over the last several years since she and Gideon married. They had not yet been blessed with a child, but whenever she remembered dear little Monta, her former adopted daughter, those thoughts turned her face into a grin.

The crack of a twig below distracted her. The wind teased Gideon's dark hair, now streaked with silver highlights. It framed his strong yet sensitive face as he bobbed into view. She was thankful for the sunlight and light breeze and especially for his smile, graced as it was by loving confidence as his eyes met hers. "Hey, glad you made it."

The lean Lakota stood beside her a moment, scanning the canyon below them. "I can't believe the cliff just drops straight off like the arm of a couch." Bending his knees, he sat near her on the rock. Settling in, he cradled his arm around her and laughed. "It is very nice to have my nephew staying with us, but I need to be alone with you."

He pulled her in for a kiss, then another.

Secora laid her head on his shoulder and asked, "How are Jeannie and Mitch this morning?"

"Jeannie has a cough, but she is still hard at work putting together the experimental water collection project, and Mitch is hot on the trail of a couple of properties in locations that would lend themselves to further test the netting."

"Hmmm, sounds hopeful." Moments later, she added, "This really *is* a peaceful setting. I'm glad we came up here one more time before you head to South Dakota for the project. How long do you think you will be gone?"

He took a piece of a small twig and touched the lichen on the rock in front of him, as he said, "Maybe three days."

"Long way to go for such a short trip."

"It's important, but I regret having to be away from you already."

"What will you fellas be working on?"

"We will test several new options for water harvesting besides the net and talk about a new housing project."

"Will the framework for the fog catcher contraption look like a badminton net, or perhaps you could wrap it around a tower structure? Would the tower be above or below ground, and would a fan help?"

"Yes, dear, that kind of thing."

After an hour's peace, while the wind sighed through the evergreens, he said, "We should probably get ready to go to work." As he stood, he offered her a hand.

Secora wondered why she suddenly felt so vulnerable. *We've had no life-threatening situations since our marriage.* Then it became very clear.

A raptor's piercing whistle sounded, and Gideon missed a step, looking like he might collapse. She grabbed his waist in time to help support his descent into a seated position. Next, she reached into his shirt pocket for the seizure medicine Guillermo and Diego had concocted for such moments. She put a few drops on his tongue and watched as Gideon panted for a moment, then sat straighter.

"I'll be okay. Wonder what's up with Wakinyan Tanka."

"Why don't you ask her? I mean, you've already taken the medicine. She must need to connect."

"Okay, hold me, please."

"No problem." Secora knew people called Gideon a heyoka because the Great Thunderbird, Wakinyan Tanka, had chosen to commune with him, and they worked as a team from time to time. Long ago, Wakinyan had opened Gideon's mind and, over time, unveiled spiritual and unseen things he had denied for most of his life.

Secora drifted in thought. *Some people referred to her husband as a contrary warrior, a jester, or sacred clown. One who functions both as a mirror of our ludicrous behavior and a teacher.*

Jimmy Lizardeye, who was Gideon's best friend and mentor, was also a holy man, a wichasha wakan, who explained that each heyoka was unique. Each would find his or her own way. It was not Gideon's way to walk backward, dare death like Crazy Horse, or use extreme behaviors. At times, he would compel cruel or unjust individuals to examine their doubts, fears, hatreds, and weaknesses—and protect whoever he could. Because of Wakinyan Tanka, his life and actions were contrary to the distractions of the material world like booze, thirst for money, random sex, gambling, and drugs—addictions that were part of the shadow life.

Her reverie dissipated when his body tensed again. The roaring whoosh, whoosh sound overcame her, as gigantic wings slowed the sacred being's descent.

The avian icon landed a few yards away and needed to take an extra step to correct her balance.

Secora shielded Gideon with her body from the dust and pine needle squall, but she could not hear the telepathic conversation between them.

Heyoka, I have come, perhaps for the last time.
I am tired.
Ancient One, you have lived nearly one-hundred forty of our years.
We will tire of this earth long before you.
It is by a special blessing of our Creator that we have shared a portion of this time together. Not many days left.

Secora noted the feathers on her body were ruffled, and the ancient bird hung her head at shoulder level. *I don't think she has long to live,* thought Secora. *The good thing is she won't have trouble leaving the cliff. She can practically lean over the edge and catch the thermals to lift herself into the upper levels.*

"Ask her if we can do anything to make the last days easier for her."

Wakinyan Tanka answered *I came to ask if you wished to stay in connection with the Wakinyan. There is a daughter who would try.*

Gideon answered *I am also willing to try. But, I wish to stay attached to you until the end.*

Secora noticed a tear roll from her husband's eye and down the expanse of his cheek as he said out loud, "Great Wakinyan, I will offer prayers for the ease of your passing. Thank you for allowing me to see you and be part of your life. Thank you for showing me the unseen things."

Thank you for healing my wounds on the high mountain. May you also have a quiet ending. Remember, I will be one of the unseen things.

Then the noble bird turned away, each of the sixteen-foot wings unfurled, leaving Secora astounded. The Old One could easily be mistaken for an aircraft. When the raptor fully extended the crest on her grizzly bear-sized head as she spied over the edge and into the canyon. Secora had never seen this before, though Gideon had mentioned the crown from his visions. The sunlight glinting off the feathers, which were tipped with glistening crimson, mesmerized Secora. Then the great thunderbird pushed off noiselessly, dipping down before lifting silently into the atmosphere until she became invisible.

The only other time Secora had been that close to the creature, the conditions were horrible. Wakinyan had been trapped by a net while trying to save Gideon in the downpour of a thunderstorm, and she suffered from festering bullet and arrow injuries. Secora and Gideon cleaned and dressed them to the best of their abilities. The Ancient One survived but did not raise her crest on that day.

As the couple descended the path, they heard a triumphal, piercing shriek echoing through the canyon behind them. They smiled in recognition of her indomitable spirit, which left them feeling extremely emotional. The path was often clouded by tears, and it took them almost half an hour to make it back to the vehicle.

WHEN THEY ARRIVED at their house, they found Gideon's nephew, Kyah, now nearly twenty, working in the garden. He had been staying with Secora and his uncle for a few days while his parents, Jane and Aparu, along with their two younger children, were visiting the Cliff City in Peru to show off their new baby. They expected the family to return home in the next few days.

Secora and Gideon invited the wonderful young man to hang out with them before he also would leave for Peru to take a six-week job on an archaeology dig. The assignment on the dig crew would allow him an opportunity to visit his buddies, the Duendes, and their taller counterparts in Bosque Alto.

Kyah also hoped to see Rocky Bernardillo, the capable ex-military chopper pilot who saved the tiny Duendes from two young thunderbirds during Kyah's first trip. His mom and Aunt Iris hired Rocky to access the remote mountain region, giving Kyah an eagle-eye view during his first flight over the beautiful patchwork of highlands dotted with llamas and alpacas. The late seventies Messerschmitt powered its way over the hills to set down between the cliffs of the Little Ones and the agricultural village of the Big Ones.

Last week, Rocky had sent Kyah ominous photos of a drought. The land around Bosque Alto was changing. It looked drier and more desolate than before. Rocky mentioned that very few of the chickens they'd dropped off as a gift at the end of their last visit had survived. And those few struggled daily to evade desperate predators. The people had applied for trees to plant a protective ring around the village, but it would take years to get them to flourish—and for that, they would need water. Kyah hoped to share Gideon's water-capturing options with the big and little folk on this journey.

If he could manage it, he would also like to fit in a visit to Isla del Sol, to see Alai, Guillermo, Rocio, and Guanaco. They were getting up in years, most in their seventies, but they still served their community as Kallawaya healers. Now, they rarely traveled away from the island for their medical endeavors. Rather, they took care of one another, and the patients who could travel to Challa on Isla del Sol for treatments.

LATER, as she watched Kyah finish his preparations for the long journey, Secora knew he'd turned into a wonderful young man. He would be missed during his first solo "away trip," and she wondered how his life would unfold. Then the song with all the animals from *Lion King* ran through her mind, portraying the limitless potential of Kyah's young life. Consequently, her thoughts turned to herself, then drifted to Wakinyan, whose earthly potential seemed spent, and again, unexpected tears welled up.

2

COFFEE WITH A FARMER

While Secora was in class, Gideon caught a late lunch at a diner on the outskirts of Ronan after listing a property. As he closed his eyes to savor a sip of black coffee at the counter, he heard a familiar voice from a few tables away.

"Hey, Yellow Thunder... bring your coffee over here. I want to ask you about listing my ranch."

Gideon turned his head and smiled as he recognized Seamus McGill forking scrambled eggs into his mouth, followed by a crunch of toast. The realtor gave a heads up to the waitress and relocated to the Irishman's table.

"What's up, Seamus?"

"Well, life has taken a few too many turns for my taste. First the drought. I couldn't put up any hay against the winter, and now I've lost a few calves. Only five of the eight cows I have left freshened this year, and two of those new calves are gone. Just disappeared—no trace."

Seamus took another bite and mulled over his thoughts. "I used to think farming was in my blood, but now I'm not sure."

Gideon's mind briefly flashed on thunderbirds as potential predators. His introduction to the possibility they might exist came in the form of a dream, featuring two thunderbirds swooping low to pick up buffalo calves, then disappearing into a storm. *That would be crazy,* he thought.

Seamus continued, "Probably bears, or so I thought. But there was no sign of a fight, no blood, tracks, or anything."

"Might have been poachers. You made a report, right?"

"Yeah, the neighbor swears it was Bigfoot, but I doubt it. I am getting to the point I don't much care."

"Oooh, that's not good."

The server brought Gideon's plate and refilled his coffee cup.

"Sorry to hear you've had such a tough time. That will leave you with only three calves to sell."

"Them and five yearlings, if nothing else happens. I might as well sell the lot."

"I'm really sorry to hear that, Mr. McGill, but if that's what you decide to do, I believe we could get a decent price for your place. Think it over. Be sure you're ready to take such a drastic step. Next year is bound to be better."

"By the way, Mr. McGill is my father. You and I are about the same age, Yellow Thunder."

Gideon laughed softly. "Give or take a decade. Until you decide, keep those calves locked up at night." His mind turned to Wakinyan Tanka. *Surely, she wasn't still alive after their last meeting. Is that even possible?*

"Sure thing. I'll even tuck them in with blankets and pillows."

"If we do this, what's next for you?"

"Who knows? Maybe I'll become a realtor," he laughed.

"You'd probably be good at it."

"Not really."

"I get the feeling you're the type of man who excels at whatever he does."

"Been doing a lot of thinking about water shortages and droughts. Maybe I'll get involved with water production technology." Seamus drained his cup, grabbed his hat, and left ample cash for a tip with his check as they stood to leave.

"Take it easy, Gideon. Maybe we can talk more about this soon."

Gideon paid and followed Seamus outside. "Have you heard about our water project?"

Seamus hesitated, appearing confused by Gideon's question.

"We're experimenting with water collection devices in a dry part of South Dakota."

"You know, now that I think of it, I have an army buddy in Afghanistan, Manzoor Nadeem Agni, who is working on something similar in the Karakoram Desert near Tajikistan, in the shadow of the Pamir Range. I haven't spoken with him in quite a while. Maybe it's time to give him a call."

"Sounds good, my friend. I will be leaving town for a few days to meet with Jimmy Lizardeye and Clive Bull Bear in South Dakota. Any chance you could free up some time to come with me?"

"I'm afraid not yet. Still a rancher. I'd have to make plans to have someone watch over the place and the animals." Then he smiled and added, "But I would love to hear the results of your visit when you return."

"I'll give you a call when I get back."

"Okay then, see you at your office in a few days."

Gideon waved goodbye from his trusty old blue Beamer, thinking *that sounded more like an opening than a closing. Perhaps our paths will intersect.*

3

A GROWING NEED

Jimmy Lizardeye set two frosty glasses on the teeny patio table that inhabited his porch.

Clive Bull Bear took a long draft, then set his lemonade down. "You know, it's a real shame about what happened to the Renfros."

After a sip, Jimmy agreed. "There's a good chance they would be alive today if they'd had four walls around them."

Clive was passionate. "That woman struggled to make a cardboard home for those kids. A solid home might have saved them from brutal deaths at the hands of those addicts. Getting to be too many crazies everywhere."

"I get it. Even if we could only help a dozen families, it would make a big impact."

Clive added, "Look at what we did with Jane, Mitch, and Gideon on these places here on the lane."

The two men sat and sipped while they imagined the possibilities.

Jimmy said, "Gideon called when I got the lemonade. He said he was almost to Porcupine Creek and would be here in about five minutes. Said he may have a lead on two real estate options in this area."

"Good, that's hopeful." Clive shaded his eyes to scan the driveway.

"That trail of dust on the road must be our heyoka." He checked his watch as he stood, then descended the stairs.

Jimmy stretched and took the now drained lemonade glasses inside for a wash before trotting down the stairs to meet Clive at Gideon's pickup. "Hey bro, welcome to Pine Ridge Paradise."

The hugs were respectful and affectionate. These three had been through a lot together. Jimmy jogged up the steps and pulled another chair up to the tiny porch table.

Clive said, "After lunch, we can show you the output log from our water contraptions."

"Yeah, we have three now."

"That's great!" Gideon smiled. He felt exhausted from the trip to the little trailer park off Bigfoot Road. It had been slow going through Oglala Lakota County on the Pine Ridge rez southeast of Rapid City, but Gideon felt revived being in the presence of his buddies and relaxing on the porch. So good that he fell asleep.

THE BOYS LET him rest while they put together chicken salad that they piled high on sandwiches made with multi-seed bread and slathered with yellow mustard. Gideon roused upon smelling the sandwiches they brought out.

THE SHORT NAP, followed by the zing of the mustard, the protein, and a glass of strong iced tea, brought Gideon back. "First, tell me about the results of your experiments. Whatcha got?"

"Over two and a half gallons of pure water a day from two of them. We just set the third one up yesterday."

"Two and a half gallons is an amazing amount of fresh water for personal use. I'm surprised."

"We're pretty sure the output will increase since we're still learning about positioning and stabilizing the upright poles."

"Yeah, right now they look more like badminton nets after a beach party some mornings."

Gideon brought out pages of design photos and instructions for them to consider. "Okay, after we look at these new capture designs, I want to hear your thoughts about building houses for the homeless parents and older people who Jimmy told me about on the phone."

"Sure," Jimmy agreed. Then he became distracted by the photos. "I kind of like the way this design wraps the net around either a triangle or rectangle. I think it would add a lot to the stability."

Clive said, "We still have a little netting left and several two-by-fours. I think we can knock one of these together this afternoon."

"We'd need another drip tray."

"Oh, right." Clive's stance deflated.

"Good thing I didn't come empty-handed then." Gideon chuckled. "New supplies are in the truck."

Once the materials were brought to the porch, they giggled like kids, trying to figure out what design to try first.

Gideon said, "If we decide to build housing out here, we'll need to average two gallons of drinking water per household per day."

"That sounds about right."

"More lemonade, anyone?"

Clive smiled. "It's gonna take Jimmy more than two gallons just to quench his lemonade habit."

Gideon said, "Yeah, I'll have another one."

That signaled a work break to discuss the tragic story of the Renfros and how even simple shelters might add to privacy, protection, and safety from the elements.

Clive stated, "Even if they're small, they'd be a much safer place for desperately poor single parents and grandparents to raise children."

Jimmy agreed, "Beats a corrugated box in an alley doorway. You're the policeman, Clive. You see more of that than I do, but as it stands now, those folks remind me of the Iraqi refugees I worked with—before they were all gassed."

Gideon brought the topic back. "Hey, tiny houses, that's a great idea. Jeannie will want to hear about this. I'll call her on the way home tomorrow. I think I told you Mitch is looking at two properties in this area."

Clive considered, "You did. Tell us more about them over dinner. I want to finish this rectangle base."

DURING A DINNER of fry bread tacos, Gideon told them about a larger chunk of unimproved desert to the Northeast and a small property west of town by the river. However, he kept drifting off, and Jimmy encouraged him to go to sleep.

Gideon said, "Thanks, guys, this trip is kind of an in and out for me. I need to leave in the early morning."

"It's a long trip back to Missoula. All the more reason for you to call it a night." Clive said, "Pleasant dreams, heyoka."

TWO DAYS LATER, Gideon was returning to his office desk after giving Jeannie a sheaf of papers to file on a new client when Seamus walked through the door.

"Coffee, Seamus?"

"You know it. Gideon, I was hoping you had time to list the ranch today."

"Absolutely, my friend."

They visited over several cups and filled out paperwork for nearly an hour when Gideon asked Seamus what he planned to do after they sold the property.

"I have been doing a lot of thinking about the ranch and my future. I'm giving up on ranching—not on life. I've read some frightening articles and books about the coming worldwide water shortage, and I think accessibility to drinkable water may become crucial in the near future."

"Already is in a lot of places."

"Right, I've decided to study water collection and dispersal technology, as I told you before. And I spoke with my friend, Manzoor Agni, in Afghanistan. We may work together for a week or so, pulling water from the desert air. After that, it's possible I might think about connecting with one of the bigger companies in the States to participate in their experiments. So, naturally, I'm curious about your project in South Dakota."

"First off, seems like you've chosen a job with a useful future." Gideon leaned forward. "It might be a little premature to make an offer but friends of mine, Clive Bull Bear and Jimmy Lizardeye are thinking about expanding their water project on Pine Ridge in order to supply a piece of arid property in a dusty expanse of land southeast of a place called Porcupine Creek in South Dakota."

"Oh?"

Gideon signaled with a beckoning finger. "Jeannie and Mitch, would you please join us?"

They all moved into the conference room.

"Jeannie is taking the lead on putting together this experimental project for us, Seamus. So, I'm going to let her take it from here for us."

Mitch looked at Jeannie and said, "Before we start, I need to let you and Gideon know that I've had a death in the family, and I need to leave for a couple of weeks to help my grandfather sort things out. I just booked a flight for this afternoon."

Gideon cleared his throat. "So sorry to hear that, Mitch." After a pause, he continued, "But I can't think of anyone I'd rather have to help me through a tough time."

Jeannie agreed, "Yes, Mitch, your grandfather will be very lucky to have you there, but we will miss you. Honestly, I can't think of a single day since I've started working here that I haven't seen your smiling face in this office." She started to tear up.

Mitch hugged Jeannie, then Gideon, and humbly excused himself to leave the office.

After Mitch closed the door, Jeannie turned to Seamus, refocused, and held out her hand. "Pleasure to meet you, Mr...?"

"McGill, Seamus McGill."

"Thank you, Seamus, for your patience. I'm Jeannie Rutherford."

She began, "We are in the early stages of planning a community based on small individual houses with tiny, fenced yards for spacing and privacy. Some parts of the project will be easier to bring together than others, but the key would be locating or developing a sustainable water source and finding appreciative and responsible occupants. One of the things I would like to share with you is that we are reviewing an underground closed turbine for collecting water and storing it below ground to prevent evaporation, but what we presently have are several net fog catchers similar to what they are using in the Andes."

After an hour of watching videos and discussing the project, Gideon said, "I think we could work well together."

"This is great. I'm pretty sure the team in Afghanistan would be interested in hearing this. I'll give Manzoor's contact information to Jeannie."

Afterward, they all shook hands and Seamus left with a new spring in his step and a grin on his face.

Jeannie said, "I'm excited about Seamus joining our team."

4
BILL'S STORY

Thinking of Wakinyan's decline led Secora's mind to images of her aging parents as she pulled into the parking spot in front of the Social Sciences Building. They were both growing frail. Her mom, L.W. Dalton, was in her late seventies and recently had a scare with her heart. These days, the renowned anthropologists were no longer traveling to speaking engagements or guest lectures on an international circuit. All that lay behind them, and they were content to spend time at home, where they appreciated visits from children and grandchildren. Sage still couldn't help spouting tales from various parts of the world. It was in his blood. But he spent the majority of his time nursing his "Olmec princess" back to health. He didn't mind. She was the love of his life.

They had earned their gray hair and, for the most part, they were content to walk along the river shore near their home, enjoying each other's company.

Sage occasionally wrote an article about ancient religions. Secora smiled at the thought. When a recent article on Central Asia caught the attention of Dr. Destiny Hawkins, the new Dean of Social Sciences, she was after him to film videos on several topics of his choice for posterity.

Sage had been putting her off, but L.W. begged him to do it, saying, "It would be good for you to work on a solid project; besides, I need more time to sleep."

Eventually, he agreed that the first topic would be the life and times of the Aryan Prophet, Zoroaster, a subject always close to his heart. The talk was supposed to be filmed at the university auditorium in front of a live audience next Saturday. But Iris had called early this morning, waking Secora to let her and Gideon know the venue had shifted at the last moment to the Hasan Resort up by Glacier. With such a big change at the last minute, Secora had doubts about the success of the endeavor.

From her office, she grabbed the materials she needed for a class on the "Coastal and Inland Salish of the Northwest." As she was leaving, a student, Bill Hoffman, met her at the door. They walked and talked on the way to the classroom, but she halted as the real purpose of the discussion became clear.

"Bill, we'll need to spend more time on this. Please see me right after class."

"I can't stay after class today. Because an animal fitting that description is attacking livestock where I live. I was wondering if there are any helpful Native American legends?"

"Large, or even gigantic, black creatures with powerful shoulders have reportedly roamed Alaska, Alberta, Idaho, and Montana for centuries, killing both wildlife and livestock and sometimes humans. Specifically, a massive creature called the *Waheela,* noted by tribes in the Nahanni or 'Headless' Valley of the Canadian Northwest Territories."

"Apparently, there's a history of humans going missing, and the few bodies that were found had been decapitated. That never seemed to make sense to me. Anyway, people have long spoken of enormous black solitary animals, similar to a wolf but much larger and more robust, with a broader head than a normal wolf, and smaller ears. They say it has relatively short, stout legs, which are noticeably longer in the front than the rear. Some say the heavily built body is almost bear-like. Its feet are described as being disproportionately large, like snowshoes with widely spaced toes, presumably to make traveling on snow and the tundra ice easier. Additionally, these paws could be used as clubs, to bat down prey, or adversaries like bears. I wonder if we could differentiate the track from that of a grizzly?"

"Thanks a lot, Dr. James. Sorry, I can't stay for class. I have to leave and go home to Bonners in a few minutes. See you next week."

Puzzled, Secora waved farewell and continued to her class.

5

GATHERING IN MISSOULA

Jimmy was sweeping the porch and moving the little tea-table when Clive arrived at the trailer off Bigfoot Road. As he moved the chairs back into place, he chose one to sit in while he waited for Jimmy to put the broom away.

"It will be good to hear from Jeannie about those house plans."

"Yeah." Jimmy went inside to get his cell phone and two glasses of lemonade, and then returned to the beautiful June morning outside.

"In case she calls," he explained as he held up the phone and slid into one of the comfortable plastic chairs while taking a long drink of the lemonade.

After receiving a text, he said, "Well, my friend, looks like it's time for us to go pick her and those blueprints up at the airport."

Clive stood, downed the last of his lemonade, and headed for the porch steps. Jimmy took the glasses inside, then joined him.

TWO DAYS LATER, Jeannie arrived back at the Missoula airport. If pictures were worth a thousand words, she had struck a gold mine. She'd been able to talk the two gents into flying back with her. She was grinning because after the landing they were acting like giddy kids.

Jimmy said, "I haven't flown since I was in the service. No wait, guess it was on the flight to South America. Either way, it's been a while, and I don't remember enjoying those trips."

"Yeah, my last flight was coming home from the army. Don't remember it being this fun."

Jimmy seemed thoughtful. "Back then, it wasn't."

GIDEON MET the trio in his BMW, and he hugged them as if he hadn't seen them in years—even though it was last week.

Clive solicited, "Hey buddy, how is the weather here in Montana?"

"Not bad. Had to scrape ice off the windshield this morning."

Jimmy chuckled. "That's right. It's June. Seems normal for Missoula."

Ecstatic, Jeannie turned to Gideon. "Hopefully, we can pull the whole team together this morning and finalize some of the details for our housing project."

When they reached the office, they were surprised by the catered lunch awaiting them.

Clive grinned. "This is too much. I feel like I just won a game show."

Gideon looked up in time to see Seamus wander in with another man. He stood and greeted them as they pulled up chairs at the conference room table. Gideon introduced Seamus as a water technology engineering student, shocking everyone who knew him as a rancher, Seamus most of all. Next, Gideon said, "Seamus, meet our crew. This is Jimmy Lizardeye and Clive Bull bear. Mitch Stevenson is still away in Minnesota. And of course, Jeannie and I welcome you."

Seamus, grinning from ear to ear, introduced the man who had come with him, a younger guy, early thirties, who seemed to look everywhere but directly at Gideon.

Seamus announced, "Hey everyone, I'd like you to meet Owings MacLeish, my wife's cousin on her mother's side. He's just in from the north of Scotland trying to get a new start in this country as a construction engineer. I figured we might need one to help us with the 'little house' project."

Gideon frowned, wondering why the young man wasn't meeting his eyes. "Possibly, Seamus. We already have several patterns in mind."

Owings replied, "I may be able to build the wee homes more efficiently. Make them a bit larger and fill them with more amenities. What would you say to that?" With those last words, he finally looked up directly into Gideon's eyes.

"Okay. Take a look at what we already have and see what you suggest."

Owings asked, "Do you have the blueprints here?"

Jeannie came with the scrolls and spread them out for the men to discuss.

After looking at Jeannie's offering, Owings suggested that the typical tiny house was not a residence but rather a temporary housing option. He had brought sensible diagrams of his own, more like apartments or mobile homes with tiny yards.

Gideon said, "I like your ideas. Before we get in deeper, let's put the blueprints away and grab a plate. I'm starved."

It got quiet while people ate. When they were finished, and the containers were rinsed and placed in recycling receptacles, it was time to put their cards on the table.

Jimmy rested the side of his face in the palm of his hand, saying, "Clive and I are thinking it's high time we build more affordable housing out there for single-parent families and homeless people who are struggling. Even dying, like refugees, without better housing and resource options."

Clive scratched his jaw. "We're hoping Gideon, Jeannie, and Mitch will help us put something together similar to what we did for the eight families who live out there on the lane, including me."

Owings wiped his mouth with a napkin and suggested, "I'm sure you know there are housing programs for that kind of thing."

"Don't you think we know that?" asked Clive.

Jimmy said wryly, "Yeah, right. We can wish for a home in one hand..."

Gideon interceded, "Thanks, Jimmy. Shouldn't it be a mix of families like we have on Bull Bear Lane?"

Jeannie was thinking out loud, "And how do we arrange the houses for the best advantage? I seem to remember that back in the 1970s, HUD built some low-income split-level houses in Montana."

Gideon said, "I remember that. My cousin Arnold referred to those as chicken coop housing." Jeannie shrugged. "I won't ask. Maybe the design was off?"

Jimmy tented his hands on the table. "I think it was more about getting something for nothing. The occupants hadn't invested anything in the process like we did. When you give people something, they don't respect it the same way they do if they have to work hard for it."

Clive concurred. "In the end, a lot of the places ended up being trashed."

Gideon recalled, "Right. A lot of them were destroyed."

Jeannie drew back from the table. "We don't want to repeat the mistakes."

Owings suggested, "I think it might be better to give each residence space, maybe a few feet of fenced yard and a shed. Those are things the owners could construct."

Jimmy pulled his eyebrows into a thoughtful frown. "Make them work for the opportunity—sweat equity. That might validate their ownership—and offer a bit of privacy. I like it."

"Two properties which might work for the construction come to mind," said Gideon. "One is a huge chunk of desert on the northeast side of nowhere. Then there is a guy selling his three-acre parcel of undeveloped land just west of town but across the river."

Clive said, "Guess the second one makes more sense for people who don't have transportation."

"It does, but I think someone may have already placed a bid on it for a shopping center. I'll see if the offer was accepted. Just a sec." He checked his phone and dialed a number while asking, "Jeannie, have you heard anything new about the Johnson property sale?"

She shook her head, then he spoke into the phone, "Hey buddy, what's up?"

While he was chatting, the others went either to tuck in another morsel, collect a second piece of cake, or grab a coffee refill.

When he ended the call, Gideon joined them at the food table to grab a slice of cake. "Hey guys, the offer on the three-acre parcel is in escrow. But I let the realtor, Joshua Bader, know that if that deal falls through in the next few days, we'd make it worth his while. Meanwhile, I've been playing with ideas about the larger piece. Perhaps we could develop on-site transportation services there."

Clive seemed riveted. "Sounds like it would be a ton of work, but interesting in that it might stimulate new jobs. We know several people back home looking for construction work. And again, maybe the families who stand to benefit could do odd jobs, the way we did."

"So, you are the team. Jeannie is developing this plan with input from all of you. Keep her posted as you connect with people who might be interested in helping or looking for housing."

Owings said, "New topic. Seamus told me the land is really dry this year. Where would we get enough water for construction, as well as water and sewer with this drought?"

Clive nodded and said, "The river is already running at thirty percent of what it was five years ago."

"You're right. So, as you know, we've been talking about harvesting water with fog nets. Recently, we added an enclosed wind turbine that collects water from the air and stores it in an underground cistern."

Jimmy said, "True, but experimental water-capture technology can only fill part of the need."

Clive offered, "I've been using mist nets to capture dew from the air behind my place. But I think that some of the new options Gideon showed us have serious potential. I think I'll add the one with the small fan blade this summer."

"Good start. How about everyone else?"

Seamus announced, "I spoke with my army buddy in Afghanistan and found that they are having significant success. His team is eager to employ more water harvesting equipment to supply other families. He suggests that participants in the process should save carafe-type juice bottles to store the water in. He says three quarts a day goes a long way to filling human and animal needs. I'm planning a trip over to the Karakum desert in a few weeks to check out their water strategy that currently supplies the majority of household water for four families, three with children. Anyone want to come with?"

Gideon considered the request. "Hmmm. Interesting. I'll think about it."

Jimmy smiled, "Don't take this wrong, but while you're thinking about it, Gideon, this old man needs a nap after the flight and a lunch like this."

"You're not old, buddy. But I rented a couple of rooms for two nights down the street. Owings, you can stay with Seamus in the second room.

"If all of you old guys want to rest and think, I guess we'll close up shop here. We can meet up later, maybe for dinner?"

"What time?" asked Clive.

"Is six, okay? I could meet you by the hotel lobby."

"Yeah, that would be great."

"By the way, I booked the rooms for two days so we could all catch Sage's talk on Zoroaster, Saturday up at Hasan's if you want?"

"Hey, thanks Heyoka."

Jimmy and Clive got up and shook hands, offering a few words to each person while looking them in the eye.

Jeannie gave them the receipts for the rooms. "Guys, the keys will be waiting at the desks if you show these.

Seamus said, "Thanks for the room. If Sage talks about Afghanistan, I'm in." Turning to Owings he said, "Right. We need to visit some hardware stores."

When they were gone, Jeannie commented, "I just love their manners. Wish I had been raised that way. How do you feel about Owings?"

"Not sure. Time will tell."

6

THE VIDEO TAPING "UR MAZD"

Saturday was a glorious June day, and the excitement held sway inside the resort. Jamal Hasan and his associate William Landsing welcomed over a hundred and fifty guests into the beautiful facility, handing each of them a compilation of notes and maps.

Gideon commented, "Seems like a lot of people changed their plans at the last minute to see this."

Vehicles crammed the parking lot and long driveway near the facility. Secora's group had to hike up the access road about an eighth of a mile.

"I think Dad pulled together scriptures from all over the planet for this talk and an upcoming series on the earliest known Prophets that the Dean of Social Sciences talked him into giving."

Gideon was saying, "It's all from his remarkable perspective."

"Yeah, this should be superb."

By the time they entered, the back doors had been pulled open for those who preferred outside seating.

L.W. was already comfortable on the patio sitting next to Jane and Aparu and their children, who had recently returned from the Cliff City. Iris and Kantun stood together a short distance away.

Sage's Guero families had all been welcomed as guests at Jamal

25

Hasan's elegant resort for the next few days. They would take in sights like Glacier Park, the ski slope at Whitefish, and the Bison Range. But they also planned several shopping trips, and of course, some of them would have their nails done.

SAGE DALTON WALKED onto the stage. Above him, a banner read:

"SMOKE ON THE ALTAR"

When the Earth-Soul cried out for a Savior, Zarathushtra was born to redeem the ancient Aryan faith.

Retired BBC correspondent and family friend, Eliot Stearns left his cameraman and came close to Sage, whispering, "We're ready."

Iris held the boom for her dad. Sage nodded to the camera.

Jamal Hasan came up to stand beside Dalton, saying, "Welcome old friend, perhaps you will come back another time to do a film on the Abrahamic Faiths."

"Perhaps, my friend. We'll see what God has in mind."

Jamal turned to the audience, "May I present the world traveler and a leading authority on the development of human religion, Dr. Sage Dalton?"

"So, you want to hear a tale about ancient religions and misty beginnings? Gather 'round now and listen with your souls."

A welcoming wave of eager applause erupted from the crowd as he drew up a seat for himself. He paused while his frame adjusted to the stumpy log chair on which he now sat. Scratching the stubble on his cheek and looking out at the eager faces in the dim candlelight of the chandeliers, he began.

"Was a time when at least three, perhaps four or five kinds of humans lived as neighbors on our planet. Nearly two million years ago, man was a relatively new arrival in Eurasia. So-called modern man followed the same paths as his forerunners, the Neanderthals and

Denisovans, and, at times, he may have even run into ol' Homo Erectus, himself.

"Must have been exciting when one group saw another. I shouldn't wonder if they each thought the other was the ugly bunch. I expect in most cases that was so. Each kind of human was separated into different sorts based on physical characteristics. Some were gigantic compared with the others. Some were stout and muscular, others reed-thin in stature, but we know they intermingled and even had children together.

"According to the most ancient priests of Egypt, there were four races. The red race first ruled our planet. Next, the black and yellow races were the forces to be reckoned with. After that, according to those priests, it would be the time of the white race. Personally, I doubt there is any truth to that. People are people, and we all have the same roots and needs.

"Be that as it may, things changed between thirty thousand and ten thousand years ago, give or take. Strange and terrible forces were at work on the Earth. First, the glaciers melted, and the land dried. When the water left, so too did the living things. All types of humans suffered from starvation, along with everything else.

"Also, I'm pretty sure Noah knew there was a whole lot more going on in His time than a simple flood when he built his floating Zoological Park, or livestock freighter, depending on which version you prefer. I once knew an old guy who put it this way." He carefully unfolded an old sheet of paper and read:

"'Consarned frozen rocks fell out of the sky, blasting their way into Mother Earth, making her feel sick—all queasy like. Her skin rotted and exploded with festering volcanoes, and she shuddered with frightful earthquakes. Fireballs fell from the sky and monstrous waves washed over the land to quench the fires that burned most everything. If all that wasn't bad enough, Mother Earth wobbled and shook for years afterward. The North and South poles shifted, and ice caps melted, re-flooding

*the land, and washing away hundreds of kinds of plants,
animals—and people.'"*

Sage refolded the paper, placing it back inside his pocket.

"One day, as I was sitting on the porch swing with my amazing wife, L.W., we were reminiscing about Zarathustra Spitama, or most of you may know Him as Zoroaster. My family and I have felt for years that He may also have been the Prophet known as the Weeping God, depicted by His followers in Tiahuanaco. This question has been a mystery that has occupied my mind during the last forty-eight years of my life.

"Who was Zardosht, Zoroaster, or Zarathustra? He was the Prophet of the Persian Empire. Let's start with His birth. A precise year for the founding of His Faith is uncertain. Dates differ wildly, but they seem to center between 3,500 to 3,000 years ago. He was born in the area of Greater Iran, now known as Central Asia, home to wandering tribes of Aryans. The little we know about Zoroaster's birth and early life is recorded in the Zend Avesta section, denoted as the Gathas. Scholars have wasted entire lifetimes arguing about what country and which time is accurate for His birth. In the end, the only important thing is what He tried to share with humanity.

"To find Him, we must look in a designated section of eastern Afghanistan and Tajikistan, in a district called Balkh, whose waters feed into the Amu Darya River. It was part of the ancient homeland of the believers in one God. They were called the Mazda Yasnis— followers of the Lord of Light. Zoroaster himself is credited with the authorship of the Gathas as well as the *Yasna,* hymns which were composed in his native language, Old Avestan.

"The Prophet tells us he was born into the Spitama clan, famous for their wonderful horses, camels, cattle, and other livestock. As a side note, this is the vast grouping of lands where horses, those magnificent creatures which captured human dreams, first stepped off the prairies and into people's homes. In fact, Zoroaster's father was called the 'Possessor of Gray Horses.' The Prophet's name refers to 'bright golden light,' or 'golden camel.' Yet, rather than a herdsman, He referred to himself as a poet and prophet. He had a wife, three sons, and three daughters–more or less. People debate. Doesn't matter.

"He acquired some knowledge from his teachers while training for the priesthood as a young boy of maybe seven years, then became a priest at fifteen. But here things become interesting. According to the Gathas, when he left his parents at age twenty, he traveled. Could he have wandered onto a ship to South America? Maybe."

A young man in the audience with long black hair stood and said with a sigh, "Never heard of these guys. You're making this up, right? Good story, though."

"Ever hear of Christ?"

"Yeah. Him, I heard of."

Laughter rumbled in the crowd.

"In the Bible, followers of Zoroaster were the first members of a previous Faith to recognize Christ's station, right?"

The young, bearded man with the question thought for a moment. "The Magi?"

Sage nodded.

"Okay, I'm with you now." Then the young man quietly sat down.

"Legend says that when Zoroaster was thirty years old, he went into the Daiti River during a spring festival to draw water. It was there he received a vision from an Illumined Being wreathed in light. It was the shining Divine Being, Vohu Manah, which means Good Purpose in English. The shining Being taught him about the Wise Lord, *Ahura Mazda,* and *Asha,* the order of things. 'The Good Path.'

"So, the riverbank of the good River Daiti," Sage tapped the map with the back of his hand and Eliot dollied in for a closeup.

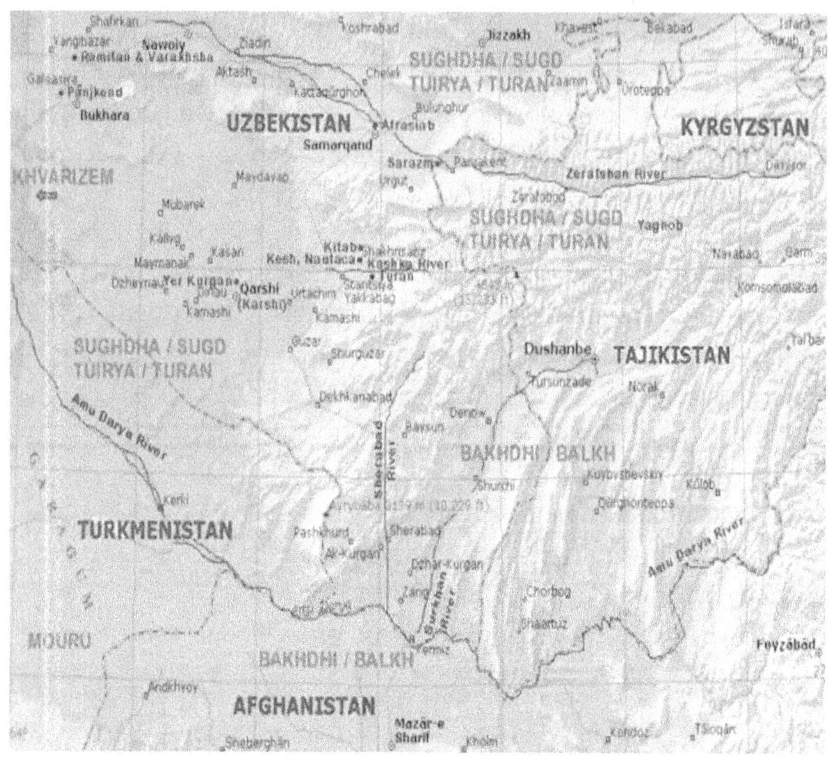

Map used by Zoroastrian Heritage site K.E. Eduljee, editor

"Folks, on this map, I can see no less than four major river drainages that could have been referred to as the great Daiti, where Zoroaster received His revelation."

He pointed to each one, saying, "They include the Syr Darya, the Amu Darya. Some think the Helmond was a sure bet for the Good River or the Balkhash-Alakol. Another prime contender is the Araxes or Aras River, which lies on the other side of the Caspian Sea beneath the Caucasus Mountains north of Iran.

"That being said, it is unlikely this was a reference to a physical waterway, but rather a spiritual torrent which had descended upon him, as another great Manifestation told us when He was anointed in the prison of Tehran in 1853.

"Baha'u'llah, whose name, by the way, means the 'Glory of God'— as in Christ's words—*I will come again in Glory, to judge the living and the dead.'*—had a dream in the dark, dank prison known as the 'Pit.'

"During the process of His transfiguration, Baha'u'llah felt as if a mountain torrent flowed from the crown of His head down over His breast, and He would burn up as if He was on fire. Then His tongue would speak words that no man could bear to hear.

"So maybe the good River Daiti was *that kind* of river." Sage rolled up the map and stepped forward to the first seats in the audience.

"After Zoroaster received His vision, Vohu Manah introduced him to six other spirits, the Amesha Spentas, from whom he received the completion of His transformation into a Manifestation of God's Word. And as such, Zoroaster renewed the Ancient Religion of God.

"Zoroaster soon became aware of another primal spirit, *Angra Manu,* the Destructive Spirit, with its opposing concept of the lie or deception. In simple terms, we could choose to believe in the One God or satisfy ourselves with deception, and follow multiple diffuse concepts like materialism, or a variety of gods who might help us achieve our desires if we placate them with rituals and blood offerings, or these days send 'it out there' to the so-called universe.

"Back to Zoroaster. The caste system, previously laid out by Rama and Krishna, was created with the intention of building strong, safe civilized societies and cities and ending the desperate chapter of starvation brought on by the climate change. Fifteen thousand years ago, as glaciers melted and land dried, famine became a reality. As it was, hungry families and clans moved frequently in search of food, at times overrunning one another to exploit decreasing supplies. It became clear that families needed to settle and somehow, laboriously, began to farm. Social relationships had to change so sedentary humans could live peacefully together.

"Rama and Krishna encouraged the development of planned settlements with a four-pronged infrastructure plan. Four castes were established, focusing on peaceful, constructive relationships in the early villages: 1) educated councils, 2) craftsmen and laborers, 3) warriors to protect villagers, and 4) humble individuals to urge spiritual development among God's children. Over centuries, settlers developed farms and useful livelihoods. By reorganizing societies, they became safer, more secure, with enough food to end the agony, and eventually lead to trade, then commerce.

"By Zoroaster's time, the caste system designed to stabilize culture and religion had become tainted and badly abused. It was now the cause of prejudice, suppression, and injustice. A cruel twisting of what was once a spiritual community vision.

"Princes called Kavis and priests known as Karapans controlled ordinary people, who relied on big ritual and ceremonial parties that lined the pockets of the priests and completely missed the point of spiritual guidance—unless the point was finding a reason to have a party. Then, as today, Aryans lay under the yoke of an oppressive community structure.

Now, we submit to a few misguided, power-hungry ayatollahs, and greedy radical factions, who may refer to themselves as Islamic—but crushing society was never the path of Islam, or the wish of Mohammad, and His *faithful* ayatollahs. Like Rama, Krishna, Buddha, and Zoroaster, He urged us to advance civilization to benefit everyone. Sharing innovations in science, medicine, and social tolerance.

"Still, some people, like those in nearby areas of Turan, believed in many gods to whom Karapans frequently sacrificed animals and drank ritual intoxicants like haoma. While focusing on day-to-day norms, they became less likely to meditate on such topics as self-awareness, accountability, uniting oneself with God's will, or enlightenment.

"Zoroaster came to set the community straight. He opposed the cruel animal sacrifices developed behind the twisted smoky veil of idolatry. Perhaps the animal sacrifices had originally been offered as a gratuity or perhaps a plea for a plentitude of meat. But this was not acceptable to Zoroaster, nor did He condone the excessive drinking of beverages made from the Haoma plant, a hallucinogenic species of ephedra. Yet, similar ritualistic disgraces continue even today in the name of religion. He offered a better way—incense on the altar. But unfocused or distracted people can misdirect even sweet-smelling smoke. Eduard Shure gave us this thought:

'Sometimes they ascended mountains clad in white robes and myrtle wreaths, to offer incense, fragrant smoke, as sacrifices to the moon, sun, and stars; as well as the winds and other elements.'

"Some of you may be familiar with the symbol for Yin and Yang—light and darkness. At any moment, we can choose to take the path of darkness or light—they are both options. The beauty of choice lies within us at every turn.

"Zoroaster believed in One God whose name was *Ahura Mazda*, sometimes shortened to *Ormuzd*—the Primary Mover of all Creation. The Wise Lord sends forth Illumined Beings, the Amesha Spentas, or whatever we on earth choose to call them. Each is a Bearer of the Holy Spirit. As one of them, Zoroaster arose and became part of an incalculable line of Prophets who progressively revealed God's Word to a gradually maturing humanity.

"He shared this exalted station with Abraham, Moses, Buddha, Jesus, Mohammad, the Bab—meaning the Gate, and Baha'u'llah, among others. Like them, He spent his life teaching people to seek Asha, the Good Path. Unfortunately, as is often the case, Zoroaster's ideas were not accepted in his homeland. A common fate of redeemers.

"The Karapans vigorously opposed his ideas. His humble purity threatened their corrupted faith and their coveted personal power. Zoroaster rejected their profitable, materialistic rituals and ceremonies. Then He downgraded the position of the Daevas, similar to saints who had come to be worshiped like gods. Their faith had become an example of paganization—a distraction from facing the Single Ordainer. They copied the ways of forefathers, idolaters who had drifted from the simple purity of submission to God, to placating one spirit or another for favors.

"For years, He had only one faithful believer, an enlightened cousin. This did not change for a long time. After years of struggle, the Pure and Righteous One wandered—perhaps overseas? The temptation arises to think He may have taken a Phoenician vessel and traveled for a few years, perhaps a decade, to the Americas.

"The Prophet, known by dozens of unique names like Viracocha, Gucamatz, Kon Tiki, and Quetzalcoatl, among others, served humanity selflessly prior to weeping as he departed His loyal followers to return to His fate in Eurasia.

"With Him, He brought harmony and grace. He was peaceful and charismatic, and rejected blood sacrifice everywhere He went, trading it instead for the offering of fragrant herbs—incense. The skilled engineers on the ships offered innovations and improvements in fitted stone construction, knowledge of Mediterranean temples, and pyramids—and improved crop irrigation technology, which had literally been a lifesaver back home. *Possibly* they even brought a written language, though the Amazon cultures did not consider it necessary, and later became lost to time.

"A grand Civilization blossomed hundreds of years after His revelation. Perhaps, the most important of its global era. Descendants of His priests and healers still serve the people of the Andes—like my beautiful Guero sons-in-law, Aparu and Kantun. I would like to introduce them now." Two slender men with bird plume-decorated hair came to stand beside Sage. He introduced Aparu, who said in English, 'We bring greetings from the Guero people of the Cliff City where we were born.' Katun then chanted a healing prayer in a beautiful language that contained bird-call flourishes.

Sage raised his arms, smiled, and said, "Kantun, Aparu, Ur Mazd!" Both of the young men stood and raised their arms skyward and respectfully repeated, "Ur Mazd."

Sage reverently echoed the name of God, "Ur Mazd. This was the greeting the people of Cliff City used when we first met in Peru. Healers, like these two men, are one of the great legacies of the southern Prophet. Is it a coincidence that *Ormuzd* is also the name for God from the Persian Creation story of the Zend Avesta? Thank you both." The young men left the stage. The appreciative audience applauded them.

"Twelve years passed before there was any acceptance of Zoroaster's teachings in His homeland. At the age of forty-two, He received the patronage of Queen Hutaosa and the righteous King Vishtaspa of Bactria. They became early adherents of the renewed Faith. Zoroaster proved Himself to the king by healing his favorite black horse. The royal couple was impressed, and they later heard Zoroaster debating with religious leaders, and decided on the spot to accept His Renewal of God's Word as the official religion for their kingdom. Their family and descendants helped to spread the Faith throughout Western Greater Iran and regions far beyond. King Cyrus the Great founded the Persian Empire on Zoroaster's principles in the 7th century BC. He was followed by rulers like Darius the Great, an administrative genius, and his son, Xerxes the Great, who ruled at the peak of the Empire, and enlarged its territory from Eastern Europe, through the Balkans and Greece, and even to Iran and the Indus Valley, forming the improved Achaemenid Empire with its centralized administration and infrastructure. By then, Zoroastrianism was well-established."

A woman with short, gray curls bounced up. "That's nice, but Christ died at the hands of the unbelievers. I bet Zoroaster wouldn't have died for the sins of His people."

Sage turned to face her, and gently said, "I would take that bet, my friend. Unfortunately, our Lord Jesus Christ was not the only Messenger of God who paid the ultimate price in order to wake humanity up and purify the spirit path toward the Lord of Life.

"Although the story of Zoroaster lies in the distant past, it is believed He lived long after Vishtaspa's conversion and established a faithful community. Some say He died at exactly the age of seventy-seven years and forty days. The Shahnameh notes Zoroaster was slaughtered in Balkh Afghanistan by a Turanian *karapan,* a priest of the old religion, named Brādrēs, who decapitated Him during morning prayers and threw the body into a well. Baha'i literature and the Qur'an also mention His violent passing. Greedy idol worshippers and misguided priests may have killed Zoroaster, and later Christ and the Bab, but they never did triumph.

"Turan and Balkh are two regions which encompassed a large part of Central Asia, as you see on the map. They fanned out to the east of the Caspian Sea in the land of the "stans." Uzbekistan, Kazakhstan, Afghanistan, and other "stans" you will never hear about. Bet you were always wondering if there was a reason for the similar names. No? You weren't wondering? Stand means 'land of.' Uzbekistan is the land of the Uzbeks.

"These lands were home to beautiful tribal peoples of a vast Aryan Nation. Their skin and hair tones ranged from pale-skinned redheads to blue-eyed blonds, to a variety of skin and hair tones throughout a vast range that eventually included Europe, the British Isles, parts of India, and even parts of China."

A hand shot up in the audience. "That's not my understanding of Aryans."

"My sympathies, but alas, no, they were not all Hitler's blond-haired boys by a long shot. They were a beautiful mix, like the Native American tribes here. Dictators make up their own rules — regardless of the truth. So, if you tend to think in terms of Hitler's definition of Aryan as blond Germans—the good news is you can just toss that out the window."

The man's jaw dropped, and he sat up abruptly.

Sage announced, "I just received the signal that dinner break will start in ten minutes. I'll take one question."

A woman in a pink knit suit and dyed red hair stood. "Mr. Sage, I am Jewish, and because of the Torah and the Bible, I thought all of the Prophets lived in or near the holy land. So, I find all of this unbelievable."

Sage nodded. "I agree that we automatically think all Prophets came from the Middle East and although that does have some validity for the last ages of men, it wasn't always like that. Plus, Mesopotamia is part of the region we are discussing, so it has never been left out, and Aryan people and events actually *are* included in the Bible. When Zoroaster died, His followers were based out of Nineveh in upper Mesopotamia along the eastern bank of the Tigris River. And I'm sure you'll agree that the earliest revelations probably occurred in Africa."

He smiled, "But today we are exploring the sacred Aryans scriptures, adding a deeper dimension to the spiritual history of our human family. I hope we can appreciate them as such."

The woman returned the smile, then said, "Very nice, but I am not giving up my Bible."

"Certainly not. This isn't an either-or concept. It is an enhancement, an appreciation of our humanity from a very different perspective, the Stone Age."

The lady said, "Cavemen? That *is* a different perspective, indeed." Satisfied, she took her seat and nodded triumphantly, her belief still intact.

Sage watched Jamal Hasan approach the stage. He invited everyone into the dining areas, saying, "Please join us now for a kosher or halal meal of steak or seafood. For those of you who still have a thousand questions, Sage will return to this venue in a week to answer one or two intriguing mysteries."

Murmurs of approval rose as the audience stirred and left for the savory delight, and fascinating conversations.

Gideon said, "I am starving after smelling the aromas from the kitchen for the last forty-five minutes."

Jimmy commented, "Yeah, I'm surprised there isn't a trail of drool on the floor."

Secora said, "That's disgusting. Way to ruin the moment."

After only a few minutes, you could have heard a pin drop as diners turned their attentions to their plates.

"I wonder what Dad has up his sleeves for the next talk?"

Gideon said, "No idea, but it should be interesting."

7

THE DEAN OF SOCIAL SCIENCES

Sleep-deprived from staying up late, talking to Gideon, Secora dragged up the stairs and stepped into her third-floor office. On the way to her desk, she eased carefully around the articulated skeleton of *Llallawavis Scagliai,* who, like Wakinyan, had defied extinction. Some referred to such creatures as "Terror Birds," and Secora knew exactly why.

This naked one stood a little over three feet tall with solidified cranial bones set atop a powerful spine that enabled it to swivel its head and stun its prey with a solid whack. Certainly, these birds could break bones, but they had other weapons. A few types scavenged, but many ran down their prey, bashed it to the ground, then shredded the bodies with their wicked beaks. Because of their excellent hearing ability, it was nearly impossible to evade them in exposed environments near streams, in grasslands, or an open forest.

She settled into her desk chair, leaning back as she recalled the circumstances of this terror bird's death. On her last visit to Peru, a flock of them had attacked Secora, Monta, her adopted daughter, and Azalea, the would-be assassin. During the battle, the women defended themselves with nothing more than a hardwood walking stick and a pistol.

Azalea hadn't survived, but neither did half of the birds, including this one.

Only the arrival of Gideon and his best friend, Jimmy Lizardeye, had allowed Secora to chase the remaining birds away and escape a similar fate.

She looked again at the skeleton. *Ah, my friend, you and your cronies should have died away completely two and a half million years ago, but I am truly sorry to have been a part of your particular demise.*

She smiled, remembering that she'd brought this specimen back from Peru as a present for her office mate, Tarkio Cyr. It enthralled him that the carcass had been a female—with an egg. He listened eagerly to Secora's gory tale, but it couldn't dampen Tarkio's zeal. He had saved genetic samples, cleaned the bones, and re-articulated them for his thesis project. Now, he was a post-graduate student whose work was stellar.

The young man had been so mesmerized by the idea of a living fossil that he made its analysis his postgraduate area of study. He even made several trips to the Imata area of Peru, hoping to locate living specimens. He couldn't find the pack which had attacked Secora, but there were persistent rumors in nearby villages of missing livestock and two missing women in the area.

Secora told him to thank his lucky stars that he didn't find them, because being in a battle with an extinct species could end up being a real downer.

SECORA NOTICED there was a message on her desk from the Dean of Social Sciences. She read enough to know that they would ask her, for the third time, to temporarily chair the department. The last Chair, Dr. Donald Chastain, was imprisoned for antiquities theft, fraud, and attempted murder.

Sighing, she picked up her phone thinking it wouldn't be long before someone of Tarkio's caliber would take the position. To Secora's dismay, Dean Hawkins happened to be immediately available.

Secora disliked the administrative aspects of the job. The red tape and pomp usually associated with being a chair were not her style. Yet, if she took the position, it would give her time to catch up on research and writing. She winced, anticipating all the excruciating meetings she would have to attend, as well as the constant struggle of securing grants and funds for the department. *Yuk, this can't happen. Retirement wouldn't be a bad option.*

She arose, grabbed her jacket, and trotted down the stairs.

BEFORE SHE KNEW IT, she was sipping coffee with the new Dean, who was in her later fifties, trim, fit, and professionally dressed with her long dark hair pinned up. Secora thanked her for setting up Sage's talk. "It was both riveting and fun. More than any of us expected, thanks."

Then Dr. Hawkins asked if Secora would be interested in chairing the Paleontology Department.

She swallowed a sip, then carefully set her cup on the table with downcast eyes. *How to say no?* "I appreciate the offer. And now, more than ever, I'm tempted to try something new. But not this. Maybe they should consider one of the invertebrate grads or instructors."

Destiny countered, "Invertebrate studies are more limited now since the great oil boom is well underway. They need someone seasoned, but dynamic, with an eye to the future."

"However long that may be, given current budget cuts."

"Oh no, haven't you heard about the new Paleontology Center they are thinking of building?"

"We need the talents of someone fresh—like Tarkio Cyr. Someone who can keep the department financially sound. That's going to take zeal, and though I'm experienced, I can't be enthusiastic about the inner workings of administration. I am not capable of departmental zeal."

"Well, Tarkio is not going to happen. He's too young and inexperienced."

"Well, you may be right about Tarkio. He is young. Dr. Hawkins, I enjoy having my office in the social sciences building and crossing over to pick up archaeology classes as needed. Until Dr. Chastain kicked me out of what had been my dad's office before me, I felt at home here. I hardly noticed I was an 'ugly duckling' housed outside of geology. Bless his heart. Tarkio offered me part of his office, and I think the poor boy is going for a dual degree as well. Inexperience might be a necessary ingredient for fervor. He almost has his doctorate. I'm getting old and bored, barely holding it together in classes I used to love."

"That's a tad disturbing, Dr. James."

Secora's mind was racing, looking for some option to offer. *This would be a long shot.*

"Research is my passion. Yesterday, one of my students, Bill Hoffmann, questioned me about hyena sightings on the way to class. He asked if there were any Native American legends regarding large black predators. One was seen attacking livestock near his home in Bonners Ferry, and I was hoping to take time off to investigate."

"Of course, you *will* look into it, and you *will publish* your findings. That could be big news."

Secora's mouth opened in shock. "Yes, of course, Dr. Hawkins."

Destiny crossed her legs. "You don't know this, but I grew up in South Cheyenne Canyon near Colorado Springs. One day I was walking home from high school with my friend, and we saw what we thought was a weird bear peering at us through the sparse pines of a vacant lot. When the animal turned to focus on us, the hair and its face were all wrong. The head was short and square—powerful, but not quite like a bear. The thing was huge—maybe even bigger than a bear with a different shape, a powerful hyena stance — something like you might see with some German Shepherds. When it turned its head to look directly at us, we could see a long fringe of mane sticking up in a ridge on its neck and down its back."

"How was the animal marked?"

"We couldn't make out its color, but it seemed to be dark brown or black. The fringe made us think it might be a giant hyena, but we didn't see any stripes or spots. The head lowered, then it started coming for us. My friend screamed, 'Hyena!' I couldn't believe it. My feet seemed to be frozen in place. I'm sure we'd have been lunch if the school bus hadn't screeched to a timely stop between us. The animal took off like a shot with its sawed-off tail sticking out behind. The tail might have curled slightly upward at the tip, but I'm not sure."

"Was it a hyena or something else?" Secora queried.

"To my friend and me, it looked similar to a hyena bear composite, but everyone we talked to shook their heads. It got to the point we doubted ever having seen it at all."

Secora drew in a thoughtful breath and rubbed her right brow with her fingers. After exhaling, she said, "I consider you to be a highly credible source, so I can't just blow this off and be done with it."

"I agree. A trip is in order. It's good to see research still interests you."

Secora winced. "Right."

SECORA RETURNED to her office and immediately called Bill Hoffmann's cell number and left a message. She hesitated, rubbing a finger across the mammoth molar on her desk, then called the number for the family home. She left another message explaining who she was and her wish to come up and investigate. Neither call was returned right away, so she tried the numbers again an hour later. Still no answer.

A little concerned, she decided to see if there was a basis for sightings of hyena-like creatures in North America while she waited.

I'm not readily familiar with the bone-crushing carnivores of the last few million years. She simply had no reason to take a closer look until Bill approached her and then later, being blindsided by Destiny's sighting.

There were red herrings she would avoid. For example, fearsome predatory mammals like carnivorous pigs and the Hyenadonts. The pigs pretty much spoke for themselves—as pigs do. The latter were *creodonts*, named for their unusual teeth. They had been ferocious wolf-sized predators, unrelated to hyenas, vanishing at the same time as the ancestors of present-day carnivores, leaving no living descendants.

Secora went to the mini-fridge to grab a cherry yogurt and took a sweet-sour bite of the creamy product. She knew hyenas belonged to Feliformia, an archetypal suborder of the Carnivora which encompassed all the so-called "cat-like" predators, including the Viverrids, a group comprised of civets, fossae, meerkats, and hyenas. She would check those before moving into the canine suborder, to look at the bears, wolves, and wolverines.

She also remembered that the prehistoric prototypes for all mammalian carnivores had once lived in forests and originally had retractable claws. When most of the early predators descended from trees in order to chase or bushwhack their prey, the cat-like creatures split into several distinct lineages in order to hunt and scavenge the rivers and grasslands along with the terror birds. Many retained their retractable, or semi-retractable claws, but she remembered that trait disappeared early on for the canines and over time for others, like the bears.

A fly landed on her desk. Looking down, she noticed the date was wrong on the calendar and flipped the page to June 2, 2008, and then spent the next few hours researching sightings.

8

THE UNUSUAL SUSPECTS

After giving a late afternoon test to thirty-three students in the bone lab, Secora returned to the office. She unlocked the door, flipped on the office lights, and eased into her chair checking for phone messages. Zip. She opened a bottle of iced tea, sipping it while gathering her thoughts. She fired up the computer to continue her search.

It had been easy to lose track of time while gazing at images and artists' reconstructions of some of the oddest members of the Viverridae, so she was startled when Tarkio thumped an armload of books and papers onto his desk.

With a sing-song voice, he asked, "Whatcha doing?"

"Background research in preparation for a field trip tomorrow. I need to check out a recent sighting of a hyena-like creature up north."

"Ooh, Ooh, can I come—please?"

"Possibly. Tarkio, were you aware that Viverridae is a family which is currently composed of nearly thirty of the most interesting housecat-sized creatures on this planet?"

He looked down at the desktop, and sounding a bit bored, responded, "Guess I really hadn't thought about it."

"Until now, I hadn't either."

Secora looked up, noticing he'd lost the sproingy blond curls of his early youth, along with the wire rims. Today, his hair was spiked into a sort of green Mohawk roach, and he wore maroon plastic-rimmed frames. *The boy is growing up. I think. His son, Frederick, must be eight now, like Monta.*

Secora's adopted daughter was back in Bolivia with her dad, who'd escaped slavery and returned to Isla del Sol to locate and claim his unmet child. The memory of losing the little girl still tore her apart. She sighed and returned to her search.

Removing his backpack, Tarkio finally slid into his desk chair and turned his printer on. "Civets and genets are cool," he said, no longer sounding bored. "They still spend much or all of their time in trees. I'm noticing several African civets have crests or manes running down their necks and backs like the hyenas, and there is an extensive range of coat colors. Some even look like the ancestral forms of hyenas except for their slender faces."

Tarkio ate a sandwich while Secora stepped down the hall for a bathroom break. When they were ready to pick up where they left off, Secora stretched her fingers and said, "Now let's take a peek at the hyenas—even though I doubt they are the culprits we are seeking, since they're not listed in brochures of North American wildlife."

Tarkio snorted and went over to the fridge to grab a soda.

Secora considered Tarkio's description. "There are a couple of things common to the Viverrids that catch my attention—a crest that raises when they are agitated and the lone hunting males. Those might fit with an animal Dr. Hawkins was telling me about. But I have a feeling they are way too tiny for most of the accounts."

Tarkio responded, "Moving on to the hyenas. As cute as the Aard-wolf is, I think it's way too small."

"Probably," she chuckled. "Also, it's built more like a tiny fox instead of a typical hyena, and it doesn't kill wildlife or livestock—just insects."

"It sleeps under the cover of bushes, trees, or rocks to avoid being overheated during the day." Tarkio added, "Oh, and here's a deal-breaker. Only a few remain in the southern part of the Kalahari Desert and in the coastal areas of southwest Africa. The range for beautiful brown hyenas is also declining. The map shows Angola, Namibia, Botswana, southern Mozambique, and southern and western Zimbabwe. Hey, all of those pieces together look just like the tip of a man's..."

"Whoa there, Tarkio. I get the picture."

"In the South, it is rare or possibly even extinct. Unfortunately, brown hyenas are used in traditional rituals and for medicine. The article says they are persecuted, poisoned, and trapped, mostly because people think they kill livestock. The author claims they don't, except maybe on the rarest occasion. But they do kill wild animals."

"There again, Tarkio, I think we can rule them out in this country, except as escapees from zoos or private facilities. Same goes for the big spotted hyenas, *Crocutta crocutta*. Although they are the largest living species, they aren't huge. Adults can weigh from ninety to a hundred-fifty pounds."

Secora grabbed another tea from the fridge, then returned to the desk.

Tarkio was riveted. "Granted. But check out these striped hyenas. They are gorgeous. Have you seen them?" He didn't wait for her response. "They live throughout northern and eastern Africa, but they have an expanded range compared to the others. They can still be found in northern and central Asia, as well as India. They even lived in the *Mediterranean* region until a few thousand years ago. The article says they can also eat the bones. That's interesting."

"They are undeniably eye-catching, Tarkio. But they are also savage killers—viciously ripping their animal or human prey apart, like the others."

Tarkio grimaced. "I've heard they go for the private parts first."

Secora's voice became unsteady. "I understand that the soul of a human being is strengthened and polished through the agency of suffering, but I don't understand why God allows beasts to undergo the agony and torment of being eaten alive."

"Are you crying, Secora?"

"Yes, I am." She cleared her throat, and changed the subject, "I think we would do well to look at extinct hyena varieties."

"You're right. And I have to say, Feliforms are a pretty interesting bunch of cousins. Who knew?"

"You did, Tarkio. At least you got the answers right on the test I gave you last fall."

"Short-term memory must be going."

"You just wait, child."

Tarkio friction-rubbed his hands together. "Okay, now it's time to look at the extinct Hyaenidae. Huh. Over seventy species developed through the ages, but we only have four or so species left."

She laughed. "The 'or so' leaves room for cryptids, right? I've looked up a few of the sightings, and from what I understand, there have been occasional accounts of hyena-like, or unidentified wolf-like creatures in both the US and Canada, and those accounts have continued right up until *last month*. No sign they'll stop tomorrow."

"Mmm-huh. And you believe *them*?"

"What reason would people have to randomly report something so outlandish?"

"R-i-g-h-t."

She smiled, "I know you aren't a fan of cryptid sightings, Tarkio, and although you may not agree, I see no reason to deny the reports without further inspection."

He grabbed his backpack. "Listen, these findings are mind-blowing. And you have found cryptids before, like Betty."

"Betty?"

"The bird here. I'm excited but torn. I have a class. Then I need to go home to Anida and Frederick. Let's continue this discussion tomorrow if you have time?"

"I will be sharing my results with Dr. Hawkins at 7:00 a.m. Want in?"

"You know I do."

"You'll need an open mind if you come with me to Bonners Ferry tomorrow. Meet me at the Dean's office. Bring your field gear."

"All Right!" He could hardly contain his enthusiasm as he bounced out of the office and into the hall.

"Happy trails." She chuckled to herself. She knew he was hooked. "Hope you still feel that jacked after we find it."

9

AHA

After Tarkio left, Secora remembered there hadn't been a return call from the Hoffmann family. She checked her watch, then tried them again—no answer. She then called Gideon to let him know she would be staying late. She stood up to stretch her limbs before returning to the computer to work a little longer.

The next few hours flew past as Secora buried herself in accounts of weird hyena or wolf-like creatures in North America.

Some articles suggested terms like "freak wolves." At a glance, she chose to eliminate those and the rest of the canids with their longer ears, tails, and snouts. Wolf-hybrids, coyotes, jackals, foxes, and dogs were genetically different animals from the family of Hyaenidae. Besides, most of them weren't as big as the animals in the descriptions, or they were the wrong shapes.

She thought, *as for werewolves, chupacabra goatsuckers, and the like, well...* she rolled her eyes—*they need not apply. They belong to an entirely **different** category.* A wry smile curved her lips. She squinted; *Maybe I shouldn't throw out the chupacabras just yet.*

Secora easily eliminated spectacular accounts of the wolf-hyena crosses and the Ringdocus, an odd-looking specimen of a "wolf" that had been shot and mounted then placed in a museum or two, because crossing a wolf with a hyena would be like crossing a lion with a hyena. Zero chance of success.

The immense size of select reported animals was also worrisome. Several of the beasts were larger than most bears: six to seven feet tall and weighing two-hundred fifty to nine hundred pounds or even *much* more. *Hmm, that rules out a lot of North American wildlife except maybe moose, polar bears, or buffalo.* Animals of this size were more in line with nightmares, rather than reality, or so she thought at the time.

A LITTLE AFTER SEVEN. It startled her when Tarkio breezed in, removed his backpack, and peered over her shoulder at the computer. "Now, what's *that*?"

"Hi. I was looking into *Chasmaporthetes* as a plausible option for recent American hyena sightings..."

Next, the clomp, clomp screech of low heels approaching the door distracted her. In popped Dr. Hawkins, with a fine smelling bag of Mexican super nachos, and a tray of iced teas. "Dinner anyone?"

Secora was astonished. "What? This is crazy... I mean in a good way, Dean."

"Enough." Destiny grabbed a beef and pico-laden chip and crunched. "Where are we in the process?"

Puzzled by the question, Secora said. "I left messages on Bill Hoffmann's cell phone, and I even tried his parents at home a few times, but I have heard nothing back."

"My next question is, don't you ever watch the news?"

"Not recently. I've been busy with the research. Why?"

Secora noticed Tarkio took what she defined as a defensive sip of tea, putting all of his attention into the effort.

After a drawn-out sigh, Hawkins said, "There was another animal attack in Boundary County, Idaho. I don't suppose your student's family lives in Boundary County."

It was Secora's turn for a distracting sip. "Yes, they do."

"So, before you leave tomorrow morning, I want to know what you have."

Secora munched a nacho. "Right. I spent the afternoon looking into so-called hyena-beast sightings reported by individuals from several cultures over a period of nearly three hundred years. Stories came from the Yukon and all across the United States, from California through the Great Plains, and from Texas to the swamps of the Northeast. Brutes in a variety of sizes, coat colors, and markings were described in nearly three dozen creature reports. The animals ranged from slightly smaller than a wolf to as large as a bison.

"It took another hour or so to divide the narratives into two categories, one for hyenas or hyena-like creatures, lumping the rest into non-hyenas who would later be divided based on one aspect or another, requiring further study.

"Really. You're going with so-called?" droned Destiny.

"Please, the accounts were credible, lucid, and sincere. They had enough descriptive information of physical attributes and actions to rule out any currently known North American animal. Yet the animals in them varied enough to come from not only separate species but entirely different phylogenetic families."

"We decided that the stories of hyena-type beasts far outweighed the staunch denials that they exist based on spotty fossil records."

Dean Hawkins scribbled a note. "You do know *you* are supposed to be one of the experts, right? Give me the Cliff Notes."

Secora looked down at her knees, and said, "Were there misidentifications? Were people describing something like a bear or a buffalo? Then I remembered you, Dean, not likely, but possible."

"This is after hours. Call me Destiny."

"Okay, then. Did hyenas escape during circus train wrecks or other transport mishaps, or could they be zoological park runaways? No doubt some were. Might they be remnants of supposedly extinct or nearly extinct hyena species? Possible. Likely, they were a combination of all these. That doesn't narrow it down much," she admitted.

"Or lies," Tarkio submitted.

Secora nodded once, then continued, "Rather than weigh in on the validity of the accounts, I decided to see where the evidence given in the descriptions would lead, and I dug into online resources and pertinent articles and publications for background data."

Tarkio stepped in. "Of the seventy species of hyenas, past and present, only four are currently recognized, and none are native to the Americas."

Secora moved forward. "But there are occasional runaways. For example, a California animal trainer recently described seeing a small hyena outside his property daily. He should have known what he was seeing. Interestingly, I found another article that mentioned a thirty-year UC Berkeley project begun in 1985. Twenty newborn spotted hyenas were brought from the Maasai Mara to California for the study. A coincidence?"

"Also, a pack of 'hyena-like' animals in New York was seen across from the Bronx Zoo. They were described as having high but crouched shoulders and low tails. The animals were three to four feet long, and they were said to closely resemble striped hyenas but didn't appear to have spots or stripes on their light brown coats. They did, however, have shaggy manes on the neck and shoulders. Interestingly, this was the only sighting of any kind that mentioned animals roaming as a pack."

Destiny surmised, "So, it seems like two or three might have been actual modern spotted or brown hyenas that escaped from private endeavors or facilities."

"Yes, other narratives bore some likeness, but were probably not modern hyenas because they were twice the size, the wrong color, or the wrong shape."

"Give me examples."

"Observers in a few sightings in Texas and the Adirondacks said the animals they saw *resembled* hyenas but wondered what else they might be. In one account, people saw two 'peculiar hyaena-look-alike beasts' chasing a deer. They had heavy forequarters and short, powerful hind legs. Other attributes mentioned were a sloped back, diamond-shaped head, rounded ears located high on the head, a mane on the neck and back, and *a long bushy tail*. The long tail isn't a modern hyena trait. And no mention of spots or other markings that were interesting and unexpected.

"The state of Indiana has also generated a few sightings of solitary, strange-looking wild animals through the years. Over a hundred years ago, there were several sightings in the midwestern states of similar creatures that seemed to defy classification. They were called by the local people *Shunka Warakin* with a silent 'n' at the end. It meant 'dog killer.' Early farmers described them as freak wolves, 'wolf-hyena crosses,' or 'hyena-like' beasts, found in forests and along roads. One was sitting back on its haunches licking its front paws much like a cat or dog. It looked at the man who was watching it from a short distance away before racing into a field of corn.

"A rancher shot a smaller freak wolf. It measured forty-eight inches from the tip of its snout to its rump, and it was twenty-eight inches high at the shoulder, about hyena-sized. There's another famous museum exhibit of a small, weird wolf shot in Montana. Its fur was blackish-brown with faint rippling stripes. For lack of another term, people called it 'Ringdocus.'

"In another description, the shoulders of a 'monstrous' creature were high, and its back sloped. The fur was dark brown, nearly black, but with lighter tan areas showing faint impressions of stripes on its flanks, like the Ringdocus. Several said it was similar to a hyena, except it had a noticeably narrow snout. Again, it was called a 'weird hyena' or 'freak wolf.'

"Coat types of these animals ranged from wiry-brindle to spotted, and fur colors included browns, gray, and black. Most were darkly shaded. Currently, only the rare brown hyena has very dark fur, but it would not be considered large."

Tarkio interjected, "We felt the term 'hyena' was used for lack of another word to describe the creatures the witnesses saw."

"A minute number of viewers described animals with sloping backs, hyena-like stances, spots or stripes, short snouts, and boxy facial features—and were an appropriate size for a living species."

Secora said, "It became clear that most of the accounts were not modern hyenas."

"So, hyenas are not responsible for the attacks in Idaho?"

Secora responded, "We couldn't be sure, Destiny, so we started with the obvious."

Secora shook her head. "Was it possible people were seeing individuals of a species that survived thousands of years longer than expected?

"Keeping with the hyena theme, we looked into an extinct American hyena with a narrow snout which was widely distributed across North America. The genus, *Chasmaporthetes ossifragus*, based on a few fossils, was found primarily in Arizona and Mexico. The name means 'He who saw the canyon,' referring to the chasm of the Grand Canyon that was thought to have formed near the same time as these fossils were laid down.

"Most paleontologists say it is the only hyena known to have crossed the Bering Land Bridge and made its way into North and South America. The interesting thing about *C. ossifragus* is that it differed from the typical hunched posture of an African spotted hyena. Fossils suggest it was the size of a small wolf with a flattened, wolf-like skull, like some of the smaller animals described before. It also lacked the stocky, hunched posture and bone-crushing musculature of an African hyena. The streamlined body aided long-distance running, and it looked more like its surviving cousin, the tiny, insect munching aardwolf."

Destiny considered, "Hmmm, could be an excellent candidate for a few of the 'weird wolf' sightings, or the Ringdocus."

Tarkio asked, "Sounds interesting. So, that's it? People are seeing remnants of C. ossifragus? Does it have to be this particular genus?"

"Well, the renowned cryptozoologist, Loren Coleman, speculated Eurasian cave hyenas might have also entered into North America in small enough numbers to elude being found in the fossil record. As for size, cave hyenas in Europe were one-third larger than African Spotted Hyenas—maybe two hundred pounds and sixty plus inches long."

Tarkio said, "Yikes, glad they're gone."

"I know I wouldn't want to face one! That's about it for the regular hyena accounts, recent or extinct."

Destiny asked, "In Idaho, what do you think we're dealing with?"

Tarkio interjected. "Probably neither in Idaho. However, it would be tough to rule out the cave hyena, since we know little about it except that it was larger than the spotted hyena. Besides, it's extinct as far as we know." He swiveled his chair to look at Secora. "What if it's not a hyena at all? Could it be something else?"

"People saw radically different types of creatures. Surprisingly, none of these animals ran in packs. They were large, dark, solitary hunters. They fell into two other categories, medium and large animals, which warrant further inspection."

"I'm with you—keep going. Wait, wolves and werewolves. Am I right?"

"Pretty close, Tarkio. I'm not feeling as negative about those classifications as I did early on. In any case, freakishly enormous wolves seem to account for a few of the animals."

"Woof, woof, woooof," Tarkio howled.

"Funny, but no. The second creature I want to mention is the North American Epicyon haydeni, a Borophagine, commonly known as a bone-crushing dog. This was the largest species at five feet long and had an estimated weight of 200–300 pounds. The compact, rounded skull featured long canines and crushing molars. This could be a candidate for nearly a quarter of the accounts, including one from the Alberta Wildlife Park in Canada, where several witnesses saw a 'peculiar hyaena-look-alike beast,' with heavy forequarters and a lowered back end. It stood around three and a half feet at the shoulder, looked like a large, stocky wolf with a hyena-like head, and massive neck and shoulder musculature.

"One eyewitness described it as a wolf on steroids, another insisted it wasn't a coyote or wolf-hybrid, it WAS a hyena, nearly black with high shoulders and a back that sloped downward. Epicyon could stay under the radar posing as a *large wolf, or wolf-hyena* cross, spot on with some of the descriptions. However, that animal is also presumed to be extinct."

"Secora, why do you say presumed?"

"As with the running hyenas, there is only circumstantial evidence to suggest their extinction. They might have been arbitrarily lumped into a mix of 'probable' exterminations. It's conceivable relic populations remained past the presumed cut-off without leaving a fossil trail. Honestly, skeletal evidence is scant and already spread over vast temporal gaps. Who's to say that the interval between the Oligocene and today isn't merely another large gap? It's guessing to say these animals went extinct along with similar predators in the early Pleistocene or Miocene simply because ecologists thought they couldn't adapt to the drying climate."

"That's reaching."

"Quite likely, but I could not afford to ignore the possibility since it so closely fits a fair number of the observations. From there, things get larger and more... interesting." Secora grinned. "I feel the Bonners Ferry beast may be one of the latter."

"Oh, here we go! What's next? I'm not going to say werewolves this time."

"Too bad, Tarkio. This would have been the proper time.

"But... Really?"

"Yes. Loren Coleman mentioned this animal, in passing, during a discussion of possible hyena cryptids. But one of America's fiercest predators wasn't any sort of hyena, wolf, or even a Borophagine. It was a prehistoric beast known as the 'bear-dog,' Family of *Amphicyonidae*. The vast majority of sightings, nearly two-thirds, were of huge, monster-like creatures. Solitary animals, whose fur was dark brown or black with occasional faint stripe patterns noted. These imposing creatures resembled a cross between a wolf and a bear, as their common name suggests.

"Amphicyons came in a range of sizes and with dimensions from a few pounds like a Chihuahua, to over 1,000 pounds, bigger than a grizzly bear. The largest species looked more like a bear than a dog. Speculation about Amphicyon morphology is limited due to the rarity of fossil evidence; one complete skull and a few other fragments.

"Amphicyon *ingens* was a typical bear-dog with its robust build and eight-foot length. These extremely large creatures displayed characteristics of both bear and wolf. It had a short face and possibly rounded ears, and bulky jaws with dog-like dentition but also sturdy flat teeth for crushing. Its stout legs ended in huge paws that could slap their prey silly. It's normally described as being covered in brown or black fur. Sometimes, long white fur is mentioned, especially thick around the shoulder area where it can stand up a couple of inches off the body like a mane when the animal is agitated."

Tarkio gasped. "Excuse me? Eight feet long? What the heck?"

Secora nodded. "You heard me. This was a solitary apex predator that could run thirty to forty miles per hour. It could hold its head up to a six-foot-tall man's waist or chest, similar to the size of a large Bengal or Siberian Tiger. But some accounts said it could look a tall man straight in the eyes."

"Yeah, I can see how that would be really creepy. What's it called again?"

"Amphicyon. As you may have guessed, they are also considered to be long extinct, dying out in the New World around two million years ago and in the Old World only 10,000 years ago. But they *could* have recrossed the bridge several times.

"An older account by the Lewis and Clark expedition tells of a rock painting featuring a giant black wolf-dog gripping a young deer in its snarling teeth with a curly shaggy mane that extended down the sloping back.

"In a more recent episode, an enormous black 'freak wolf' was shot in Idaho's Boise National Forest. A Wikipedia article noted that in addition to its enormous size, the body was covered with heavy black hair resembling the coat of a Newfoundland dog, but heavier and coarser, and the animal was bob-tailed. This is similar to reports of the Waheela, who decapitates people in the Nahanni Valley of the Canadian Northwest Territories."

Destiny's eyes were wide. "Wow! That's..." She was at a loss for words, so instead, she took a sip of tea.

"There are other reports, including a very large hyena-like animal the size of a big hog, weighing between four and five hundred pounds, with its tail tucked between its legs. Witnesses supposed it would measure between five to six feet tall at the shoulders. Another report told of a 'terrifying giant.' If it stood upright, it would have been over seven feet tall. In fact, one man, who stood six feet plus, saw a beast from the seat of his truck, at a distance of thirty feet. He said it was the size of a cow, and a genuine, life-threatening fear seized him. He explained that if he stood toe to toe with the brute, its head would be taller than him."

"Two others involved attacks on vehicles by a giant wolf-dog or ferocious hyena-like creature. One ran out of the forest and bit a truck tire, causing the vehicle to swerve while the assailant fled back into the woods at a high speed. In a second incident *an enormous prehistoric-looking, almost horse-sized hyena, as tall as the car and about half as long with a ridged or humped back, had rings around its body that culminated at the top of its head. It was hunched forward in stature, almost like a hyena, but not quite. It had wiry, dark, grey hair and walked in a kind of slinking motion with its back about five to five and a half feet off the ground.'* Of course, the viewer had seen nothing like this.

"In the last few years, there were a couple of reports of massive, hyena-like creatures spotted in rural Illinois along Route 37. One really opens the can of worms. A witness was driving near midnight in an area that has had sightings for over fifty years when a deer raced across the road in front of the car. A gigantic creature that took up a lane and a half slinked across the road like a stalking cat following it. The front haunches were like a hyena."

"Quote, *'I couldn't tell if it had a tail... I would have to say it reminded me of a werewolf, like on 'American Werewolf of London. That's what it reminded me of.'* After passing the point where the creature crossed the road, the driver turned around to see if they could see it again. *'No luck. I did see the deer trying to hide in a yard behind a few trees, laying there shaking as if it was terrified of something.'*"

"Destiny, do you know how many reports of werewolves there are?

Maybe this bear-dog explains the physical form attributed to such creatures, and there you go, Tarkio—the werewolf connection."

"Outside of Bigfoot, Amphicyons are the only creatures large enough and dangerous enough to freeze a human's blood from fear. Over half of the sightings fell into this gigantic beast sub-set."

"How big did you say?"

"If you put a six-foot-tall human next to a grizzly who stands on its hind legs at eight-feet-tall and weighs six to eight hundred pounds—then added an Amphicyon which stands on its hind legs at nine or ten-feet-tall and weighs nine hundred to one thousand pounds, the man probably should run and let the two animals fight it out."

Destiny put a hand over her mouth and nodded vigorously. Looking increasingly anxious, she crossed her legs. "That's big. That's what I saw!"

Tarkio, stunned by Destiny's admission, swallowed hard but said nothing. The room became quiet as everyone thought about the ramifications.

"As you see, there has been less of a break in sightings than in the fossil record—by far." Secora inhaled and closed her eyes for a moment. "Initially, I wanted to rule out the stories of monstrous creatures with impossible proportions. But, in the end, they made up the majority of the sightings. It's possible an Amphicyon is the large black predator Bill Hoffmann's family saw in Idaho."

Remembering her own experience, Destiny stopped Secora. "Oh, my God. That's enough. I'm not sure you should go out there at all."

"Are you okay?" Tarkio asked.

No answer from Destiny.

"This is why I am not as eager as I once was to find Megafauna in the field."

Destiny took a deep breath and stood, saying, "It's after midnight. Be careful tomorrow. I pray this is not what our student's family is dealing with. I'm looking forward to your report. Let me know if you need anything from me."

10

CONFRONTATION OF DOOM

Early the next morning, with two coffees and before meeting Tarkio outside of Dean Hawkins's door at 6:50 a.m., Secora printed copies of her findings.

The young man arrived wearing hiking boots and lowered a duffel bag to the floor.

"I couldn't stop thinking about the 'extinct' animals we talked about. You're right, Secora. There could be pockets of survivors that persisted until the present or that might have died out fairly recently before being officially recognized."

Secora shook her head. "It's frustrating that people parrot back what they learn without investigating things for themselves. It bugs me when they deny the existence of documented individuals without demonstrating a compelling end in the fossil record. They find two teeth and speculate about their range, what they ate, and when they became extinct, yet are hesitant to accept very specific descriptions in a variety of reports given by people who have no idea they are extinct."

Both turned when they noticed Dr. Hawkins had joined them.

"Very interesting." She changed her coffee to her left hand, dug keys out of her pocket, and jingled them into the lock before ushering her guests inside. She smiled. "Breathe, Dr. James."

"Thanks. It's just that I'm finding *way* too much descriptive information about supposedly extinct animals in modern sightings. Most folks don't know their names, let alone that they've passed their expiration dates."

"What do you mean?"

"Witnesses offer details unlikely for anyone to know regarding these long-vanished creatures, like size, coat color, white guard hairs, manes, and stance. A few even described habitats and foods they ate from pronghorns to prairie hens. How could anyone know that?"

Tarkio said, "It would be pure speculation. Unless they saw one."

Destiny suggested, "Okay. Let's focus on today. If you're right, you are about to make a discovery that could be devastating."

Secora inhaled deeply. "True, if you don't mind, I'd like to text my husband to come along. He's good with a rifle."

Destiny looked surprised. "Definitely. Go ahead."

Tarkio excused himself to make a bathroom stop while Secora texted Gideon.

When he returned, Tarkio said, "I met the motor pool guy in the hall and got the keys from him." He swung a high-five Secora's way. Then, picking up his duffel bag and backpack, he urged, "Time to go."

"Listen, I've got another meeting... Keep me posted."

Secora hefted her worn sorrel leather backpack over her shoulder, said, "Goodbye," and gently closed the door.

At the stairwell, Tarkio turned to say, "We should probably think twice about looking for an animal that can cause someone grief just by thinking about it."

"I think it goes far beyond that when you see the animal of your doom."

Secora was already tired from rising at 4:00 am for the meeting with Destiny, but nearing the parking lot, the fragrance of a rose in bloom enlivened her. She took a breath of the perfumed air and stretched. Her phone rang, breaking her focus on a deep bend.

The call was from Iris, who wanted to remind her that their father's second taped talk would be this Saturday at the university auditorium.

"Listen to me, sis, I agree this is important, but I have to drive to Bonners Ferry today, and it may take a day or two to track down an animal. If I don't get back in time, I hope to help you with the next one. My boss is adamant that I go, or at least she was yesterday. Hopefully, I will be back tomorrow—or the next day at the latest."

She ended the call. "Okay, love you too, bye."

Anida and young Frederic arrived with an extra lunch and snack bag for Tarkio. They stood off to the side of the street, saying their goodbyes. Anida kissed Tarkio. Then he kissed both of them twice, and they left the parking lot.

Tarkio walked toward Secora with a determined look, maybe tinged with a touch of sadness.

"Are you nervous?"

"Kinda weird to say goodbye to your wife before heading off for a long drive to find an imaginary animal, at best. At worst, something more like a fierce werewolf."

Secora smiled. "You're right. Not every job offers such amazing perks."

Gideon pulled up and parked his truck. He grabbed his backpack and a rifle boot with a 30.06 rifle inside. After stowing them in the back of the university passenger van, he kissed Secora and then hopped into the front seat with Tarkio, who was already at the wheel.

"Did you pack a lunch, Gideon?"

"Of course. For both of us. Our favorite travel food—PB&J."

Secora had brought her other PB&J lunch from the fridge at the office. "Okay, then we're covered."

Secora preferred to ride in one of the middle seats for a better 180-degree view. She thought they could pick up anything else they needed along the way. Briefly, she imagined herself asking a perky gas station attendant if he could sell her a howitzer.

AN HOUR DOWN THE ROAD, Secora noticed Gideon had become still and eerily quiet. "Honey?"

There was no response. So, she asked Tarkio to pull off the road. She hopped out and opened Gideon's door. It was as she thought. Assisted by his counterpart, Wakinyan Tanka, Gideon was having a seizure/vision. She reached into her backpack and pulled out one vial of seizure medicine that Guillermo had prepared for her husband. Then, with Tarkio's help, she drizzled some on his tongue.

As he recovered, Gideon told Secora he hadn't understood what the ancient bird was showing him. "There was a thunderstorm and strange animals in a strange land. She dived toward one of the creatures the way she had before, and it made me feel terribly sick."

"Could you tell if it was in the past or the present?"

"I don't know. Maybe the future?"

"Does that make sense if she is dying?"

"No, it doesn't. At least, not yet. I'm okay now. Let's keep going."

THE DRIVING distance of two hundred forty-one miles between Missoula and the ranch outside of Bonners Ferry took them over four hours via I-90 and US-95 with one gas stop.

The little town had grown from its beginnings as a river crossing in the 1860s, serving the prospectors who were heading out to discover gold in Canada. It was now the seat of Boundary County and had a population of about 2,500 of "Idaho's friendliest" residents.

When they arrived at Bill's neatly maintained manufactured home, they stiffly tumbled out to stretch and give the Hoffmann family a chance to prepare for company. Tarkio placed the camera around his neck, then the trio wandered up to the cranberry-colored door of the doublewide and knocked. No one answered. They knocked again and Secora peered into the darkened kitchen window.

"Hmmm, there's a car in the driveway." Secora pulled out her phone to call the number. "No bars."

Gideon said, "Looks like a truck pulled out of here. Fresh tracks."

They wandered around the property looking for clues. Gideon and

Secora checked inside the barn, where the only animals they found were cats.

Tarkio hollered from outside. "I think I see something."

The couple hustled over. He was shading his eyes with his hand, and when they followed his gaze, they noticed a sow bear with cubs eating a cow carcass.

Tarkio asked, "Maybe that's what has been bothering their animals?"

Secora was hesitant. "Could be, I suppose. But we have to remember Bill is a paleontology student. Hopefully, he would know if they were seeing a bear with cubs."

Suddenly, a large dark blur rushed from the woods into the field and swatted the sow's head, flipping her body, and she lay still where she fell. Gideon drew up the rifle and prepared to shoot.

Secora grabbed his arm, stopping him. "What if there are two? We need to get away from here right now."

Safely back inside the vehicle, she said, "Take some pictures, Tarkio. Gideon, can you use your Satfon to call 911? We can't do this by ourselves. Shooting it would likely piss this creature off."

Gideon looked shocked to see Secora scared. "I have never known you to back away from anyone or anything." He immediately called 911. Dispatch would send the game wardens.

Tarkio surmised, "If that animal wanted to open this van up, we'd be like waiting sardines."

Gideon rubbed his jaw. "Yeah, I doubt that mobile home could withstand a full-on attack from an angry—whatever that thing is. I'm guessing that's why the family is not here."

"Maybe." Tarkio tried a few photographs from this side of the pasture. When he looked at the results, he said, "Even with the telephoto lens, I doubt this blur will be sufficient for an identification."

"Just another blobsquatch?" Gideon referred to the requisitely bad photos people took of Bigfoot.

"It will have to do. We aren't going any closer until it's gone. Too bad."

When she looked out again, the animal was dragging the whole cow carcass away in its powerful jaws. "Okay."

The crew drove slowly to the kill site in the meadow to see if they could record tracks or recover any kind of evidence.

Secora stared into the trees. "I think it is watching us," she whispered.

Gideon shrugged, "Probably."

When they crept forward together in tandem and peered into the woods, they saw the rear of the animal trotting away from where it had been watching from the trees. Before disappearing from sight, it looked back at them over its shoulder, deciding to leave the carcass remnants behind.

A barn cat walked over and wound its way through Gideon's legs, startling everyone.

Tarkio said, "I'm half afraid that if we look too hard, we'll see human body parts out there. Secora, I'm beginning to understand the dread you must have felt with those terror birds."

She didn't answer right away as she thought about it.

Gideon spoke, "We're getting too old for this kind of thing. Except for you Tarkio—maybe."

Tarkio nodded. "But if we don't collect some data, this creature will be tracked down, killed, and erased from the record without much more than a footnote saying a wolf-like creature was shot near the Canadian Border."

Gideon concurred, "True. No government agency who denies the existence of Sasquatch will allow rumors of something like this to escape into the news." He walked to the van and started the engine. When he returned, he said, "Maybe that will intimidate the creature while Tarkio takes his photos."

Secora nodded and checked the drag trail through the grass. As she was doing so, the rickety-looking barn cat rubbed against her leg. "Hey kitty, you need to be careful out here. You'd barely make a gourmet snack." Then, her eyes followed Gideon, who was on his way over to check the sow who lay still on her side.

"She's alive."

Secora and Tarkio came over to see her panting in unbearable pain. Her small cubs cuddled beside her. It was a miserable sight.

"Her spine must be broken. She doesn't even try to lift her head." Tarkio was using the video camera as they discussed the situation. Gideon was prepared to put her out of her misery when they noticed a vehicle joining them in the meadow. At first, they thought it was the family returning to find the university van in their pasture. But it was a Fish and Game vehicle.

Two wardens approached the trio and asked what happened. Gideon related how the animal rushed out and hit the sow.

Gideon offered his rifle to one of the wardens to put the poor creature down. It was at that point the family truck also joined them, followed by a sheriff's SUV.

The game wardens questioned each of them about the death of the sow grizzly. One noted the tag number in her ear. Gideon told them he hadn't shot her, which the warden confirmed by inspecting the gun and the carcass before he ended the suffering. "We'll be doing a necropsy. I'll need your contact information just in case we need further info."

Then the sheriff rechecked Gideon's rifle. The game warden had fired the only shot.

The Hoffmann family remained in their vehicle. From the driver's seat, the father rolled down his window and asked, "Did you get him?"

Secora asked Tarkio to join her as she walked over to introduce herself. He said he would join her as soon as he finished filming the wardens as they tranquilized the cubs and loaded them and the dead sow into the back of their vehicle. Instead, Gideon went with Secora to meet the traumatized family.

"I'm Dan Hoffmann, my wife Elena, and of course, you already know our son, Bill. Is that the beast?" He nodded toward the dark lump he couldn't see in the grass.

"Afraid not, sir. I'm Secora James and this is my husband, Gideon Yellow Thunder. When we arrived, we saw a sow grizzly with her two cubs at a carcass out there."

The Hoffmanns' faces drew back in protest.

"We were wondering if she might have been the source of your vexation when a dark blur—much larger than a wolf, larger even than the bear, flew out of the trees and charged the sow smacking her with a paw and breaking her neck and spine," Secora said.

Tarkio walked up to join them, capping his lens. Secora introduced him as he took out the sim card and replaced it, dropping the case with the used card into Secora's backpack.

He explained, "In case the camera gets confiscated."

The others nodded.

Bill said, "Hey, let me see the camera."

Tarkio happily greeted Dan and Elena, then he reached through the window with the camera. Bill took some quick shots of the barn cat, the forest, the meadow, and a trio of vultures in the sky.

"This will look better. It won't be such an obvious dodge."

Tarkio grinned and nodded before he excused himself to return the camera to the van.

Bill asked. "So, you saw it?"

"Yes, from the other side of the meadow—but we all saw it," Secora replied.

Elena wrinkled her nose and asked, "Well, what is it?"

Bill said, "I have a crazy idea."

Secora encouraged him, asking, "What do you think it is?"

"I don't think it's a wolf."

"I think you're right. Go on..."

"Could it be... an Amphicyon?"

"Darn good question." Secora stared at him a moment, then said with all sincerity, "Bill, I believe you are right." She smiled. "Thinking out of the box like that just earned you an 'A' for my class."

Bill seemed shy in front of his parents but pleased, nonetheless.

Gideon added. "But don't get attached to being right. I doubt anyone else will believe us."

Elena sighed. "It does feel like we have been threatened by the animal on the one hand and the government on the other."

Dan said, "I imagine they'll send out hunters, and we'll hear no more of it. At least I hope so."

Tarkio joined them and added, "If Amphicyon still exists, it is *the* apex predator. If they can dispatch it or chase it away from the area, that should make your lives a lot easier."

"Even if many paleontologists insist that it's extinct," muttered Bill.

Secora looked up from the grass by the truck tire and said, "Yeah, well, you aren't the only people to have seen this type of animal recently, but it will take hard evidence to go public with a statement about it."

Tarkio said, "We collected a few samples and photos which may or may not be of value in this effort. Bill will know if anything definitive comes from what we've found. In the meantime, we'll put game cameras all around this pasture and your barn."

Gideon counseled, "Whatever you do, don't go out on foot or alone when you feed or check the cows."

Elena looked exhausted. "I dread living in fear of this thing. I can hardly sleep at night thinking it might tear our door down."

Dan placed his elbows on the steering wheel and let his forehead drop onto them.

"We can't keep losing stock. I don't have much of a financial cushion. We might have to sell out."

Gideon sympathized, "That's understandable. This animal is no joke. But there is a good chance the game wardens will track and kill it, or at least chase it away from the area. I doubt it will be back anytime soon."

Dan shook his head. "This *thing* and the bear both attacked in broad daylight. It's not like sticking the cows in the barn at night helps very much. Maybe there's a pack of them living in the area. I took a shot at one two weeks ago on a hilltop while it was eating my neighbor's sheep."

Secora was curious. "Do you have any blood drops, pictures, or anything from that kill?"

"No, but I'm pretty sure it died. It dropped to the ground after the shot, but it was gone by the time we got to the sheep carcass. There was a blood trail. I followed it until I got creeped out. Felt like it was watching my every move. My blood chilled, and I left. Don't know what my friend Sam will do. He can't take these losses either."

Secora asked, "Dan, could you see if Sam is willing to answer a few questions for us?"

"I'll give him a call."

Tarkio ventured, "I have another favor to ask."

Dan nodded and lifted his hands in helplessness. "Anything."

"If you wouldn't mind, I'd like to stay with you here tonight. Could I bunk on your living room floor?"

Dan looked to Elena, who said, "Yeah, sure. Maybe we'll sleep better."

"Me too?" requested Gideon.

"Great. There's room for all three of you."

LATER THAT AFTERNOON, the sheep farmer came for a visit, but in the end, there was little information to add to what they already suspected. Everyone seemed so 'down' that Secora offered to take them all out to an early dinner in town, which they gleefully accepted.

After dessert, Sam said, "If you do get a good picture, I want a copy."

"Sure, if we live to bring it back," Secora laughed.

Nobody else laughed.

THE DEN

The next morning, Secora woke early. She looked over at Gideon and gave his forehead a gentle kiss. He fidgeted but did not wake. She remembered how he had bravely remained beside her throughout all of her most frightening moments in the past, like when the assassins were preparing to make their moves to dispatch both of them at the Cliff City.

Sighing, she had just closed her eyes again when she heard Tarkio creep over, awake and excited. She rose, and they exited the house. They sat on the patio quietly listening to a late cricket and a few frogs while Secora combed her hair.

"In a parental sense, I'm very much against you staying here without us, Tarkio, while we look for that carcass over at Sam's place today."

"Secora, I am old enough to make my own decisions, and besides, I will be with two well-armed game wardens."

"I know, but Anida and Frederick... I worry."

"Boy, that's new for you. The Secora I know would salivate at the opportunity to join me."

"My path has crossed with dangerous beasts before. The outcome of such interactions is murky. Not everyone who meets these creatures makes it out alive. Survival—that's a bonus."

Gideon joined them, rubbing both eyes with his knuckles. "Secora, you should give him your Satfon. Tarkio, my number is programmed into it. Call me if there's the slightest problem." He sat on the step and stretched. "We'll be looking for the carcass of the beast on the neighbor's property." He yawned and blinked, waiting for Tarkio to nod.

Soon they noticed Elena at the door, inviting them in for scrambled eggs, sausage, home fries, and biscuits. They followed her and the delightful aromas into the dining room and dug into a wonderful breakfast that for a moment allayed Secora's concerns that this was likely to be an ominous day.

When the dishes were dried and put away, Secora wandered through the dining and living rooms, fascinated by lovely photos which had been blown up and hung as wall art. There were a series of deciduous tree panels showing closeups of leaves in the full range of fall colors that any child would wish to capture in her hand as she walked down an autumn street. The collage of purple, maroon, several shades of red and orange, green, gold, and yellow hues made her smile. Next, she noticed some evening horizon shots of black rocks against a layered blue-purple sky, featuring stars and meteors.

In the hall on the way to the restroom, she stopped at a black and white photo that captured a team of Belgian horses plowing a field, and inside the bathroom, she found a dramatic photo of white bear grass plumes shooting up from a super-steep green slope surrounded by clouded mountains that took her breath away.

She asked, "Bill, are these your handiwork?"

"Yes," he said shyly.

They heard a knock at the door, and Elena ushered the game wardens inside.

Introductions were brief, as the wardens shook hands with the family. Gideon and Secora hugged Tarkio, who by then felt like he was part of their family.

The senior warden, James, smirked, and said, "Don't worry,

ma'am. We handle wolves and bears for breakfast. We can handle him."

"Them, I'm not worried about. I'm afraid this is something far more dangerous."

"Like Bigfoot." They both laughed.

"More like a tiger. It may hunt you. Just be careful."

Both James and Frank, the other warden, chuckled again, but perhaps there was a slight edge to the laughter this time.

Tarkio said goodbye and followed them out the door, promising he'd give them a blow-by-blow account of the excursion. Secora sighed from her heart but smiled. It was time to let the crew move out.

Secora hollered after him, "You have bear spray on you, right?"

"Yes, Mom. Two cans."

"Okay, use my Satfon. Please keep in touch."

Gideon added, "Tarkio, Secora and I will be only a few miles away."

She turned to Gideon and said, "You'd better call Jeannie and Mitch to update them."

"I already did."

Gideon turned the vehicle around, then stopped. "Was there something just at the edge of the woods?"

Secora rolled her eyes. "Oh, I imagine there was."

He said, "I hate to leave."

"Didn't you say that thing probably wouldn't be back?"

"I don't feel so sure about that now."

While the Fish and Game vehicle was heading across the meadow toward the forest fence line, Secora said, "I understand. But being with them probably won't change the outcome. This way, we can be available to help if we're needed."

As they left, they noticed the family was already in their pickup, crawling down the two-track road towards town.

WHEN TARKIO and the other men climbed over the fence, everything appeared normal enough. Birds were singing, and Tarkio noticed a purple butterfly flapping erratically past their faces. The wardens walked ahead at a good pace, occasionally bending over to look at imprints in the pine needles.

Frank commented, "Looks like a grizzly paw print."

If it weren't for the remnants of the cow carcass, they would have found very little else.

At one point, Tarkio collected a sample of two-inch dark fur caught in tree bark. He wondered about where this thing had been taking the carcass. *Did it have a den? Could it be a female with cubs? What kind of den would such a creature have? Would it be underground?* Den choices in the open pine forest were, of course, limited. He thought about coyotes, then bears. *They go underground, but that doesn't mean this girl would. Pumas and other big cats might den up in the rocks.*

The men he was with had almost twenty years on him. They were puffing and took a break in a thick patch of conifers. The surrounding air turned chilly. Tarkio could see his breath as he sat on a rock and put his hands in his pockets. That wasn't enough, so he pulled his coat tightly around him. Little sunlight penetrated the thickly foliaged forest. He again put his hands in his pockets and pressed his elbows toward his ribs to conserve heat.

Finally, he said, "Guys, I'm feeling eerie, and I am cold all of a sudden."

James agreed, "Yeah, me, too. Frank, maybe we should call it a day."

Frank smiled. "I have a 30.06 that says you guys are making a mountain out of a molehill."

Tarkio continued, "Listen, this beast could easily be a female with cubs. Why else would she be dragging that cow around?"

"We don't want to be around a hungry sow with cubs, do we, Frank?"

"Okay James. What say we take the rest of the day to explore closer to the ranch area?"

James slowly rose, unholstering his pistol. Relieved, he whispered, "Yeah, that sounds sensible."

At that moment Tarkio felt an utter dread. Had he seen eyes flashing between twigs?

James said in a harsh whisper, "Frank, get up and walk behind us with your rifle at the ready. We are going to need eyes in the backs of our heads."

"What are you talking about?"

James whispered, "We're being hunted."

"Why are you whispering? Talking is better with bears."

They moved out towards what they felt would be the direction of the vehicle and the ranch and heard a definite snarl.

Tarkio popped the cap on the bear spray. Then he remembered the GPS on Secora's Satfon. As a precaution, he dialed Gideon.

"We're in a pickle here and heading back toward the vehicle at the ranch."

"Keep sharp."

"I have the bear mace."

"Maybe you should spray a little of it around you and on your pant legs and boots. Hold your breath."

"Good idea. If it doesn't like the smell, maybe it will back off long enough for us to make it."

"Hope so."

Tarkio could hear Gideon tell Secora to grab her coat and head for the car. He heard her answer that she was dialing 911. The young man sprayed the pant legs and boots of his companions. When he finished and could speak, he said, "Okay, I think we are safe to breathe."

Frank's bravado had left, and he had become noticeably shaken as they went forward again. "I've listened to YouTube Bigfoot stories for years. This feeling of being watched, and everything going too quiet could apply to this thing as well. Even the air is still—breathless."

Another snarl came from their right. It was all Tarkio could do to keep from running full out like a crazy man.

Frank asked, "Don't they have stories of wolfmen or some other large wolf creature that can stand on its hind legs and be seven to twelve feet tall?"

James said, "You don't think this thing can be that big?"

"I don't want to, but the lady is right. How many animals drag off a cow carcass rather than eat it where it falls?"

"Frank, get a grip. This is the last time we'll take a civilian into the field."

"Okay James, maybe so. But would you still be out there if you were alone?"

James's breathing was becoming a little ragged. "Hell no," and he began to trot.

"Now, there's something off to our left, too!"

"Whoa! What is that *stink*?"

"James, I think I shit my pants."

"Me, too."

There was a snarl, changing to a guttural growl down to their right. Then a deep roar with a subsonic tone erupted from the hillside to their left. Tarkio's head whiplashed from one side to the other.

Gideon said to Tarkio, "I've noted your location. You are only two and a half miles from the ranch but on a direct line. We'll be there soon."

"That's good." He relayed the information to the others. Then suddenly Tarkio was hit from behind. As he fell, he heard both the pistol and the rifle fire.

TARKIO FELT GROGGY. His sleep had been disturbed. Now he felt like he was being dragged off his bed, and there were muffled noises. No, they must be voices around him. He didn't want to open his eyes. He was afraid to open them. Instead, he called, "Frank?" Then after a pause, "James?"

There might have been a groan. Tarkio was still lying on his back and couldn't open his eyes. Without warning, he was picked up and carried off—not by puncturing jaws he was relieved to discover, but like a potato sack. The air reeked. He was uncomfortable bouncing along, and he allowed darkness to overtake his agitation.

12

HIGH RESOLUTION

"Hurry, they're under attack," Gideon yelled, getting into the vehicle.

Secora hit the gas. Sam's ranch was ten minutes from the meadow. "I hope the sheriff is closer, and he arrives before we get there."

As if by magic, they heard a siren crescendo. Secora saw the lights and pulled over for the cruiser to pass.

Gideon told her he'd heard a roar on the phone and a scream for "Help." Three shots were fired before the Satfon went quiet.

Moments later, the university van pulled up to the forest fence, but Secora and Gideon couldn't see any people—just the cruiser with its lights still on and doors left wide open. Secora sniffed the air. "I smell a faint, pungent odor."

"Me, too." Gideon passed through the gate, his rifle at the ready. There were no other sounds.

"Everything is too quiet."

They followed the path of bent grasses when they could. Occasionally, there was a partial heel indent. Gideon stopped to look at the Satfon GPS. "We seem to be heading in the right direction. We're about a mile out from where the phone fell, and I last heard Tarkio with the game wardens."

There was no mistaking the snarl they heard off to their left. "Almost sounds like a bear," noted Secora, as she whirled to face that direction.

Gideon stopped with her. Then they crept toward the noise, all their senses alert.

"Honey, I'm seeing drops of wet blood on the grass. I'm going to collect a sample for DNA testing." She took off her backpack and put on a pair of gloves to swab a sample, while Gideon hollered, "Tarkio. Tarkio, where are you?"

There was no response for a second, then they heard a call from the direction of the game warden's path. Gideon jogged toward the noise while Secora noted where and when she had collected the sample and followed him.

Suddenly, someone was shouting from behind her. She turned again and squinted back toward the fence. It was Bill, running full out toward her and yelling, "I heard the sirens and knew there was trouble, so I took the pickup and came back as quick as I could."

He reached her puffing and anxious. "What... what happened?" He puffed again. "Is anyone hurt?"

"Gideon is up ahead. Let's catch up and see. Be aware, Bill, I think there's a large animal off to our left. It growled a warning for us to stay away."

"G-r-e-a-t, no problem. I don't have a weapon."

"Me neither."

Secora smelled the dry pine needles as they crunched their way through the brush. It was about three minutes before they could see Gideon through the shrubs. He was standing near a clump of trees with the deputies. Secora couldn't hear what they were saying, but she took a careful 360 degree look around before approaching them.

Bill looked terrified. "What's that horrible smell?"

Secora shook her head but said nothing. The deputies looked them over and asked them to identify themselves. They showed their IDs, and Gideon vouched for both of them.

Secora bent down to examine the evidence.

Bill pinched his nose and said, "That's a crazy amount of excrement."

One deputy asked, "How many men did you say were here?"

Gideon replied, "Three men—two game wardens and a paleontologist from the university."

"And one Bigfoot." Secora looked up when no one commented. "I think the Bigfoot was using excrement as a weapon to deter the animal which originally attacked the men."

"Okay, ma'am, do you understand how ridiculous that sounds?"

"I do. You got something better?"

Bill said, "That would explain some of this... but where are the bodies?"

"We've called into dispatch for a search team and dogs. Until then, they are officially missing."

"There have already been several disappearances in this county and across into Canada this spring."

Another deputy said, "That's none of their business."

Secora took a step toward him. "Well, it kinda is. The university expects Tarkio to teach classes on Monday, and I'll need to call his wife and son. Surely the game wardens also have families."

Bill advised, "I think Secora and Gideon should go in while we wait for the search team."

Gideon sensed a hesitation with the deputies, so he pushed a bit further. "It would be like having a tracker go in before the search teams."

"We can't let you do that. You could ruin the trace evidence."

Three knocks rang out as if someone was sending a signal by whacking a tree with a chunk of wood.

Secora said, "One or more of them might be alive. In that direction. We could check it out without messing up the evidence. You can direct the search from here."

Bill said, "By the way, your dogs might want to check out the blood drops on the grass about a mile back and to the South."

A deputy said, "That's probably from the cow carcass."

Secora asked, "Do dead cows snarl? I heard a warning growl off to my left at that position, and the blood was wet."

The deputies' faces registered disgust and possibly a little fear. One said to Gideon, "Hey, use your Satfon and keep us updated." Then the two of them headed back toward the farm.

Secora asked Bill to photograph the attack site while she and Gideon took samples of excrement and blood, marking their positions at the scene. She pointed out deep claw marks on a nearby tree to Bill, who photographed them. Then she took a swab from the fresh scratches. They headed uphill toward the west-northwest, toward the knocks. The trail was fairly easy to follow as there were occasional deep impressions of a large human foot, along with beaten-down grass and other signs. It became clear there was more than one creature passing through.

Gideon sniffed the lingering pungent odors in the air. Secora wasn't the only one who noticed. They stopped to listen. Things were perfectly silent until Bill snapped a photo of a rare mountain orchid. She smiled and said, "Send me a copy of that, will you?"

Then another set of three knocks came from several miles away. However, they continued to follow the tracks and the scent. When they arrived at the base of a hill to the North, Secora thought she could smell blood. "Wait. Just a moment." She closed her eyes and tried to use telepathy to let everyone know these three meant no harm. *Please let us help our friend and any who live.* There was a single knock above their position.

THEY ARRIVED at the biggest tree in the area and found two bodies surrounded by a circle of what must be urine and feces.

Gideon explained, "To ward off dangerous intruders." He bent down and checked for signs of life. One warden and Tarkio were alive but unconscious. "No sign of the third man."

"I should call the deputies to bring medics. Why don't you two say prayers and leave offerings up a hundred yards or so?" She took a PB&J and a baggie of dried apricots out of her backpack and gave them to Bill. Gideon took a sandwich and raisins from his lunch, and they left. She called after them, "Be sure to put them in a tree—preferably high enough to be out of reach for a dog or man."

She dialed the number she had been given. As she spoke to the deputies, she could hear the men climbing over rocks and fallen trees above with their gifts and their gratitude.

It took a half-hour for the rescue crew to arrive. The warden, James, regained consciousness on site but had nothing to say about what had happened. Gideon and Secora found out later that Tarkio roused on the way to the hospital.

The search dog found the third man partially devoured. Frank lay with his head knocked away from his body in the area where Secora had heard the growl. Nothing further was noted about the attack or any of the unseen creatures in the official record.

LATER, after checking out of the hospital, Tarkio would say, "That was the weirdest thing! How did I ever make it out alive?" He remembered the eerie feelings they had of being watched—no, hunted. Something had rushed in from the left, the side James was on. Both men fired at a dark blur. Tarkio remembered being hit from behind. "Why wasn't I killed?"

Secora iterated, "Don't overthink it. If you survive, it's a bonus."

Tarkio scratched his head. "It was because I had help, wasn't it?"

Gideon chuckled. "Looks like you had a friend or two in high places and us."

A DAY LATER, in Secora's lab, Bill was helping her prepare the samples to send in for DNA testing. He asked, "Do you think they'll figure it out?"

"Not much chance we'll get back anything definitive, but I'm pretty sure we can rule out bears or wolves."

"My folks are selling off the cattle and the ranch."

"Where will they move?"

He shrugged. "Still up in the air."

She started putting equipment away and picked up the mailer with the samples. "Too bad. I think they have powerful friends in the area. The sort that won't take guff from most predators."

"Yeah, my parents don't know that. Don't take this the wrong way, Dr. James, but I don't want to study Pleistocene megafauna anymore."

She smiled at him and said, "Let's close up here and head over to Montana Pies for a slice and some coffee." She hit the light switch and closed the door. "I'd like to talk to you about photography." As they started down the hallway, she said, "You seem to have a gift."

13

WEAH WASHTAY

Secora needed time for rest and recovery after the crazy week that ended in chaos near Bonners Ferry. Everyone, even Gideon, thought she was tough enough to handle anything life threw her way, but she hadn't fully processed her feelings about what had happened to those around her. She craved an opportunity for reflection. Enter her dear uncle-friend who called her with an invitation.

Jimmy Lizardeye was a sweet wichasha wakan, a Lakota holy man with a sacred gift of sight and extraordinary prayers, who had earned both her love and respect many times over. He seemed ageless, but the truth was Jimmy was entering the "I don't remember ever owning a droid" stage. Recently, however, he'd found a lady friend. Or rather, she found him. He described her as "a seeker extraordinaire," and this was the day he invited Secora over to his home off Bigfoot Road to have a glass of iced tea and meet her.

She was enjoying the ten-plus-hour drive to South Dakota. Even without the trauma and drama of last week, school had become fatiguing toward the end of the quarter, and she was happy to leave town. The next rest stop, just up the road, would present an opportunity to breathe the fresh piney air and hear the wind rustle the branches.

She found a parking space near a picnic table adjoining a large

82

ponderosa. Taking a sip from a bottle of water and a mouthful of a PB&J, she relaxed and smiled. She'd learned to love this type of sandwich from her dad, who almost always had one in a baggie stashed somewhere in a pocket or a pouch during his traveling days. She thought about Sage's upcoming discussion on the 'First' Prophets. *Ought to be a good one*, she thought.

A squirrel caught her attention as it hopped onto the bench beside her. She pinched off a piece of sandwich and tossed it about midway between them. Any closer might scare the creature. *Enjoy the peanuts.*

Secora's mind wandered to Bill. She pushed the button next to his number. "Hey, I hope you have time to finish our last conversation."

Bill told her he'd been staying at the mobile home on the property until they sold it. He asked what she wanted to do about the game cameras they had left behind. He could bring them by the lab next week if it would help. There was a picture, or perhaps two, which he wanted to show her.

She told him there had been no results yet from the testing. It was a long and very expensive process. She'd been filling out applications for grant funding to cover part of the outlay. Maybe they would hear something in six months at the earliest. Even then, the samples would likely be 'inconclusive,' as they probably didn't have type specimens for Bigfoot or bear dogs yet.

He said he had been to a shrink and was feeling better about the event. Would he come back? He didn't know. But there were classes at the university that still interested him. As she hung up, she harbored hopes of seeing him around campus, even if he pursued another course of study.

The squirrel had scampered off. It was now early afternoon, and the azure sky held no clouds. There was a light breeze, and it was pushing eighty-three degrees. Secora walked to the car on a mat of pine needles, thinking, *this is heaven*. One last deep breath of pine-scented air, and it was on to the last leg of her journey.

A plethora of thoughts occupied her mind during the rest of the drive. In particular, Jimmy. *Must have been the wedding bouquets he caught at our wedding.* She chuckled out loud, remembering his embarrassment and a slight smile as he headed for the sanctuary of the men's bathroom afterward.

Jimmy had recently told her he ran into this delightful woman one day at a gas station and from the moment he'd spotted her, his eyes never wanted to leave hers. This turned out to be a good thing since she had made the trip to Pine Ridge specifically to find him.

He referred to her as 'Weah Washtay'—a good woman. Strike that, a remarkable woman in her early fifties, with the verve and exuberance of a twenty-five-year-old. It made Jimmy laugh to watch her. "And she likes animals," he'd assured Secora over the phone.

According to Jimmy, Weah Washtay was born in the mountains of Colorado, and though a Christian family raised her, she'd studied the Bhagavad Gita and turned toward Sri Krishna as God's representative. Although some people she grew up with made fun of her ways, she was a down-to-earth servant of God—not the whacked-out hippie girl or wannabe that some accused her of being.

Apparently, she was working on personal growth, trying to banish the 'insistent ego' when she read a book on the life of Black Elk by John G. Neihardt. Naturally, she became interested in Lakota spirituality, and the way warriors called heyokas tried to remind people they were spiritual beings living in temporary bodies in a foreign place. Heyokas warned people should not blindly follow the information they heard from others. They should personally seek the spirit of the world around them and the creatures in it. Heyokas encouraged them to remember they were children of the Great Spirit, our 'Grandfather.'

Not surprisingly, the spirituality of South Dakota appealed to her. A few months ago, she took a trip to wander throughout the state during spring vacation. She stopped to eat at a diner in Rapid City where she heard someone talking about a hermit named Lizardeye, who spent his early years in a southwestern pueblo, later moving to South Dakota after a traumatic stint in Desert Storm. Now he lived with the family out on a lane off of Bigfoot Road who had saved him.

After their first magical meeting, Weah Washtay had returned to her job at the university in Western Montana. She came over on weekends to see Jimmy, and conversely, he saw her when he'd drop by to visit Gideon and Secora in Missoula.

If this meet and greet went well, Secora was thinking of offering to drive both of them back to Missoula to stay at her home as guests, so they could be present for Sage's talk on Saturday. She would soon discover that they had made their own plans for the trip.

Her car was crawling down the lane to the trailer when she spotted Jimmy sitting on the porch, raising a hand that held a glass of lemonade in greeting when she pulled up and parked. The radio weatherman had said, maybe over ninety degrees outside. The scorching sun smacked her face when she left the car and walked up the five steps to hug her uncle.

His arms gently encircled her. "Thought you'd never get here, Kimimila."

The door creaked open, and a woman came out balancing a small tray of iced tea glasses. Her hair lay in long waves. The burnished thick mane, nearly black, was streaked with a few silver strands that glistened in the strong sunlight. Her eyes were a striking light color of brown and the irises looked like cross-cuts of logs to Secora. Long twisted silver hoops hung from her ears, and she exuded an uncommon grace. Dimples appeared when she smiled or laughed, which, Jimmy said, happened a lot.

Secora met her with a smile as the realization dawned that she knew this enigmatic woman. "Wow, this *is* a surprise."

"Have a seat." Destiny Hawkins laughed almost shyly as she seated herself beside the little patio table that held the tea tray. "A genuine surprise for me, too. Jimmy was mentioning you as 'Sloth Girl,' and 'Kimimila.' I had no idea."

"Hard for me to picture you as a whacked-out hippie girl."

Jimmy chuckled, "I take it you two know each other?"

Secora shaded her eyes with her left hand. "Yeah, Jimmy. She's, my boss."

14
ARYAN PRE-HISTORY

After picking up information packets by the door, Gideon and Sage entered the auditorium to find an audience charged with excitement. They quickly found seats to hear Sage begin his discussion. It took an extreme dimming of the lights to get people to simmer their conversations. The banner above the stage read:

> *Like radii of the same circle, all these traditions indicate a common center... long before the India of the Vedas, before the Iran of Zoroaster, one sees the first creator of the Aryan religion emerging from the forests of ancient Scythia.*
>
> — SCHURE, THE GREAT INITIATES, 1889

Footlights came up on Sage as he walked to the end of the stage and said, "Humankind has been on our planet for almost six million years and so-called modern man, for only a quarter of a million years in Africa. So, it is no surprise that the vast majority of our Prophets were not Homo sapiens, sapiens."

He scanned the crowd and smiled. "Good. It doesn't look like anyone fainted."

That got some great laughs and a few confused looks.

"Prophets not only spoke in different languages and dialects but also with the tongues of different kinds of humanity. The great Zoroastrian scholar, K. E. Eduljee, disclosed to us the fact that ancient human varieties have occupied sites in the Central Asian area now known as Tajikistan for as long as 900,000 years. That is nearly a *million* years of both human prehistory and history, folks. But in 1991, a skull found in Georgian cave, at Dmanisi, about ninety miles southwest of Tbilisi in the river valley of Mashavera took the date back to 1.85 million years in Eurasia. That, my friends, is nothing short of stunning! Some of us stepped out of the African homeland almost two million years ago. When I went through college, we were excited to say 42,000 years ago —*big* difference."

The gasps and sporadic laughter from the audience sounded like a release. These people were getting used to Sage's zingers.

"This means what we can dig from the prehistory of the Zend Avesta and other Zoroastrian literature such as the Bundahishn and the Epic Shahnameh of Ferdowsi, is humanity's history—and it includes several distinct forms of human beings, united by their faith in God, their culture, and language. We will look at all three topics today."

Dr. Jane Roanhorse came forward dressed in deerskin and beads, hair in braids.

"I'd like to share with you a breathtaking early prayer on behalf of all the tribes covering the earth. The Svetesvatara Upanishad is hauntingly beautiful, and it rings as true as if it was written yesterday, rather than the Stone Age! I suspect it came from around 14,000 years ago when the first monuments and cities were built. It might have come from Rama, but the actual time or name of the Prophet doesn't matter. This spiritual treasury was part of an oral tradition protected by pure-hearted Rishis, ancient sages, who bore these Eternal Truths in mind until they could later be placed on paper. Bless them forever!"

"Here are excerpts of the—It is a long poem, a deep rendering of God's relation to the cosmos and its creatures in the heroic Aryan tradition. In that way, it reminds me of the elf ballads of Tolkien—but better. It is a candidate for the world's oldest remembered, and eventually recorded prayer."

> *O Brahman Supreme! Formless art Thou, and yet Thou*
> *bringest forth many forms; Thou bringest them*
> *forth, and then withdrawest them to Thyself. Fill us*
> *with thoughts of Thee!*
> *Thou art the fire, Thou art the sun, Thou art the air,*
> *Thou art the moon, Thou art the starry firmament,*
> *Thou art Brahman Supreme;*
> *Thou art the waters—Thou the Creator of all!*
> *Thou art woman, Thou art man, Thou art the youth,*
> *Thou art the maiden, Thou art the old man tottering*
> *with his staff; Thou facest everywhere.*
>
> *Thou art the dark butterfly; Thou art the green parrot*
> *with red eyes. Thou art the thunder cloud, the*
> *seasons and the seas. Without beginning art, Thou,*
> *Beyond time, beyond space. Thou art He from*
> *Whom sprang the three worlds.*
> *Maya (material Creation) is Thy divine consort—*
> *Wedded to Thee…Many are her children—The*
> *rivers, the mountains, Flower stone and tree, Beast*
> *bird and man—In every way like herself.*
> *Thou spirit in flesh, Forgetting what Thou art, Unitest*
> *with Maja—But only for a season. Parting from her*
> *at last, Thou regainest thyself.*
> *Forgetting his oneness with Thee, bewildered by his*
> *weakness, full of sorrow is man; But let him look*
> *close on Thee, know Thee as himself, O Lord most*
> *worshipful, and behold Thy glory—Lo this heavy*
> *sorrow is turned to joy.*

*Changeless art Thou, Supreme, pure! In thee dwell the
gods. The Source of all scriptures Thou art; Yet what
shall scriptures avail if they be smooth on the lip but
absent from the heart?*
To him who knows Thee comes fullness—to him alone!
*The Source of all scriptures Thou art; and the Source of
all creeds.*
One Thou art, one only. Born from many wombs,
Thou hast become many: Unto Thee all return.
*Thou Lord God bestowest all blessings, Thou the Light,
Thou the Adorable One. Whoever finds Thee finds
infinite peace.*
*Thou art Lord God of all gods, all the worlds rest in
thee; Thou art ruler of the beasts, two-footed, four-
footed: Our heart's worship be Thine! Thou art the
blissful Lord, subtler than the subtlest. In Thee alone
is there peace.*

*Thou, sole guardian of the universe, Thou lord of all. In
the hearts of Thy creatures, Thou hidest thyself.
Gods and seers become one with Thee. Those who
know Thee die not.*
*Of all religions thou art the Source. The light of thy
knowledge shining, there is no day nor night, nor
being nor non-being—Thou art alone.*
*Thou the Light imperishable, Adorable; Great Glory is
thy name. No one is there beside Thee; no one equal
to Thee.*
*Invisible is Thy form, invisible to mortal eyes; the seers
alone, in their hearts purified—*
They alone see The
*Neither male nor female art Thou, nor neuter; whatso-
ever form Thou assumest, that Thou art. Thou dost
pervade the universe, Thou art consciousness itself,
Thou art creator of time.*

Thou art the Primal Being. Thou appearest as this
universe of illusion and dream. Thou art beyond
time. Indivisible, infinite, the Adorable One—let a
man meditate on Thee within his heart, let him
consecrate himself to Thee, and Thou, infinite Lord,
wilt make Thyself known to him.
Thou womb and tomb of the universe, and its abode;
Thou Source of all virtue, destroyer of all sins—
Thou art seated in the heart. When Thou art seen,
Time and form disappear. Let a man feel Thy pres-
ence, let him behold thee within, and to him shall
come peace, Eternal Peace—to none else, to none
else! Let a man devote himself to knowledge of
Thee: All his fetters shall be loosed.

OM . . . PEACE—PEACE—PEACE.

"This was translated from Sanskrit by Swami Prabhavananda and Frederick Manchester in 1948. Even though 14,000 years ago seems primeval, the concepts are clear and distinct. The Revealer uses concepts with which we are familiar today. For instance, the *Universe — matter uniting with spirit then parting,* or *O Thou womb and tomb of the universe—and its abode. The Source of all scriptures Thou art; and the Source of all creeds.* Did you expect that sort of complexity from a stone Age Prophet?

"It shows us early forms of man were capable of knowing God as the source of all. Human religion didn't begin with fear of thunderstorms or eclipses. It was conscious awareness of a Creator in a life of illusion and dream. If you chose to embrace a religion, you would recognize sacred words from each and every Prophet—Krishna, Christ, and even Baha'u'llah as if they belonged to your savior. Because they are one, united by the Holy Spirit." She bowed her head, and the spotlight dimmed.

SAGE CAME FORWARD as Jane left. "Let's jump back twenty thousand years. To a time when the icepack began to melt and recede. Wave after wave of Proto-Indo-Europeans was freed from arctic lands. They descended through the snow-forested taiga, and wind-blown, grassy steppes of Siberia and northern Asia, to take advantage of opportunities provided by the changing climate.

"Over the next seven thousand years, the land became drier in the more southern latitudes, game dwindled. Hunger inspired domestication. Later, increasing herds prompted people to find fresh pastures for horses, camels, sheep, goats, and cattle."

A man in the audience, who stood about six-foot-seven-inches, unfolded himself to ask, "Excuse me. I did two tours in Afghanistan and became fascinated by the locals in the Helmond. One family I met told me about a book I could read, by a Porus somebody. Have you heard about that, Dr. Dalton?"

"Thank you, sir, and welcome home. In 1995, a semi-fictional historical novel on the origins of the Aryanpeople, entitled *The Saga of the Aryans*, was written by Porus Homi Havewala. It is interspersed with heroic verse in the great Aryan tradition. Think again of Tolkien's elven folk.

"It deals with the lives of the ancient Indo-Europeans about twenty thousand years ago who proudly called themselves the 'Noble Ones,' and considered themselves the first *Mazda Yasnis*, or worshippers of *Ahura Mazda*, God in the ancient tongue.

"In volume one of five books, he describes the Great Migration of the Aryan ancestors from their homeland in the Arctic Circle, where they had been debarred from moving further south due to glaciation. Although it was an Ice-Age, they lived in an arctic area surprisingly devoid of ice. Also, in the Vendidad, a historical part of the Zend Avesta, that great journey is authenticated."

"I have a quote." Sage flipped open a book he'd removed from a shirt pocket and read: "Trials and tribulations befell the ancient ancestors on their passage southward, as it unfolded towards Turkey, Greece, Poland, Germany, and the other nations and islands of Europe... They displayed great heroism against the bitter cold and blizzards, savage animals, and occasional barbarians whom they overwhelmed."

Sage looked to the audience. "Probably referring to local pockets of different types of humans—hunter-gatherers who were tragically fighting for their livelihoods, and unfortunately were overrun, probably with little regard.

"In other words, they completely covered Western Europe and Asia.

"These tribes seeded many civilizations, including the Hindu, Hittite, Persian, Greek, Russian, Roman, German, Celtic, and English, among others. We know this because all of these ancient people share the same ancestral Proto-Indo-European language base, as well as a similar religion and culture.

"Eventually, ice melt allowed them to go further south and west into a vast region of Central Asia that was sometimes called Greater Iran, or Greater Armenia - bordered by the pinnacles of the Pamirs, the Karakoram Range, and the Himalayas in the East, the Indus River in the south, and Turkey in the West."

Sage spotlighted a map at the back of the stage.

"You are aware that a major aspect of culture is our language. Early proto–Indo-European words are recognizable in many of today's languages.

"Let's look at the English word 'new.' In Old Irish Gaelic it was 'nue,' and in Sanskrit, 'navas.' In Hittite, 'newas,' in Greek 'neos,' and in Tocharian 'nuwe.' And 'naujas' in Lithuanian, and of course 'novus' in Latin. Is that not cool? *It's amazing!*

"Sometimes I'll be reading a passage in Sanskrit or another language I don't know, and still get the gist of what's being said.

"Here's another example. The word 'brother.' Twenty-thousand years ago it was 'bhrater' in Proto-Indo-European. "In the Germanic languages, 'broder' or 'bruder,' and 'phrater' in Greek, also 'frater' in Latin, and in Sanskrit, Celtic, and Avestan, 'bratar.'

"By the way, dokhtr meant daughter. Even today, Turandokht is a female Iranian name meaning daughter of Turan.

"Notice, if you will, an Aryan theme is developing: Turan, Eran,

Iran, Aryan, Eire, Airyanem. Even all of the 'stans' end in 'an'. You'll notice there are dozens of similar place names used in Europe and Asia today.

"The purity and unity of Airyanam Vaejo, the ancient Aryan Homeland, was its belief in Ahura Mazda—One God! Not in a purity of skin tone or hair color. There were dozens of shades. Take your pick. I'm sure that some of you were able to make out the word 'Viejo,' meaning 'old' because both English and Spanish are derived from the ancestral tongue.

"Rather than blond Valkyries, the Aryans were known as 'the Noble Ones' because of their submission to the will of God, plain and simple.

"At one time, we humans were a big Eurasian family. Pastoral tribes wandered all the way from China to the Western Sea, sharing a belief in one unique God—our Source, Sustainer, and Destroyer. At least, we did some of the time."

"During times of idol worship and again in more recent times, the Aryan Nation split into two or more main camps. Turanians occupied the upper areas of the region. South of Turan lay the ancient kingdom of Balkh, which encompassed lands from northern Iran, to Afghanistan, and to India. This is noteworthy because Zoroaster was killed in the storming of Balkh by a Turanian idolator. It was like Idol Worship had *temporarily* triumphed over the belief in One Creator.

"Those who are curious to find out more about these people can read the *Oxford Introduction to Proto-Indo-European and the Proto-Indo-European World*, by Mallory and Adams. Don't worry. It's in your information packet."

Mr. Hasan stepped beside Sage and put his hand in the air. "Dear guests, we have ten minutes before we are ready to serve dessert. Thank you." He left the stage.

Sage continued, "In summary, the early Aryans, rather than being a specific race, were tribes united by the ever-present Faith of God, rather than skin or hair tones. Layer after layer of prophetic revelations over many millennia became the roots of the Avestan and Vedic texts."

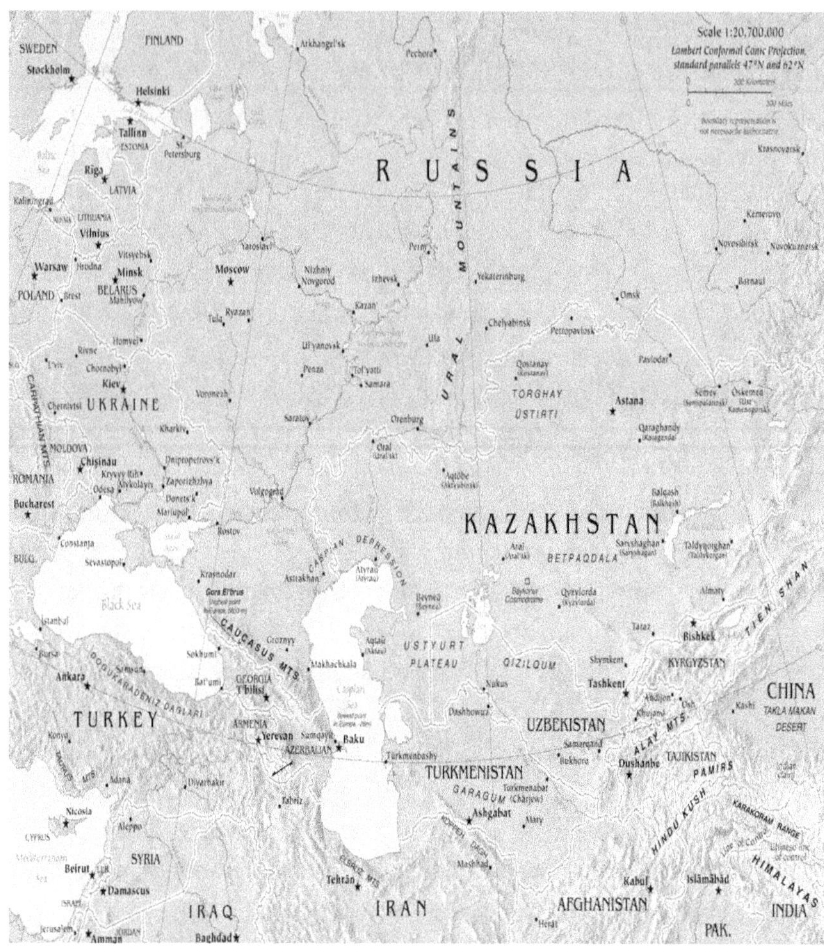

Russian and Central Asia Map

He looked directly at Secora, then said, "When we look at these earliest revelations, we see a sequential record of human development just like paleontologists and geologists peel through layers of the earth's history. The Aryan Prophets' names, with which we are most familiar, include Yima, Rama, Krishna, and Zoroaster. But we can unwrap the names of others and cross-reference them with bits from the Bible, the Chinese scriptures, and elsewhere, to lay out a framework for the northern continents over the last two million years. Thanks for listening. I appreciate your interest."

William Landsing came to the stage as Sage left. "Next Saturday, at ten in the morning, Dr. Dalton will present another topic, 'Creation and the earliest Prophets.' Enjoy a delightful breakfast. Then delight in a day-long mountain hike-and-ride, ending with a campfire meal on the trail. For those who are interested, join us back here for dinner."

There were whistles and cheers from the appreciative audience, who then eagerly embraced bowls of ice cream and a variety of cakes and pies.

L.W. had saved a seat for her beloved Sage, and his family gathered around, thanking him for such a meticulous and insightful explanation. After desert, Sage, L.W., and other family members remained to relax at the resort. Secora and Gideon said goodbye, hugging their loved ones, and left for Missoula.

On the way home, Secora received a call from Bill, which she put on speaker for Gideon's benefit. She answered with a smile. "Hey, what's up?"

"Just calling to get an update on Tarkio and to see if you've heard anything from the DNA lab."

"Just to let you know we're coming back from Glacier and will probably get cut off."

"Not a problem. Is Tarkio, okay? I think about what happened to him a lot."

"He's happy to be alive and seems to be coping fairly well. There is no lasting physical trauma. Mentally, it's a lot to process, even though he was unconscious through most of it. Like you, I think he has a different understanding about interacting with Pleistocene megafauna."

"Is he going to quit?"

"He has the summer to decide, but I doubt it. Hey Bill, we're coming to a place with almost no connectivity. I'll call you tomorrow if we get cut off." She sighed when she realized she was talking to no one. "I didn't even ask how he was doing."

"You'll lead with that next time," Gideon said to comfort her.

15

PEACE

The next week Tarkio arrived at Bill's trailer for a visit and to walk the grounds for an upcoming article on the Amphicyon events. He left the car and began stretching. A couple of barn cats greeted him before Bill met him at the door.

It was a sunny summer morning, and it wasn't long before they had hopped the fence between the pasture and the woods and began walking along a path into the timber.

"I found the game camera with the interesting photos about a half-mile in this direction." Tarkio nodded and noticed that the skinny old barn cat had not only followed them, but she ran out ahead on her adventure. Another fifteen or so steps toward the hill on their right, she stopped and hissed, fluffing, and arching her back. Tarkio heard a low, guttural growl which reverberated at an almost subsonic level.

As the men turned in that direction, they were astounded to see a large bear dog with its lips pulled back into a snarl not thirty feet away. Directly beneath her head was a cub that appeared to weigh three hundred pounds or more, bristling with its back arched like the cat.

Tarkio wilted in utter defeat, but oddly, neither of the gigantic animals moved a muscle. He could see that the adult's eyes, level with his own, were looking past him and Bill. Making infinitesimally small moves, he ventured a peek to the left and became rigid as he saw a large male Sasquatch, maybe twelve feet tall, with possibly 900 pounds of muscle fixing the predatory creatures in a non-verbal threat.

When he could find his voice, Tarkio whispered, "Bill, are you seeing this?"

"I seriously want to snap that picture, but I'm getting a distinct '*no*.' I'm setting the camera on the ground as a gesture of trust. Part of me reasons it would be worth my life to take that shot, but breaking his trust is unthinkable."

"Can you get the bear dogs with your camera on the sly?"

There wasn't a verbal answer, but Tarkio thought he could hear the click of a cell phone camera.

With eyes fixed on the threat, the bear dogs backed up, then turned, walked cautiously and stiltedly away from the standoff. By now, both men were in a submissive squatting position not looking directly at the forest man, until they heard *leave* in their minds, and *don't come back.*

They rose slowly to comply, and the man was gone. Bill snapped a photo of the fresh prints where the forest man had stood, and then they obediently turned to walk out of the woods.

"I'm going to make a big warning sign for the fence."

"What's it going to say?"

"Toxic chemical dump—guaranteed death for trespassers."

"What do you think the EPA will say?"

"I don't care," he laughed. "We got lucky twice—that's it!"

The skinny barn cat raced into the field ahead of them, having returned from whatever grass patch or cranny in which she had been hiding.

"Damn, she's brave!"

Tarkio said, "I'm thinking of adopting her in case you move. What will happen to the other cats?"

Bill shrugged. "I hate to think."

"Let's round them up and get them neutered. How many do you think there are?"

"Sure, we can do that. Guessing six or seven. I'm actually thinking of keeping this place. At least for a while."

Once they were safely inside, the men made a bunch of sandwiches, which included everything from Swiss cheese, baloney, and mustard to peanut butter and jelly. They threw in a couple of apples and two oranges, then packed everything in a bright yellow towel, suspending it from a tree that overhung the fence line for their benefactor. When they returned that afternoon, the towel, and its contents were gone, but there was a perfect smoky quartz crystal on the fence pole beneath the branch.

Bill said, "Okay, how about we get started on that article?"

"We?"

Bill grinned. "You heard me; I have photos."

16

TROUBLE AT WORK

Gideon climbed the stairs to his Missoula office thinking about Clive and Jimmy, who had been holding down the fort, so to speak, on the water projects near Porcupine Creek. The population of the area was only a few hundred residents, soon to expand with the low-income housing that was finally beginning to take shape.

His thoughts quickly vanished when Jeannie offered him a pastry on a napkin as he passed by her desk, saying, "This is going to be a wonderful day! I can feel it."

Gideon nodded. His phone rang as he sat down, chewing a bite before answering.

"Hey Yellow Thunder, this is Joshua Bader. You were looking at one of my properties in South Dakota for building low-income housing a few weeks ago."

"Yeah, Josh, I remember the piece, three acres, close to town. The owner had accepted an offer."

"That sale fell through, Gideon. And I'd like you to have it if you are still interested."

"Not so much Josh. I'm knee-deep in another project now."

"I understand, but how about an investment for the next project? I was counting on turning this property over without having to put money into it. You see, I picked it up for a friend, but their mortgage fell through and now there's no money to cover the payment."

"Ouch. I'm spread thin, myself."

Josh said, "I'm not gonna lie. I'm in a real pickle here. There must be something we could work out."

"That's sounding a little dangerous. Josh, let me text you a couple of numbers for realtors in California who are desperate for property outside."

"Okay man, thanks."

Gideon set the phone down as Mitch asked, "Who was that?" He had returned to Missoula after helping his grandfather adjust after losing his grandmother.

"Just a weird call. A little unsettling. The guy who had the other property we were considering is desperate to sell. The escrow fell through, and he doesn't want to get stuck with the payment."

"We've got our hands full with what we have, G."

Jeannie joined them. "And we are having trouble getting the drain field okayed by the county."

Gideon frowned. "Add to that, Clive says a few people have already squatted on the land."

Mitch joked, "Literally?"

Gideon smirked. "Both. Literally and figuratively."

"County won't like that."

"No. Jimmy is looking into getting an outhouse company to set up a couple of units on the land."

Jeannie pulled over a chair so she could sit. "We'll have four tiny houses to set up by next week—and no water."

Gideon's hand rubbed his brow. "Bottled water will work for cooking and drinking, but we need shower facilities and we don't..."

Mitch cut him off. "I know. We still need permits for the wells and the drains."

Jeannie said, "I'm trying to work with housing to find our first four homeless families and get the down payments escrowed. Right now,

Clive is outlining a row of yards, but without permits to dig, the fencing will have to wait."

Secora popped in with an early lunch, carrying it in a cardboard box. "Hey, everybody. Fried chicken, Cobb salad, Pecan Sandies, bottled grape, *and* grapefruit juice. Any takers?"

Mitch laughed. "Where are the fries?"

She smiled and pulled out a brown paper sack. "Have 'em right here, boss."

Things became quiet for a few minutes while everyone ate, then Gideon asked, "How are the finals going?"

"As you might expect. Bittersweet. An end to another year. Tarkio is grading papers for his first carnivore class and still working on the article with Bill."

Jeannie returned to her desk, grabbed a note, then asked, "Who owns the mineral rights for our property?"

"Why?"

"I received a call right before you came in telling us to stop construction until we test for uranium and other rare earth minerals."

Gideon could feel his usually calm nature transitioning into hot lava. "You have got to be kidding."

"No way." Even Mitch was caught off guard.

"There are nearly 170 abandoned uranium mines that operated in the Black Hills from the 1950s through the 1970s. We fought for them to stop. It's radioactive, it's toxic. It poisons creeks and our groundwater."

Jeannie looked down at the note. "I was told the United States nuclear power plants produce about 20% of our electricity. They need 100 million pounds of uranium annually, mostly imported from Canada, Australia, and Kazakhstan. They would like to investigate local sources."

"What's the deal? This didn't just happen out of the blue."

Gideon's office phone rang. Jeannie answered and handed the phone to him.

"Hello?"

"Hey, it's Josh again." Gideon hit the speaker button. "What's up, Josh?"

"I just heard mineral tests might delay your construction."

Jeannie bit her lip, and Secora listened intently.

"Is that something you did, Josh? Not a good way to win friends."

"Not me. I just need half a million for the other property. It's a bargain. Water and sewer are already in and a power line was dug."

"Josh, do you know anyone with half a mill sitting around collecting dust?"

"I'm desperate. How about your wife? Doesn't she work at a university?"

Silence reigned for a few moments. Secora wrote a note and showed it to Gideon.

"How much are you into the lenders for?"

"I'm already on the hook for half. Two hundred and fifty thousand. By the way, I think I can make the testing go away. I didn't start the trouble. It's some political wannabe. I know his family."

Exasperation showed in the faces of the Treasuremont crew.

"Sounds like blackmail. Call me in ten." Gideon hung up.

Secora said, "I have enough in my IRA, but the tax penalty would be massive. My dad has that kind of money but no desire for property. Any chance you could flip it?"

"I couldn't guarantee anything at this point, and now I don't trust this guy."

Gideon's phone rang again. On the speaker, Josh said, "I scraped up fifty-thousand. Any luck on your end?"

Secora signaled for Gideon to put Josh on hold.

"Dad is in town. I could give him a quick call and ask. It might get that guy off of our backs."

Gideon reddened and his face twisted with the words he wanted to say. He tried to muster patience before resuming the call. "Josh, you should come over, and don't pull anything like this again, or you will pay the consequences for the blackmail."

"I understand. I'll bring the papers over, and I'll see about canceling the uranium tests."

"Great." Gideon hung up, and turned to Mitch and Jeannie, saying, "Guys, I need to walk this off." They nodded and Jeannie put back the chair she'd borrowed and returned to her desk to do battle. Mitch started dialing, and Secora left to meet with Sage.

An hour later, Secora called Gideon, saying, "It's a go for Dad. He sounded entertained by the concept. Meet you back at the office."

17

JOSHUA BADER

Gideon was finishing a call on the speakerphone with Clive and Jimmy when Mitch sat down across from him. Gideon cradled his forehead with his left hand. "Mitch, do you think we can pull this housing project off?"

"Sure, we can handle just about everything that comes our way."

Sage and Secora arrived, waving to Jeannie, who was deeply engaged with someone on the phone. They took seats near Gideon's desk after Secora pecked Gideon's cheek. He looked up and kissed her on the lips.

As Sage plopped down, he said, "I'll settle for saying 'hi,' if you don't mind."

Mitch smiled and said, "Hey Sage, we were talking about the state of the 'Porcupine Desert' project."

Sage nodded. "Secora says you're making."

Gideon tapped a pencil eraser on the desk. "Clive and Jimmy have the first four tiny houses on site, and the yards are being surveyed."

Mitch added, "Once the wells, septic tanks, and drain fields are in, we can move the houses to their permanent locations. Right now, they're raking the sand and rocks with a harrow while we wait for the go-ahead."

Secora rose and filled two cups with coffee for Sage and herself. She held the pot up to get people's attention. "Anyone else want a top off?" No one responded. She sat down after offering Sage his cup.

Mitch quickly grabbed the half-full mug from his desk, then said, "I think the next five structures are slated for transport this week, and Jeannie's working with Clive to fill the four we have on the ground with the neediest families."

Sage sighed. "Oh, brother. Then the headaches will begin."

Mitch looked at his knobby knees. "No kidding."

They all turned as one when the front door opened and a young man with glittering dark eyes and curly hair blew in.

He offered his outstretched hand. "Hey guys, I just wanted to thank you for saving us."

Gideon stood to look him in the eye, temporarily ignoring Josh's proffered hand.

"Why did you need saving, Josh? Were you trying to shank us? Do you have a gambling problem, or is it something else?"

The man lowered his hand. "I don't. It's my wife. I love her, but our lives have to change. As we speak, she's in the crisis center after trying to commit suicide. Our very future depends on her successful rehab."

Jeannie thoughtfully drew up a chair for Josh, then, brandishing a pastry, set it down in front of their guest, who looked up in surprise.

"Thank you."

"You're welcome." She reseated herself, arms folded across her chest.

"Her addiction has cost us nearly everything. Seriously, *I'm* applying for one of your tiny houses." He bit into the treat.

After a pause, Gideon said, "Okay, let's look at the paperwork on your property—see what can be done."

There was a catch in Josh's voice. "I have nothing left to back this property. Our house is on the market, and we've had a nibble but no other assets, really. The car is a '92 Ford. If I lose Sokhela, there is literally nothing left but our cat."

Sage stepped over and, in a fatherly gesture, put his hand on the young man's back. After introducing himself, he said, "I've thought about picking up a property from time to time. What exactly are we talking about here?"

"It's a three-acre parcel at the back of an old subdivision west of Porcupine Creek. I picked it up as a favor to friends. Right now, it's a weed patch. Too small to interest most investors. I thought it might work for your low-income housing. Then a buyer put earnest money on it, and I didn't think it would be available when Gideon called. But their mortgage fell through, and, at the moment, I have nothing with which to cover the payment."

"What-say I buy the land and you be my contractor? If covenants allow, we'll build a dozen modest homes on it. With luck, sales will cover our monthly payments, provide you with housing, and a small stream of income until you get back on your feet."

"Thanks, Dr. Dalton, but I have no money. Not even to pay Sokhela's medical bills, let alone build us a small home."

"If I float you a construction loan, will you promise to pay me back? Every cent?"

"W... sure. I would be thrilled with a pre-fab tiny house or even a tent." He laughed, but his nerves jittered the sound. "I have nothing to put inside it but me and the kitty." His demeanor sagged with defeat. "I thought we were doing so well, until..."

Secora shook her head. "That's heartbreaking, Joshua. If Sokhela spent her time at a specific club, you might call them to see if they offer rehab support. A friend of mine had her medical bills paid by her regular casino."

"They can do that?"

"The good businesses do."

Jeannie looked at Gideon and Mitch. "I could order another tiny house for immediate delivery to the new location today."

Sage answered, his face beaming like that of a cheerleader. "Sounds like a plan, Jeannie. But Josh, do you want to move to South Dakota?"

"I'd rather stay in Missoula, to be perfectly honest. We are tribal,

I'm Armenian, and she is Chechnyan, but I'm not sure we could make it in South Dakota."

"Perhaps you and the cat could lodge, temporarily, with L. W. and me in our basement apartment. Closer to your wife's rehab. We could set up the tiny house on a lot, for when Sokhela returns. Of course, I'd have to run that plan past my wife."

Gideon frowned while he considered. Then he said, "That is an unbelievably kind offer, Sage. But before we move forward with details on living arrangements, perhaps you and Josh should put your heads together and take control of the Porcupine Creek property. Didn't you say water and sewer were already at the site?"

"I did. Let me follow up on what it would cost to tie in with the water and sewer, and to finish bringing the power in."

"Is it tied in with the *city* water and sewer?"

"Yes."

"Mitch, do you want to put this sale together?"

Mitch grinned. "You bet I do." He grabbed his mug and moved back to his desk. "Gentlemen, please step into my office."

Sage and Josh scooted their chairs over, and Mitch began preparing the purchase documents.

"I'll see about subdivision restrictions and permits in Oglala Lakota County," Jeannie said. She hurried back to her desk before Gideon could even answer.

Secora drew him out of his chair. "You and I should take a five-minute walk." She hugged him and led the way. Outside, hidden by a large fir tree, their kisses became passionate. He called Jeannie to mention they would return later than expected. He could almost hear the smile in her voice as he hung up and said to Secora, "They've got this."

After everyone but Mitch and Jeannie left the office, her call to the tribe regarding subdivision and covenants took an unforeseen turn. The tribal council had just received a proposal to build a resort that included a dinosaur museum complete with animatronic creatures, celebrating the rich dinosaur fossil deposits in the Dakotas, and an adjoining water park.

They were trying to find out who owned the property. Based on what they stood to make, they agreed to pay the 500 thousand plus a finder's fee of five percent to Josh, but Mitch would only agree to the deal if they made the ridiculous inquiry into rare earths go away on the Porcupine Desert project.

Done and done. After grins and 'high fives,' Jeannie and Mitch began calling Gideon, Sage, and Josh with the astounding news.

18

"CREATION STORIES"

Gideon gently woke Secora. "It's time to rise and shine. I already made breakfast."

She was so grateful for his attention to detail. As she munched, she noted he had already packed their bags and was eagerly waiting to begin their four-hour trip to the Hasan Resort. A week had passed since the taping of the story of the ancient Aryans, and they both were excited to see how today's finale would unfold.

They arrived late due to heavy traffic, and as usual, parking near the resort was almost impossible, even though a new lot had been opened east of the mansion.

The guests were wearing jeans or comfortable slacks, as many would be hiking and riding up beyond Black Mountain after breakfast was over.

All the bustle and hustle Iris had put into the preparations was paying off beautifully. As before, information packets had been prepared and were waiting for distribution in the lobby. Panting from the exertion, Secora and Gideon scooted into two of the last indoor seats. It was time for the event to begin.

This morning's banner read:

Three things came into existence at the same time: God, light, and freedom.

— ATTRIBUTED TO SRI KRISHNA

"For He dwelleth in the ark of fire, speedeth, in the sphere of fire, through the ocean of fire, and moveth within the atmosphere of fire. How can he who hath been fashioned of contrary elements ever enter or even approach this fire? Were he to do so, he would be instantly consumed."

— BAHA'U'LLAH, GEMS OF DIVINE MYSTERIES,
#110

Jimmy Lizardeye stood with the beaded pipe raised to offer a prayer.

"Grandfather, Source of all things, please assist our under-standing of the ancient peoples' ways and bring about harmony between our, past, present, and future. From the Earth, our mother, and the four directions—we ask a blessing for the people here today in their endeavor to understand one another as they attempt to live in grace with other human beings, the plants, the animals, and the minerals of the earth—as one family and one community."

Secora wiped tears from her eyes. Jimmy always touched hearts with the exact words people needed to hear. Upon noticing his wife's tears, Gideon, whose eyes were also glistening, put his arm around her.

Jimmy finished, "May the six grandfathers honor our prayer. Hetchetu 'alo. Thank you." He then quietly took the seat next to Destiny.

Sage rose from his stump chair on the stage.

"The tapestry of human progress described in sacred texts is one of the most intriguing mysteries in the house of civilization. We are

110

blessed and honored in this computer age to be able to compile documentation of a trio of 'First' remembered Great Prophets. Scriptures of Central Asia would include Gayomart and *Yima, followed by Siamak and Hooshang.* In the Bible, of course. It is Adam and Eve, followed by Seth and Enoch. If we look to China, the first would be *Fu-Xi*, followed by Shennong and Huangdi—together known as the San Huang Trio.

"The first of the three stages include early Stone Age Prophets who might have lived a long, long time before glacial melt when the land was still lush, and they could hunt without the assistance of horses for what they needed. Second, we have what little is remembered from a desperate time of starvation and die-off caused by global warming. And finally, the beginnings and early glimmers of domestication and plenty. A remedy for the famines and the onset of communal society, cities, and trade—before the flood.

"And in Africa, we find an extremely early reference to an Educator called *Nu Wa*. Each of these Beings has a variety of names—spelled differently due to the passage of time, evolving languages, and differing cultural regions. So don't be fooled if you find differences in spelling or titles.

"There are also references to a number of others who at one time or another have been called the *First*. I won't take time here to go into details about Rama, Deucalion, Atrahasis, or Gilgamesh. Truth be told, every Manifestation of God's Word is equally the 'first' of their age, and we will never know the names of the thousands of 'firsts' sent to humanity throughout the last several millions of years. Not important.

"We'll offer fragments of a story regarding the earliest remembered Prophets and their Revelations throughout the day. We've scheduled the first portion to coincide with breakfast, the next piece will be on the mountain after a half-day trail ride, and the conclusion will be back here tonight with dinner.

"First off, Iris will speak about Nu Wa from Africa. Next, Destiny will share some Biblical pre-history, then Jane will share early references from the Chinese scriptures. I will end with a few words from Avestan and Vedic texts—but I will not be including Lord Yima this morning since his story spans so many thousands of years and is so full of human and communal development, that it would need an entire day in itself."

That idea must have tickled one or two individuals in the audience because they laughed out loud, and everyone turned toward them.

A chuckling man stood and said in self-defense, "Exactly! I am a historian who has never known quite how to deal with the tales of Yima or Yama. I believe I will take you up on your offer and schedule a date to hear more about Him, if you don't mind."

Everyone then turned to Sage, awaiting his response. He smiled. "Sir, I have a hunch that Yima or Yama is yet a fifth creation story that has been included among the early Aryan scriptures so as not to be forgotten. But exactly where or when it began is beyond what I can say... Well, I guess it came from God originally. Baha'u'llah said, 'There were a thousand Adams, nay a thousand times a thousand.' We could safely say that Yima's name was applied to quite a number of them." This time, the laughter was contagious.

"I will say this. Long before Zoroaster, who was sent to humanity approximately 3,500 years ago, Yima likely represented a separate classification of humanity, different from that of the more recognizable names of modern Prophets. Different even than other kinds of humans, like 'Gaya Maretan,' whom we call Gayomart. For imagery's sake, we can pretend Yima might have been Homo Erectus, Gayomart—Neanderthal, Siamak, Denisovan, and Hooshang, a more modern human form. But that is merely to give an image to the differences of form."

The historian said, "Actually, now that I think about what you are saying, I agree that Yima's extended reign could be an entirely separate Creation story somehow mashed together with the rest of the Persian Avestan story. And, if you look with a searching eye, the Avesta recognizes that Gayomart and Siamak were different types of humans than Hooshang, Mashya, and Mashyana. That's brilliant! We *have* to talk later, thank you."

Sage nodded as the man sat, then continued, "The individual reign of an Aryan Prophet-king might seem to last thousands of years, but in general, the sequence coincides with one of humanity's historic ages.

For instance, Gayomart is said to have worn animal hides and lived in caves. He is referred to as Gar Shah, the *first* we remember from an early Stone Age hunter-gatherer society.

"Similarly, Adam is considered the 'first man' in the Bible, but he was part of the starvation, and is also a parent or ancestor of farmers during the times of herd and crop domestication. Keep the real-time references in mind as we say a few words about these remembered 'Firsts.'"

Secora and Gideon glanced at the surrounding audience. They murmured their approval.

Sage announced, "First up is Dr. Iris Snowden, who will share thoughts on ancient African memory."

Sage offered his daughter his hand in a gesture of welcome. As Iris clipped on her mike, he said, "We have a unique bit of human prehistory from Africa which begins with a social order not much different from that of our earliest human ancestors who began to explore life beyond the safety of trees nearly 5.6 million years ago. Similar societies exist among the great apes and even non-primate mammals."

Iris began, "The Remote One was said to have brought humanity to the humans. This female, called Nu Wa, as well as other names throughout Africa, would most likely have nurtured mankind from primal human memory, perhaps even back to the Australopithccincs nearly four million years ago. Well before several newer sorts of people fanned out from Africa. There was, as yet, no complex moral or social order. Infants and small children were cared for by their mother, siblings, and other available individuals, not specifically including nuclear fathers.

"When they were hungry, Nu Wa's people searched for food and ate what they wanted on the spot, throwing away the remnants without regard for the next meal. Like many animals, they devoured their food hide, hair, blood, and whatever. We can easily speculate that they made nests, beds, or simple shelters, and used convenient tools. They may have used animal skins, leaves, bark, and mud or rushes to protect parts of their bodies.

"In some ways, those people were more primitive than the much sought-after Bigfoot families who probably eat similarly and are not thought to need much 'clothing.' However, Sasquatch appears to live in more structured, nuclear groupings that include fathers. Photos suggest they construct wikiup-like structures and take advantage of cave shelters in which they may build nests of boughs and leaves. Communication between them and other species may include body language, vocalizations, wood knocks, defecation, and telepathy. There are also references to the occasional use of fire, simple tools like clubs, and hammers. Bowls fashioned from mud, and medicines have been mentioned, and a few observers claim nature, art, and shiny things like crystals also fascinated Sasquatch. Apparently, they mourn the loss of family members, and sometimes, human friends. This doesn't seem like a stretch when we know that even elephants miss and honor those who are departed, including human friends.

"Nu Wa came to bring a sense of community and moral, social structure to early humanity. She started them on a path that one day would lead them toward civilization. A path we are still learning to walk.

"According to some Tao texts, Nu-Wa was also Fu-Xi's wife or sister. Some think these two were the only survivors of a great flood. Yet these suggestions make little sense, given Nu-Wa's primitive event line. Fu-Xi's timeline, as you will soon hear, was far more recent and sophisticated. However, both may have lived long before the cataclysmic floods. Occasionally, Taoist depictions show the lower bodies of Nu Wa and Fu Xi, resembling serpents intertwined like a double helix or a caduceus. Some of you may recall that a similar creature, an ancient half-serpent woman, was depicted in the movie *Big Trouble in Little China*."

There were a few whistles amid the applause from the audience.

"Yeah, that was a cool movie, wasn't it?" She grinned and looked at the floor, then lifted her head and said, "Nu-Wa was said to have brought humanity to our ancestors. She provided an expanded social and moral context and an appreciation for the Creator. This scrap is the most ancient specific religious reference to the early human condition I have yet seen. That is all I have. Thank you."

There was clapping and a whistle or two from the audience, and a "Yeah, man!" also floated from the crowd. Iris winced as she noted that one of the whistles came from her big sister, Secora, who was now laughing.

Sage smiled. "Thank you, Iris." When things quieted, he loudly snapped his fingers. "Now let's skip *forward* to the 'Beginning,' at least the version most of you think you know. But first, a familiar prayer."

William Landsing walked to the mike stand on the central platform and composed himself.

"Our Father Who art in heaven, hallowed be Thy name. Thy Kingdom come, Thy will be done on earth as it is in Heaven. Give us this day our daily bread and forgive us our debts as we forgive our debtors. And lead us not into temptation, but deliver us from evil, for thine is the kingdom, and the power and the glory forever—Amen."

There was a murmur of echoed "Amens."

Sage enjoyed the effect on the audience. "Take it away, Dr. Destiny Hawkins," he said, smiling.

The attractive and dignified woman walked up, smiling to greet Iris. She then shook her shoulders, flicking her long hair away from a white satin blouse as she attached the mike.

"In the Bible, as with other scriptures, we begin with a Creation piece. When some of us were young, we may have learned from the Old Testament that, 'In the Beginning was God, and the Word was with God.' Then follows the story of the design and construction of the earth and its features.

"But what was this 'Word?' And how do we recognize it? You might respond in any number of ways: 'Jesus told me He was the Word made flesh.' Moses clearly said so. Well, certainly Adam, as the Bearer of God's blessed Word and His representative on earth would know, wouldn't He?

"But what do we know about Adam? As one to whom God spoke

directly, most of us Christians see Adam as the first man that was created—but was that was 3,000, or 13,000 years ago? Or was it 6,000,000 years ago?

"Do you see where this is going? I'm asking these questions so we might consider that the extensive story of Adam, as with the early Persian Creation, and the prodigiously long timeline of Fu-Xi in China all refer to only one select name which people handed down for millennia, even though events attached to that one name could cover countless centuries of cultural prehistory. We have to start somewhere. Certainly, nobody can remember all the layers of God's educators, and like Sage keeps reminding us— 'Not important.'"

She needed a sip of water, after which she continued, "Some renditions say that Adam and the other 'Firsts' had to leave Heaven or Paradise to become mortal earthly Beings. The Quran says that Allah sent both Adam and Eve away from heaven down to the earth where they became His representatives. Also, in the Torah, God banishes Adam and Eve from Eden, a heavenly state, and sent them to earth.

"But, if we take into consideration that Adam is also the ancestor or parent of farmers, maybe it was closer to 13,000 years ago, before farming started to become an industry. The timeline attributed to Adam is understandably confusing in that it spans millions of years. But saddle up, people. I think the same type of scenario exists in *each* of the ancient scriptures and tales.

"Genesis mentions that Eve, wanting to please God, gained knowledge of the difference between good and evil represented by an especially wonderful apple, only later finding that such knowledge, or rather the *choice* between good or evil, was a distraction from knowing God alone. In other words, she ate of the forbidden fruit offered by the tempter, a dragon or a snake with legs which were later taken away as God's punishment so that he had to crawl on his belly." She read...

*And the great dragon was cast out, that old serpent, called the Devil,
and Satan, which deceiveth the whole world: he was cast out into the
earth, and his angels were cast out with him.*

— FROM THE KING JAMES BIBLE, REVELATION.

"This is similar to the description in the Avestan story of
Gayomart, who also preceded the creation of the earth and descended
from Paradise. With help from the moon-white bull—a symbol of
domestication, He fought the evil of Angra Manu who came in the
form of a snake with legs."

A hand went up along the aisle, then a dignified woman in a mint
green knit suit; her hair hanging in brown curls, somewhat reminiscent
of Jackie Onassis, stood and said, "I thought Eve ate an apple and
pissed God off. That's it."

There was a definite rumble of agreement from the crowd.

"But in the Qur'an, it is claimed that *Adam* gave *Eve* the forbidden
fruit from the Tree of Knowledge of good and evil. Either way, she and
Adam became enmeshed in the conflict between Good and Evil on
earth, kind of like getting sucked into a reality show. Maybe Adam
forgot the Revelation was the purpose for their existence. I mean, they
had reasons. People around them were starving to death, fighting over
scraps, and resorting to cannibalism. Quite possibly, Adam and Eve
starved to death along with them.

"Let's address the famine of Masha and Mashyana from the
Adamic point of view. Something happened on earth at this crucial
point in time. Droughts and famines increased due to post-glacial
drying of the rivers and land. Climate change. Life became unstable.
Until that time, people had sustained themselves as hunters, fishermen,
and gatherers of fruits and vegetation for their diets. Similar crises also
pop up quite graphically in Atrahasis' and Gilgamesh's stories, where
the disappearance of the fishes is specifically mentioned. In all the
accounts, people suffered horrendous famines. Starvation seemed to be
the only choice. People killed and ate family members to survive,
starting with the young and the old."

The audience shifted about in their seats, visibly uncomfortable.

"After they left Eden, Adam and Eve also suffered from a horrible famine very similar to that experienced elsewhere in the world. She read...

"When they were driven out from paradise, they made themselves a booth and spent seven days mourning and lamenting in great grief. But after seven days, they began to be hungry and started to look for victual to eat, and they found it not. Then Eve said to Adam: 'My lord, I am hungry. Go, look for (something) for us to eat. Perchance the Lord God will look back and pity us and recall us to the place in which we were before. And Adam arose and walked seven days over all that land, and found no victual such as they used to have in paradise."

— KING JAMES BIBLE, GENESIS

"Leaving Eden means so little as a sentence, but understanding the real-life drama gives significance to the words. Our ancestors could no longer satisfy their needs from the forests and the waters. Starvation was the engine that impelled humanity to tame plants and animals in desperate hopes of survival. They eventually learned to raise herbs, vegetables, grains, and fruit. Painstakingly, they confined animals in small flocks to meet basic needs. Some endured. Perhaps Adam and Eve did not.

"I know the thought of mass starvation and its attendant bullying, violence, and conflict hurts our hearts. But it gives us perspective. This is *our* human history—and God forgive us—maybe our future, too.

"At that particular point in evolution, perhaps humankind was meant to become more consciously aware of themselves, and the consequences of their thoughts, choices, and actions.

"The Story of strife between Cain and Abel also bears this out. We must be held accountable for our actions. Perhaps that was the most powerful teaching of Adam's Revelation. If there is no accountability, how can human society become civilized?"

The woman in the audience looked at the floor for a moment and then said, "Actually, that makes a lot of sense. It's a clearer way of looking at the story. But why did God punish them and make them leave Eden?"

"Some accounts say it was *they who* turned away from *their Creator*, turning towards something more worldly for a time. They grieved the loss of connection when they realized their mistake and knew His great disappointment and displeasure.

"Haven't you ever felt like you were a bad person? Shut yourself away from everyone—even God. Closed your heart, and probably your bedroom door, hiding from the light, your friends, and family?

"Was this the first sin? Probably not. Given a choice, sometimes a Prophet or any of us will put *something or someone* before God. In fact, Yima changed his mind a couple of times about how he wished to serve the Source and humanity. He decided not to be a Prophet but to be a king who would bring prosperity back to humankind. Probably, much like Adam in that respect.

"Even so, God cherished him at every turn. God gave us free will, there's no reason to think this doesn't include the Manifestations. They are, after all, just men at times. Scripture from every faith shows us that the great Prophets are severely tested and they question their calling, as we saw in Gethsemane and in Baha'u'llah's plea, not to mention the forbearance of Mohammad when his daughter was run through with a spear.

"In Adam's case, it led to corruption when people sacrificed to the rain god, or the fertility goddess in desperate times, or by choosing idol worship, praying to elements, saintly figures, or personifications for specific help or favors."

One gruff man stood and said with all sincerity, "You better not be talking about Our Lady, Mary, when you condemn praying to saintly figures."

"Sir, it is in no way my intention to tell you what to believe, or offend or condemn Mary, or you, in any way. Our service to God is all about the purity of our hearts, isn't it? That is not the same as serving the god of death, or wealth, right?

"The 'snake' represents human frailty, attachment to the earth, and material existence. In tough times, it is tempting to take a shortcut that is too good to be true, an easy path—instead of keeping to the high, or noble road, painful as that may be.

"In fact, the name of the American Prophet, Quetzalcoatl, represents that choice very well. At any moment, man may choose the bird of the spirit, 'quetzal' flying toward heaven, or the snake 'coatl,' ignoring the issue, and binding himself to the day-to-day of earthly life. Just getting by, not making a difference."

She then turned outward toward the audience.

"Let me leave you with this beautiful piece—a reduced quote by Baha'u'llah from the *Tablet of the Immortal Youth;* about how difficult it must be for the Manifestations of God's Word to descend from Paradise to an earth where they are beset by contrary winds, suffer, and perhaps die in the quest. You may wish to close your eyes and think about your particular Savior, who is the return of the Holy Spirit."

Lo, the gates of Paradise were unlocked, and the hallowed Youth came forth bearing a serpent plain. Rejoice! This is the immortal Youth, come with crystal waters...This is the immortal Youth, come with a mighty name. Upon His brow there shone a beauteous crown, which cast its splendour upon all who are in heaven and all who are on earth...

On His right hand was a ring adorned with a pure and blessed gem. Rejoice! ...Upon it was graven, in a secret and ancient script: "By God! A most noble Angel is this." And the hearts of the inmates of the eternal realm cried out: "Rejoice! This is the immortal Youth, come with an ancient light...This, verily, is the Horseman of the Spirit Who circleth round the fount of everlasting life." ... He stood, even as the sun in the midmost heaven, arrayed with a beauty at once peerless and transcendent...

This is the immortal Youth, come with a mighty trumpet blast...

come with a mighty glance. He hath rescued all who are in heaven and on earth from the perils of death and extinction, clothed them in the garment of true and everlasting existence, and bestowed upon them a new life.

No sooner had this hidden Word shone forth from the Realm of inmost being and absolute singleness to illumine the peoples of the earth than a breeze of mercy wafted therefrom, purifying all things from the stench of sin and arraying the countless forms of existence and the reality of man with the vesture of forgiveness.

... Wherefore, O ye lovers of the beauty of the All-Glorious! ...It behooveth you to be free from all attachment, whether to yourselves or to others; nay, ye should renounce existence and non-existence, light and darkness, glory and abasement alike...that ye may, pure and unsullied, enter the realm of the spirit and partake with radiant hearts of the splendours of everlasting holiness ... Cast off the burden of love for this world and every attachment thereto, and, even as luminous, heavenly birds, soar in the atmosphere of the celestial Paradise and wing your flight to the everlasting nest.

The audience sat silently for several moments.

When the enchantment wore off, Destiny once again took control. She looked out the windows, then back into the sea of faces.

"As followers of diverse faiths, you will probably have recognized pieces from the quote. For instance, those of you who follow the Norse Eddas will probably recognize the phrase, 'This, verily, is the Horseman of the Spirit Who circleth round the fount of everlasting life.' as being very similar to the thirteenth century Edda, that describes Odin riding Sleipnir up and down Yggdrasil, the Tree of Life in every age. Or, if you are Christian, you may recognize the horseman and the Trumpet Blast from Revelations. The Holy Spirit is one and the same."

Smiling, she said, "Thank you for your attention." She unclipped the mike and returned it to Hasan. She calmly walked away to a roar of applause.

Jamal asked, "Wouldn't you fall before any Manifestation of the Holy Spirit after hearing this?"

The applause turned into a standing ovation. As the clapping quieted, he invited the crowd to take a break and grab breakfast and beverages in the dining area.

Several people sought out Destiny to ask questions, but Secora and Gideon headed straight for the goodies.

"That will be a tough act to follow," Gideon said.

"Oh, I imagine Jane will come up with something pretty special." Secora's phone rang. It was Tarkio. He was asking if he and Bill could write a second article about the events at Bonners Ferry based on the game camera photos. "Sure, see what you can make of it. I'll take a look at it when I get back."

After finishing their meal, Secora and Gideon returned to the auditorium. After people settled back into their seats, Jimmy Lizardeye walked onto the stage and said, "This quote is from Ban Gu, a Chinese historian, politician, and poet who lived during 32–92 AD."

Then came Fu-Xi and He looked upward and contemplated the images in the heavens, and looked downward and contemplated the occurrences on earth. He united man and wife, regulated the five stages of change, and laid down the laws of humanity.

"Now we will become aware of the vast ages spanning the historic events of Fu-Xi in China, and for that, we call up Dr. Jane Roanhorse."

Secora noticed some folks were respectfully standing and reverently acknowledging Jimmy. She joined them, as did Gideon.

Jane approached the standing microphone and began. "Thank you, grandfather. As with the other *First*s, there are many parts to Fu-Xi's story, arguably, too many. It is a tale that begins as far back as humanity itself. Perhaps because of His seemingly endless event line, Fu-Xi is known as the first Supreme Ruler and God-Emperor of China. He shared with us an extraordinary stream of events that crescendoed around 6,000 to 5,000 years ago. A time also associated with the deeds of Lord Krishna.

"Similar to the virgin births of Mary and of Krishna's mother, Devaki, Fu-Xi's virgin mother was made pregnant by the vision of a rainbow and a white elephant. It would seem that three nymphs came to do some washing in a river and suddenly a garment bore an image of a lotus in full fruit. The child born of this virgin was a boy, radiant as a rainbow. In the parallel tale, Krishna is also called the Radiant One. We can assume there was contact between China and India during that time. The mountain sanctuary where we are told Krishna resided in later life was visited by, and I quote, 'yellow-skinned' people."

The audience chuckled uncomfortably.

"Even the archers who shot Krishna were said to be 'of yellow and black skins.' It is highly conceivable that His East Asia disciples returned to grace their homelands with tales of Krishna as the mighty Fu-Xi—at least for that part of His timeline.

"He spurred many innovations, like inspiring us to farm silkworms 5,500 years ago and to use the eight trigrams of the I Ching or Pakua, that are said to be the basis for Chinese writing around 5000 years ago. According to Ban Gu, in order for Him to gain mastery over the worlds, Fu-Xi had the arrangement of the trigrams revealed to him supernaturally on the shell of a turtle's back.

"Music flourished because He showed us how to create beauty on a stringed instrument that looked like a short clarinet with seven strings known currently as the guqin zither. It originated about 5000 years ago. The arched harps also date to that time as noted in Egyptian funerary art and relics, along with the long-horn (didgeridoo or alphorn), and wood-knocking (drumming) that was universal in all early cultures across Africa, Asia, and Europe. So, it makes sense that these musical tools, along with Neanderthal's flutes, were already in use tens of thousands of years earlier.

"The harp was a broad wooden or hide-covered soundbox, joined with a curved branch of appropriate dimensions. It is still used as a revered accompaniment to the performance of oral history and myth in Africa and eventually became the lute that was used by the minstrels of

Europe. The number of gut strings varied anywhere between three and ten. Players are depicted as kneeling and using both hands to pluck the stringed instruments that may have originally developed from the bow.

"Later in history, we tip our hats to Fu-Xi who was also busy during the Iron Age, helping mankind to hunt with weapons made of iron 3200 years ago and during the Bronze Age when people lived in thatched huts, made pottery, and fashioned iron jewelry, as well as a wicked assortment of weaponry. Without such comprehensive guidance that spans the entire time range of the first *three* remembered Prophets—indeed, where would humanity be?

"Incongruous highlights of His many gifts to humanity include teaching Homo erectus to cook with fire—1.8 million to 300,000 years ago, showing us how to offer our first sacrifices to heaven, and to use fasting for physical and spiritual cleansing—earliest dates unknown. Nearly 80,000 years ago, He showed us divination by the use of yarrow stalks, and the use of medicinal plants, which were also utilized by Yima, Rama, Abaris, Asclepius—and even by ancient humans, presumably, Bigfoot and other mammals.

"He helped us tame wild animals 30,000 to 6,000 years ago, and evidence of fishing goes back to Paleolithic times, at least 40,000 years ago. But nets made of willow wands date only to 10,300 years ago, and sinkers have been found at several sites 10,000 to 5,000 years ago. At some point, Fu-Xi instituted marriage and personally chose the one hundred Chinese family names, decreeing marriages should only take place between persons bearing different surnames.

"Dear friends, in China, Fu-Xi is one name remembered for most of human prehistory. Clearly, His story, like Yima's, is an intricate accumulation of divine revelatory gifts. Because He endowed humanity with social laws, art, and inventions to help civilization advance over tens of thousands of years, we honor Him today. Thank you."

She left respectfully, and Jamal Hasan closed, "These first remembered Prophets added with Nu Wa, paint for us a tremendously long prehistory. They bring a richness and noble beauty to the development of human religion, society, and culture. We will now hear from Dr. Sage Dalton."

Applause erupted, and Secora heard versions of comments like, "I knew none of that. Did you?" She stood and applauded Jane's presentation and again added a whistle or two.

"She did such a marvelous job. I'm proud of her."

Mr. Hasan was saying, "I do not know a prayer from Gayomart, so I will offer instead this warning from the first remembered Prophet, as noted by the historian al-Tabari."

Pay heed to what is said, not to the speaker. Look up to advice and wise words, no matter who says it. Acknowledge the truth, no matter of what provenance.

The most recent Prophet, Baha'u'llah has echoed this same message.

Man must be a lover of the rose, no matter in what garden it may appear. He must be a lover of the light, no matter in what lamp it may shine.

Secora felt the audience hold its collective breath as Sage approached the stage, not knowing what to expect.

"The honor of being 'first' in the memories of the earliest Aryans was bestowed on 'Gaya' meaning life and 'Maretan' meaning mortal, later shortened to Gayomart. You may be more familiar with the name, 'Keyumers,' at times, simplified to 'Q-mers' in Farsi. Again, the reason for the variety of spellings is that the Aryan languages have changed over the tens of thousands of years of their history.

"Zoroaster's Avesta unequivocally states that Gayomart preceded Creation. He was eventually sent to earth in noble beauty, His purpose being to oppose evil. He was considered to be the 'First' Prophet, as well as the first human Ahura Mazda created—outside of Yima." He joked, "By now, that probably doesn't surprise anyone."

Satisfied with the audience's reaction, he continued, "In ancient texts, Gayomart... Yes, you have a question, sir?"

A boy who didn't look like he was out of high school stood and posed, "Dr. Dalton, I am a Mormon Elder. Are you saying that the first Aryan prophet was the first man—like Adam?"

"More or less, but you bring up a complex point. Science tells us mankind's earliest branches originated in Africa. The oldest representative we recognize lived 5.6 million years ago. It would be highly unlikely that the earliest name we currently have for any of our Prophets would be the very first. Maybe they were the first for a particular stage of human development. But let's try not to get hung up on a name because we can't possibly know the names of thousands of anonymous Prophets over millions of years. Does that sound reasonable?"

The young man looked puzzled—perhaps even shaken. He seemed to think it over, then nodded.

"Thank you, sir, for your patience and excellent question."

The young man, still looking a bit stunned, took his seat and Sage moved on.

"From the Avestan Yasnas 9 through 17, and the Bundahishn, which is a collection of pre-Zoroastrian beliefs, we have an accounting of 'Primordial Creation' somewhat similar to Genesis in the Bible.

"'First the sky was created from rock crystal in the shape of a hollow sphere, both above and below where the earth would be. Water was created and then earth.'

"The first plant was the mother of all trees. It was called the Saena, Gaokerene, or ox-horn. In its physical form, it offered healing properties. But spiritually speaking, it was probably no less than the 'Tree of Life,' also known as the Word of God. Its crown provided a place for the first nest for the first bird, a falcon. When he beat his wings, the dropping tree leaves became the first plants. After plants the animals appeared, then the first mountain, Alburz, also known as Mount Hara, or Harbatz, grew.

"So, could that be today's Mt. Elburz? Unfortunately, place names from ancient times are not even remotely likely to be the same ones we recognize today." Sage chuckled. "For all we know, this might be a reference to somewhere in Africa, or even at the North Pole from 30,000 years ago. Again, it's not good to be distracted by details. We must savor the bits we think we know."

He smiled. "The first animal that came into existence, or more likely, that became important to early Stone Age humanity, was represented by a primeval aurochs, bright white as the moon that lived across from Gayomart's cave above the banks of the Vah Daiti, the Good River that flowed from the center of the world.

"Gayomart, in His radiant beauty, was created spontaneously in the middle of the world by the Force of Creation to assist 'Ahura Mazda, The Wise Lord, in His fight against the Evil Spirit known as Ahriman or Angra Manu, during the sixth 'Gah (pronounced Gay), meaning sixth Day of the Creation.

"His body was created from earth and its divinity was fashioned from the light and brightness of the sky. He measured four medium reeds in height and in breadth. He was round, white, brilliant, and shining as the sun.' Perhaps this visual was inspired by the supernal Farr, that glowing sacred aura which surrounds God's emissaries as they bring His Revelations to earth."

A man from the audience yelled, "Sounds like an orb to me."

Sage nodded and continued, "Could be, sir. Here, it gets interesting. At first, Gayomart had no flock to preach His Revelation to. He was created as a fifteen-year-old boy with physical features *similar* to the men who *would later be born of his seed*. This suggests He was a pre-modern form of human. Time-wise, this could have been anything from Australopithecine times two to four million years ago, to Neanderthal or even later Stone Age. Doesn't matter." Sage grinned.

"Referred to as the 'Gar-Shah', the 'King of the Mountains,' He lived in caves in the stony hills above the fertile valley along the Daiti River and wore the skins of leopards. His followers, also cave dwellers, wore leaves and the hides of animals. Geographically speaking, this cave *might* have been along the Aras River, also called the Araxes, that flows from Turkey along the border with Armenia on to Azerbaijan. Or the area might have been literally anywhere in the

Carpathian or Alburz Mountains. Again, an actual location is irrelevant —but I'll admit, it's fun to speculate.

"Because Gayomart was the Righteous representative of God on earth, He took it on himself to contend with evil, depicted as Angra Manu, the distractor, and his minions. This is likely a reference to the uncaring, materially wealthy, or idol worshipers of that time. Unkind people relied on giving and getting favors. They were dangerous manipulators.

"When Gayomart and the bull appeared, the source of evil and darkness was laid low in awe. He was more than a king, as Christ was more than a mere king. He embraced the Will and commandment of Ahura Mazda and was granted the shimmering Farr. Such an effusion, brilliant like the sun, is reserved for luminous Beings. Between the bull and Gayomart, we have the brilliance of both the sun and the moon. Those heavenly bodies are pertinent to many cultures, especially Mexico, Central, and South America.

"However, the white bull is still revered among followers of Hindi sects, and this ancestral tale is a good bet for the origin of the taboo station of cattle. Ironic, since the bull's first appearance was likely instrumental in staving off starvation. In the early days of domestication, there were surely bans on killing the breeding stock until meat became plentiful once again, and famine was a distant memory. Some laws that once had a purpose, like aversion to pork, linger too long. But enough about old wine in new skins.

"Gayomart brought spiritual wisdom to humankind. His name, like the others, is associated with a range of millions of years. It doesn't matter. We understand He is remembered from our most ancient times. He ruled over men and beasts by His gentle but potent nature and unparalleled wisdom. Gayomart, the Pure and Righteous, was a peaceful and pious King who rendered the primitive world prosperous and habitable. Perhaps another reference to domestication? He was also known as the first man to practice Justice and was called the Lawgiver. To be fair, so were Yima and Jamshed.

"In this way, Gayomart's story is similar to that of Adam, in that it begins prior to domestication, at a time when the people were hunters and gatherers of fruits and vegetation. In both accounts, climate change resulted in the drying of the water and land, reducing the amount of available food sources. Populations began to suffer horrendous famines, as will become apparent a bit later when we speak of Masha and Mashyana.

"Starvation or cannibalism seemed to be the only choices until domestication became well established. Later, herds of cattle and goats grazed pastures which were ringed with the awe-inspiring pinnacles of Inner Asia that protected Gayomart's people from cruel raiders who attacked them and their herds every few years. It's a story of humans successfully surviving a world disaster."

A man in a yoked shirt with his hat in his hand arose and asked, "Excuse me. Before Creation, after domestication... how long did this fella live?"

"According to the legend, Gayomart, or more likely his lineage, 'lived for 3,000 years in peace. He did not pray, eat, or talk. He meditated the whole time, until' Angra Manu, the Evil One, was awakened and arose in the form of a fiery dragon. Perhaps this meant personal idols did not distract the people for that length of time as also validated in the Atrahasis and the Gilgamesh epics.

"But the 3,000-year period during which Angra Manu had been stunned ended when 'Jeh,' or 'Jahi,' similar to the Hebrew 'Lilith,' and the Babylonian 'Lilitu,' the archdemon whore, or more likely a powerful idolatress *yelled*. This temptress woke the fanatics up! She promised to help Angra Manu destroy Gayomart and the creatures of God.

"The minions of Angra Manu were called the divs, which, like demons, battled with the Light. On the first day of spring, the Evil One, himself, leaped onto the earth as a dragon, a snake with legs. He created darkness with sloth, lust, thirst, hunger, death, and a thousand diseases among the life forms, and he unleashed the pesky kyrm, a category of evil beings—at times humans depicted them as bugs and snakes who were then considered unclean. So, were the famine and ensuing disease the consequence of distraction? Could be.

"A pure-hearted tenth-century Persian scholar, Muhammad ibn

Jarir al–Tabari, wrote the *History of the Prophets and Kings* around 1,099 years ago. He ascribed to Gayomart, a collection of apothegms, maxims, or wise sayings, ancient wisdoms which return repeatedly, verbal traditions like Mother Goose stories, easily remembered lessons since there was no form of writing. 'Know thyself' is one such gift from Gayomart. Another example is 'Hear no evil, speak no evil, and see no evil.' Clearly, we could add 'Think no evil' and of course 'Do no evil.' A form of this golden rule has been repeated in every Revelation throughout history. Baha'u'llah gave us the same admonition thousands of years later in Persian Hidden Word number 44."

> *O COMPANION OF MY THRONE! Hear no evil, and see no evil, abase not thyself, neither sigh nor weep. Speak no evil, that thou mayest not hear it spoken unto thee, and magnify not the faults of others that thine own faults may not appear great; and wish not the abasement of anyone, that thine own abasement be not exposed. Live then the days of thy life, that are less than a fleeting moment, with thy mind stainless, thy heart unsullied, thy thoughts pure, and thy nature sanctified, so that, free and content, thou mayest put away this mortal frame, and repair unto the mystic paradise and abide in the eternal kingdom for evermore.*

"Gayomart, like all Revealers of God's Word, renewed the ancient Faith. But from the early Aryan beginnings, two spirit paths developed: The roots of *Hinduism* and *Zoroastrianism* spread. *Ahura Mazda* was the Avestan name for God, but in the Rig Veda of Hindu scriptures, God was referred to as *Asura Varuna.*

"Like the Prophets who followed, Gayomart had one goal—for humans to worship the Supreme Creator and purify their hearts, to turn away from the materialistic devas or polytheism, to refrain from making offerings to various elements, talismans, idols or icons in order to get something in return.

"In closing, revelatory Prophets are all related in a special choir of souls: Nu Wa, Gayomart, Rama, Krishna, Abraham, Moses, Zoroaster,

Buddha, Jesus the Christ, Mohammad, the Bab, and Baha'u'llah are treasured Emissaries of the One Source—never competitors. They are literally soul brothers as bearers of the same Holy Spirit. They always had each other's backs... praising the Blessed Person who came before and mentioning at least One who will come after them. For example, 'the Glory,' or the 'Spirit of Truth,' or, 'He will come again from Sinai.' The clues are in the scriptures if you use a seeing eye.

"Given all of that love and respect, there shouldn't be rivalries or arguments between faiths, right? I'm afraid the disputes, murders, crusades, and wars are all on us—caused by greed for control or material benefit. In essence, materialism is *why* the Ancient Religion of God must be renewed and cleansed, from age to age."

Iris pulled another map down.

"This beautiful map shows how close the Aryan holy land is to the Middle East *and* Africa. Meditate on this. Many of these Prophets walked along the Tigris and the Euphrates River."

"Thank you all for sharing your time."

Jamal Hasan rose and raised his hands. "All right everyone, Sage will continue his talk on the mountain. Have another bite of brunch, then find us outside as we prepare the horses and the Jeeps, which will take us to your next destination for lunch and tidbits on the second remembered names of the early Prophets."

TURKEY
Karasu River
Murat R
Kayseri
Adana
Gaziantep
Diyarb
Tigris R
Euphrates
Aleppo
Latakia
SYRIA
Homs
Beirut
Damascus
Golan
Heights
Jerusalem
West Bank
Amman
Dead Sea
(lowest point in Asia, -408 m)
JORDAN
Al
'Aqabah
BibleStudy.or

ARMENIA
AZERBAIJAN
Yerevan
Baku
Caspian Sea
Van
Tabriz
Lake Urmia
Rasht
Zanjān
Qazvin
Erbil
Kirkuk
Kermānshah
ZAGROS
Arāk
Baghdad
IRAQ
Ahvāz
An Nāşiriyah
Abādān
Al Başrah
Kuwait City

THE CLIMB

Secora grabbed a warm croissant while Gideon munched a cream cheese bagel before joining the guests, who were eager to continue the trip into the mountains to hear the next piece of the story. Most of Secora's family followed Sage down the long driveway to the main road. For her, it felt like a mile and a half hike to Ken and Sue's guest ranch. She broke into a sweat along the way and, turning to Gideon, said, "I guess this will work off some of the calories from the crepes and scrambled eggs."

He smiled. "The ponies probably conspired with Ken and Sue to help us lose a pound or two before we mount up."

Sage, who was walking beside Gideon, chuckled. "Too right, as our friend Eliot would say. Wonder how he's doing in Kensington?"

L.W. smiled at the thought. "Don't know, but I miss him. It was good to see him briefly last weekend when he filmed the Zoroaster piece."

Sage looked at her lovingly and said, "Oh, I'm sure he'll pop up again one day. He often does when something exciting happens."

Secora thought her parents were doing very well for folks their age. She could see that several people arrived way ahead of Sage and his extended family and they were already being paired with horses. The rest of the animals were still waiting at the tie rails, twitching their ears, and slapping their tails at flies.

Within minutes, almost everyone was mounted and patiently waiting to leave for the trail. Sue led a big light-colored bay over for Gideon and a smaller paint for Secora. The squeaking of the oiled-saddle leather was music to her ears.

L.W. and Sage waved their goodbyes from the ground, saying they would ride in a Jeep with the crew, as their bones were too old to enjoy a four-hour horseback ride.

Once everyone was set and waving goodbye to their hosts, William Landsing led the way on a red mule named 'Carrots,' his long-time companion from his mammoth hunting days. As was his way, Gideon joined William at the front of the line. Secora fell in with others toward the rear.

The string of riders passed down the main forestry road, then took the cut-off up toward Black Mountain. About four hours later, they would wind up at a hunting campground complete with restrooms, picnic tables, and a corral for the animals. It was there they would enjoy lunch and Sage's second installment of the great Prophets. Later that evening, he would finish with the *Thirds*, probably the most prominent and influential of the great remembered Prophets.

Billy led them off the logging road onto a deer or cow trail that was sometimes a single path. At other times, the path split for a while, then came back together. Dust of hoof-ground granite, manure, and leaf litter covered the track. The grass along the sides was tall due to heavy fertilization throughout the years. All this made the passage of the hooves soundless—no clopping or clunking unless a hoof hit a downed log along the way. Then the knocking sound carried and echoed through the standing timber. Staccato blows from a hunting woodpecker seemed to startle a few of the dreamy riders, including Secora, as the trail climbed the right-hand side of an abrupt hill.

Suddenly, a slight breeze jittering the aspens. The effect was calming and beautiful. At one point, the white tree trunks closed in, almost pinching the steep path shut. Secora had to lift her knees to keep them from rubbing on either side.

She was surprised at how many mosquitoes were buzzing beneath the quaking leaves where the air was moist and was glad Jamal had reminded them to use bug repellant before leaving. He'd provided several dispensers on a table by the door.

About an hour in, the trail turned a corner to fit the terrain, and riders could see the river flowing in the canyon below them. The sides of the hill were precipitous, and quite a few boulders had rolled down to create sections of white water. Secora could hear several guests discussing a return to the canyon to throw in a line.

Off to the side, there were outcrops of mushrooms which delighted Secora, as did the little birds flitting around dung piles for insects or worms. Sacred scents of the forest filled the air, and she thought of her husband, wishing he wasn't so far ahead in the line.

At a rest stop, Gideon tied his pony to a tree with a halter and lead rope that it wore beneath the bridle for such occasions. Secora dismounted, then watched as he came over and pulled her in for a kiss, saying, "This is so amazingly beautiful. I could live here forever." He smiled and kissed her again. Everyone sat and rested a few moments but not so long as to let stiffness creep in.

On the last leg, the trail to the campground led them across a fairly flat meadow and into another piece of aspen forest. Everyone remained silent. Secora couldn't even feel the breath of a breeze. The only sound was the occasional knocking of a hoof against a dried log that had fallen across the path. If the log was too large, the trail simply diverted around it.

There was a perma-smile pasted on her face. What a pleasant break from everything at the university. No fierce Amphicyons could possibly live here. Only birds and deer and summer grazing cattle. When a breeze finally picked up, every breath felt refreshing; every passing tree recharged her energy. Her horse stomped at a large bot fly that was biting her shoulder. Secora smashed it as a service to the beast.

When they finally arrived at the campground, the sight of a Jeep and two large trucks, already parked in the meadow, happily surprised them. A huge, white-speckled blue enamel coffee pot was already brewing over the fire along with boxed lunches atop the picnic tables, and a cooler containing water bottles and soda cans.

Sausages, bacon, and hot biscuits sizzled in a large pan over the fire. The smells could put one into ecstasy.

Luckily, there were hand wipes, a washbasin, and paper towels to remove the caked horse sweat and grime. Secora saw Sage, who, with a cup in hand, making his way over to the ranch-sized coffee pot. Secora chased a buzzing fly, then gratefully sipped from her cup.

Smiling people gravitated to the box lunches which contained two sandwiches—one baloney and one PBJ, fresh-cut veggies, and cookies; or they chose plates of biscuits and gravy with sides of sausage and bacon. Chatter quieted when everyone dug into the amazing offerings. As some prepared for seconds, praises to the cooks echoed from nearly everyone's lips. It wasn't long before the plates and cups had been gathered, and people sat around comfortably to hear part two of Sage's talk, aptly called, "Seconds Please."

As they nibbled and waited, several wranglers unsaddled the horses, then loaded them and the tack into the big trucks for the return trip to the ranch. Several passenger vans also pulled in to wait. After the talk, they would collect the sore, stiff riders and return them to the sanctuary of their rooms.

2 0

"SECONDS PLEASE"

Sage sat on one of the tabletops with a portable mike and pointed to the stack of notes and pencils on the table beside him. After people had settled and scanned the notes, he began.

"There is much less material regarding the reigns of the second remembered Prophets worldwide. Probably because a lot of what they brought to the world was either lumped into the extended reign of the 'First' or had been lost to history due to the famines and droughts of global warming that decimated the populations. During this time, Stone Age mankind struggled to build a few temples and monoliths to honor the Creator and his creation. What we do have are the names of Siamak, Seth or Shiith, and Shennong. This afternoon let's begin with the Central Asian version, then the Bible, and follow up with the Chinese scriptures.

"Commencing the second cosmic stage, Gayomart and the bull were attacked because they withstood the idolaters' attempts to spread worldwide destruction. The ensuing combat between the forces of light and darkness ended, it is said, by the arbitration of angels. But the bull had been mortally wounded. Still, this was not enough to defeat the forces of good. Next, Angra Manu sent the demon of death, Astovidat,

138

to spy on Gayomart, but he could not kill the Prophet because His fate had not yet come. Gayomart lived thirty years longer before Angra Manu, in the form of idolaters, finally killed Him.

"The cave dwelling Prophet foretold as He died that despite His death, a more modern human race would be born. Subsequently, the Word of God and prophetical counsels were revealed to Masia, His wife. Later, they were disseminated to all mankind through their son or descendant, Siamak, and thirdly through Hooshang, a grandson or later descendant.

"Siamak was beloved to all except the devil, called Angra Manu or Ahriman, who raised an army under the command of his own demonic son, to kill Siamak. An angel named Soroush warned Gayomart of the danger, but the noble Siamak led an army of His own and accepted the challenge of hand-to-hand combat with the evil son of Ahriman. So, it was that the beloved king died at the hands of that demon. Is this reminiscent of the story of Cain and Abel? Or the battle of the Kurukshetra Plain, where two descendants carry on the fight between evil and good?

"Siamak's descendent, Hooshang, led the army that ultimately defeated Ahriman's son, who was eventually bound and beheaded. One might imagine that idol worship was quelled and humanity again turned to peaceful worship of a single God.

"But there is an incongruous time break between Gayomart and other types of humans. Where He was slain, Gayomart's seed fertilized the earth, and forty years later a rhubarb plant shot up. The top of it split into two branches and it gave forth two persons, a male, 'Mashya,' and a female, 'Mashyana.' They were known as 'Ask' and 'Embla' in Norse Mythology, and some call them 'Adam' and 'Eve,' which became the first mortal couple. Perhaps the first *modern* human couple? Okay! Rhubarbs! Yes! But is that any weirder than coming from a rib, or earth, or mud? All the same in my book.

"After fifty years, the first humans of that latter age had twins. Unfortunately, Angra Manyu, the Evil one, took the form of a snaky, fiery dragon, and he tricked Mashya and Mashyana into worshipping him instead of Ahura Mazda, the One True God. They, like Adam and Eve, failed, and because of their sin, things changed.

"Humanity suffered horrible famines, and starvation forced them to eat their precious children. There are pervasive global memories of tremendous famines where game and fish and perhaps even the rivers disappeared. Outcomes included the cannibalism of the weak, young, or debilitated as mentioned in Biblical scriptures, and Egyptian texts.

"The Akkadian Epic tale of Atrahasis, thought by some to be the oldest account of prehistory and the Great Flood story, begins like Yima's, in layers that precede the creation of mankind. Before the flood, Atrahasis was not simply an earthly king. His name meant "The Wise," also known as Ziusudra in a Sumerian version of the Epic. He was sent to earth to be the Stone Age king of Shuruppak, possibly the city of Enoch, 'the Healing Place.' At one time, it was a bustling capital city built along the Euphrates River and influenced an area of commerce that included the lower Tigris and Euphrates Rivers.

"Atrahasis' people flourished. Their numbers grew to the point of overpopulation and noisiness—eventually becoming 'as noisy as a bellowing bull.' At this point, they were struck by a plague (similar to the one striking Rama's people) to curb the population size. The king prayed for relief. Enki heard Him and told Him to have the people stop praying to personal gods and pray only to the Almighty God, specifically, to have the plague ended.

"Now there was one, Atrahasis, whose ear was open to Enki (God), and he spoke to His Lord. *How long will the gods make us suffer? Will they make us suffer illness forever?*

"Enki responded with a 'me,' an edict, a universal decree of divine authority. He heard, and his voice spoke to his servant. *Call the elders, the senior men! Start an uprising in your own house, Let the elders proclaim... Let them make a loud noise in the land: Do not revere your gods, do not pray to your goddesses...But search out the door of Namatara. Bring a baked loaf into his presence.*"

"Through prayer, people had survived the initial plague, but the noise came back. The gods ceased to perform their duties, and all of nature's bounty disappeared. There came a horrible drought and grue-some famine during the second 1200 years.

When the second year arrived, they had depleted the storehouse. The people's looks were changed by starvation. When the fourth year arrived their upstanding bearing bowed, their well-set shoulders slouched, and the people went out in public hunched over. When the fifth year arrived, a daughter would eye her mother coming in; a mother would not even open her door for her daughter... When the sixth year arrived, they served up a daughter for a meal, served up a son for food.

—Dalley, Stephanie *Myths from Mesopotamia: Creation, the Flood, Gilgamesh, and Others* (Oxford World's Classics 2009)

"Children had been a source of joy and a fulfillment of love during the ancient conditions of marriage and childbirth. The famine brought utterly horrible conditions in which Mashya and Mashyana ate their first children, and hunger smote Adam and Eve. It finally ended when Enki sent rain and a large quantity of fish into the rivers.

"The die-offs may have encouraged a new type of human to step to the forefront.

"After a long, long time, Mashya and Mashyana bore another set of twins from which humanity developed. Enoch refers to them as twin Giants in His Book of Giants. Finally, according to the Persian Creation story, when modern humans, the most recent of all creations, were born in the seventh creation fire, all was done and the Creator rested.

"Siamak obviously predated this piece. He was a variety of human who live prior to the arrival of Mashya and Mashyana and the giant twins. Later still, the throne of revelation passed to Hooshang.

"Control of animals and other crops became imperative, placing Adam squarely at the onset of domestication. Husbandry was feebly set in motion during the starvation times of Seth."

"Here is a view of the Prophet Seth (Shiith) from Muhammad Ibn Ishaq."

Years and years passed, Adam grew old and his children spread all over the earth.

When Adam's death drew near, he appointed his son Seth (Shi-ith) to be his successor and taught him the hours of the day and night along with their appropriate acts of worship. He also foretold to him the flood that would come.

"And according to a hadith narrated by Abu Dhar...

Muhammad said, 'Allah sent down one hundred four psalms, of which fifty were sent down to Seth. When the time of his death came, Seth's son Anoush succeeded him. He, in turn, was succeeded by his son Qinan, who was succeeded by his son Mahlabeel, who reigned for a period of forty years.

"Persians claim that Mahlabeel was King of the Seven Regions. He was the first to cut down trees in order to build cities and large forts, which sadly, may have contributed to the devastating droughts. He is credited with building the cities of Babylonia."

When he (Mahlabeel) died his duties were taken over by his son Yard, who on his death, bequeathed them to his son Khonoukh (Enoch), who is Idris according to the majority of the scholars.

"Upon Adam's death, his son, or more likely a descendant, Seth, took over the responsibilities of prophethood. The 'first scriptures,' mentioned in the Qur'an 87:18, agree that Seth was *the Receiver of Scriptures,'* perhaps the fifty psalms. Medieval historian al-Tabari and other scholars say Seth buried Adam *and* the *'secret texts'* in the 'Tomb of Adam,' referring to it as the 'Cave of Treasures.'"

"Unfortunately, because of cultural distance, Egypt's distant memory of Seth, or Set, no longer bears any ties to reality, only fanciful tales in which he was debased to a mischievous, composite-animal creature, or, at times, was forgotten altogether."

"In *Antiquities of the Jews,* Josephus refers to Seth as virtuous, and of excellent character. He states...

'His descendants invented the wisdom of the heavenly bodies, and built the 'pillars of the sons of Seth,' two pillars inscribed with many scientific discoveries and inventions, notably in astronomy, in order to protect the discoveries so they might be remembered after the destruction. One was composed of brick, and the other of stone, so that if the pillar of brick should be destroyed, the pillar of stone would remain, both reporting the ancient discoveries, and informing men after the coming flood, that a pillar of brick was also erected. Josephus reports that the pillar of stone remained in the land of Siriad in his day.'

"Seth's descendants built them based on Adam's prediction that the world would be destroyed at one time by fire and another time by global flood.—as noted by William Whiston, a seventeenth/eighteenth century translator of the *Antiquities.*

"Worldwide destruction would again occur. Humanity, at least part of it, would survive. In summary, the lesson to put the Great Being first has been difficult for humankind to retain. It bears repeating at every age. Let's now turn to the Far East for guidance from Shennong."

Sage took a drink of water before continuing. "Even though Fu-Xi is remembered for taming animals between 30,000 and 6,000 years ago, obviously, severe famine and domestication fit in there some-where. At that point, He was succeeded in his mission by Shennong, the second of the three Noble Emperors and ancient forebearer of modern humans.

"Shennong disseminated a mass of medicinal lore, but His greatest contributions lay in agriculture and farming innovations. His food production and storage techniques allowed humans partial control over the periodic, horrifying famines, and, eventually, provided an excess of products, anticipating the glimmers of commerce.

"Shennong, like Yima, taught humans the use of the plow, an ard. Oxen, hooked to a simple shaft, dragged an angled stick through the soil to loosen it. The farmer grasped another stick, projecting from the top of the shaft for guidance control.

"Shennong graciously shared other aspects of basic Mesopotamian types of agriculture as well. He is associated with growing barley, beans, hemp, millet, oats, peas, rice, sesame, and soybeans. Huangdi, His descendant, would continue the farming enhancements.

"According to *'Baihu tongy,'* by Ban Gu of the Han Dynasty, people in ancient times only ate animal meat. By Shennong's time, there were too many people, and animals were insufficient. He taught them farm techniques, and the people called him the 'god of farming.'"

Sage folded his hands. "I have no recorded knowledge about what happened in Africa during these times except in Egypt, where the great Sahara Desert began to eat up greenery, lakes, and rivers about 11,000 years ago after the domestication of goats. The land dried, people and animals died, and travel out of southern Africa must have been curtailed for a time.

"In the Americas, people followed fish and game along the coast and through the ice corridors, seeking fresh water and pastures where they could survive. But by the time of the European invasion, many indigenous people seemed to be at a cultural crossroads between hunting and farming.

"In conclusion, friends, the names of the 'Seconds' are remembered from dangerous and dramatic times. There may not be many enduring references, but it is clear everyone was suffering. The good news is that some humans and animals did survive. Tonight, after dinner at Hasan's, we will investigate what happened with the 'Thirds,' before the Flood."

Secora stiffly rose to her feet. Her joints, along with everyone else's, were sore after four hours in the saddle and a large lunch. Still, she walked over to give her dad and mom hugs. After they said good-bye, Gideon sighed. "Guess I'm ready to get back to the resort to take a hot shower and a nap before Sage takes our breath away again with his finale."

She agreed. "I hope I can revive my legs in time." It had been several years since she's spent hours on a horse's back. "All in all, it had been a fantastic day." Her mind reviewed the highlights as they traveled the dirt road back to the resort. "Wish we could visit the parts of the world where so much growth took place."

He responded, "Maybe we will. You never know."

"AGE OF METAL"

Forks laden with the seafood dinner provided by the resort moved from plate to mouth amid loquacious and robust conversation. Secora pushed her plate away after finishing a trout. When Gideon took the last bite of crab salad, she opened her mouth to speak, but was hushed when the lights dimmed, and an unseen kettle drum began to rumble and quiver. Floodlights flashed revealing Sage on his stump, holding a microphone.

"Did you know that names, times, and stories of the Prophets do not register across the globe at the same rate? They are disjointed, depending on how far removed the culture is from the actual Revelation—by either time or geographical distance.

"What we can say is that the third remembered Prophets take us into more plentiful times, featuring agricultural surplus, metalwork, and trade routes. Communities are developing great cities and fortifications. Society is more organized and civilization progresses."

Sage stood and approached the audience. "Upon Siamak's demise, the 'throne' passed to Hooshang. His name is spelled either with two 'ohs' or an 'ou.' He was a powerful Manifestation of God, who then became the third remembered leader or king of men. He was able to beat back the oppression of cruel deva worshippers and greedy idolators. For a time, the world was renewed, purified by love and virtue. People would be kind to one another and, especially, to the poor. Men of goodwill were once again able to live in peace. Such is the rhythm of religion. Purification, then degradation, sects, and dissolution caused by the wills of men—then purification once more.

"Horses, donkeys, and oxen plowed fields and carried loads. They transported people during daily chores, marketing, and warfare. Sheep and cattle herds flourished allowing meat, dairy products, and hides to become plentiful. Besides surplus bounties provided by the animals, grains, fruit, bread, and woven goods could be marketed, providing a way to pay taxes for maintaining infrastructure like roads, irrigation canals, and aqueducts to enhance the crops. Abundance led to the establishment of trade networks like the silk road.

"Smiths melted metals from ore, producing household and farming tools like saws, axes and hoe-like mattocks, and knives, as well as weapons. The Shahnameh mentions that gold was used in ancient times to make the surgical knives for performing Caesarean operations well before Caesar's time.

"Hooshang began a hereditary kingship and a royal line that ruled with justice and grace. This is the beginning of the Divine Right of Kings since the first kings were bearers of the Holy Spirit. Hooshang's titles included first King and first Lawgiver—yet to be fair, this was also granted to Gayomart. Law was the concept of common justice. In this system of governance, the kings had a sacred responsibility to protect the people, establish and uphold just laws, and encourage community development and the advancement of society. Kings who maintained this sacred trust were said to rule the ethical path in *grace.*

"Unfortunately, those who later traded belief in Ahura Mazda and the Lawgivers for Idols instigated battles for territory and material gain. Central Asia split into bellicose regions like Balkh and Sugd in Afghanistan shattering the perceived unity and leaving the people and social strata open to invasions by domineering nations and fanatic sects for thousands of years to come."

The Caucasus and Central Asia

Wiki Commons Map

Again, the kettle drum thundered from an unseen station, and the house lights rose to full glow, but Sage had disappeared.

Jane was now at the mike wearing blue and gray beaded earrings with red accents at the base of tubular beads that gave the impression of porcupine quills. They shone brightly against her dark braids and a lovely deep maroon dress.

She smiled, then said to the audience, "Huangdi is referred to as the Yellow Emperor, named after the Yellow Phase, which represents the earth, dragons, the center point, and up and down. A reference to Him appears in a Chinese text on an early bronze vessel in the Warring States period prior to 2,475 years ago. He was both a cosmic ruler and lord of the underworld, known for many inventions and innovations, and for being a patron of the esoteric arts.

"According to tradition, the Yan Emperor fought the evil force of the Nine Li tribes under their leader Chi You, who is described as—get this—a bull-headed, iron-skulled man with sharp horns and a bronze forehead, four eyes, six arms, and a human body! He was considered to be an unbelievably fierce, cruel, and greedy tyrant—a corruptive force who may also have been a wayward descendant of Shennong.

"The story goes that the evil Chi You defeated the good Yan Emperor and fled to beg for the Yellow Emperor's help. During the ensuing battle, Huangdi employed his tamed animals, but the evil dude gained the upper hand by darkening the sky, breathing out a thick fog that confounded his adversaries. To overcome this, Huangdi invented the South-Pointing Chariot, a compass of sorts, a small two-wheeled vehicle that carried a movable figure with an outstretched arm as a pointer to indicate south. No matter how dark the skies, the chariot turned unerringly to lead his army out of the fog."

Jane took a sip of water. She capped the bottle, and William whisked it away as she continued.

"Huangdi's homeland is thought to be the Sheep's Head Mountains just North of Goaoping in Shangxi Province. He brought to humankind a dizzying array of innovations, which included carts, boats, and elaborate clothing. Other inventions credited to the emperor include the Chinese diadem, throne rooms, early astronomy, math calculations, and 'cuju'—an early Chinese version of football.

"Huangdi is regarded as the father of Chinese characters, said by some to be the oldest continuously used system of writing in the world; an oracle bone script found on animal bones or turtle shells, that was used in divination during Bronze Age China. His principal wife, Leizu, taught people how to weave silk and dye clothes that were also attributed to Fu-Xi, as mentioned before.

"As was His right, as a Manifestation of God He invented the Chinese calendar and a sound code of laws. Huangdi was known as the originator of the degree of unity known as the centralized state, and He is regarded as the initiator of modern Chinese civilization.

"His teachings are said to be the basis for the Five Phases, the Five Virtues, also the Five Cardinal Points or Five Elements. The elements, wood, fire, earth, metal, and water are used for describing interactions and relationships between phenomena and are employed in fields of early Chinese thought, including geomancy, Feng Shui, astrology, traditional Chinese medicine, music, military strategy, and the Shao Lin martial arts."

Gideon turned to Secora. "The directions and colors of the cardinal points remind me of our Lakota philosophy." Secora nodded her agreement.

"The Yellow Emperor lived for over a hundred years before meeting a "phoenix," a symbol of high virtue and grace, and a "qilin," a hooved, lion-headed, horned horse creature—sometimes depicted as a giraffe. These animals are known throughout various Asian cultures to signal the imminent arrival or passing of a wise sage or illustrious ruler. Then, Huangdi, the Yellow Emperor, died.

"At times, Shennong and Huangdi were considered to be friends and fellow scholars, despite the 500 years and seventeen or eighteen generations between them. It is said all Manifestations know each other intimately and sympathize with the sufferings the others must bear because of their exalted stations. So, undoubtedly, they were spiritual friends.

"Together they shared with humanity alchemical secrets, the making of gold objects, improved practice of medicine, and of course, immortality. Each is credited with improving the livelihood of the nomadic hunting tribes, teaching them how to build shelters, and tame wild animals.

"Shennong and Huangdi were Fu-Xi's spiritual descendants. Together, the three legendary Emperors Yao (Fu-Xi), Shun (Shennong), and Huangdi (Yu or Yenti) were known as the **San Huang Trio**. They ruled by virtue and wisdom and dedicated themselves to creating a remarkable political culture based on responsibility and trust.

"Interestingly, Jesuit missionaries, most notably Matteo Ricci, tried to find common ground between Christianity and traditional Chinese spirituality during the late 1500s and early 1600s. These Jesuit Figurists viewed Fu-Xi as Enoch, the biblical descendant of Adam, as the Giver of writing. They also considered Confucianism's moral teachings as compatible with Christian beliefs. They viewed Confucian rites such as the veneration of the dead who truly continue to live and influence the fortunes of earthly inhabitants as essentially moral basics rather than conflicting religious doctrine.

"When addressing the European public, the China-based Jesuits like Ricci, strove to present Confucianism as represented by its *Four Books*: *The Great Learning*, *Doctrine of the Mean*, *Analects*, and the *Mencius*, as well as the Five Classical Chinese texts of Taoism in a most favorable light.

"Though Confucius was not himself a Manifestation of God's Word, he summed up the laws and practices of Chinese Faith. We can describe the Five Classics in terms of five visions: metaphysical, political, poetic, social, and historical."

Destiny joined Jane. They respectfully bowed and shook hands, after which Jane took a seat.

Destiny stepped into the spotlight, looked down at the stage, then up into the eager audience, and opened with, "In Neolithic times, there was a bold and brilliant pre-flood Messenger born of the line of Jared. He was referred to by many names around the world, including Enoch, Khonoukh, Hermes, Thoth, and Idris. Although the name, Enoch, was also Given to the son of Cain, Enoch the spiritual and literal King was a son of Jared, and the father of Methuselah who was the father of Lamech and grandfather of Noah. This Enoch was the first of the 'children' of Adam to be given prophethood after Seth. Later on, He was called Hermes Trismegistus, or 'thrice great,' excellent as a great king, a legislator, and priest. It is everything He said and did that sets Him apart.

"He renewed His forefather's (Adam) religion for the Babylonians, but only a handful listened. As normal, the majority turned away. They forced him to abandon the land of His birth, where people failed to grasp His revelation, but His teachings succeeded famously in other parts of the world.

"He fled to Egypt where, as Thoth, He was the first to invent a basic form of written language. There, He was also called Hermes by the Greeks, who visited Egypt in search of wisdom. Edouard Schure gives us this glimpse."

*Leading his brave followers out of Babylon, he headed for
Egypt. There, as Thoth to the Egyptian, and Hermes to the
Greek, He carried on His mission, (having) His greatest effect
on mankind from Egypt, where the effect of His Illumination
was gargantuan and mysterious.*

*Beneath the seeming idolatry of its external polytheism, Egypt
preserved the ancient foundations of esoteric theology and its
priestly organization. In Assyria royalty controlled and crushed
the priesthood... whereas in Egypt the priesthood disciplined
royalty, and never abdicated even in the worst times, standing
up to kings, driving out despots, and always governing the
nation... for over 5,000 years Egypt was the stronghold of pure
and exalted teaching.*

*He bade people to do what was just and fair, teaching them
certain prayers and instructing them to fast on certain days and
to give a portion of their wealth to the poor. He shared a vast
amount of divine knowledge.*

Destiny cleared her throat. "He must have been a supreme Manifestation of God, destined to leave a prominent mark, even past the
destruction of the flood and the millennia beyond. He still influences
our society today. You might be interested to know that Enoch not only
laid the foundation of philosophy but filled libraries in Egypt with
scientific volumes. Enochian knowledge and Hermetic ideas were
basic to the turn of the last century's secret societies like the Illuminati
and social fraternities that began with the Greeks and Egyptians and
continue even today with the Masons, the Benevolent and Protective
Order of Elks, the Rotary Club, Lions, etc. Incidentally, He is known
for hermetic sealing techniques." She smirked.

Scattered laughter showed an appreciation of the reference. A
young woman stood and said, "Dr. Hawkins, that is absolutely amazing. But didn't he also influence black magic and sorcery?"

"I'm pretty sure the introduction of the sciences appeared to be
nothing short of magic to many. The concept of dark magic, as seen
today, forms in the realm of a twisted or influenced human mind."

"In The Gods of the Egyptians (1899) E. A. Wallis Budge adds:"

In Egypt, Thoth is considered to be Ra's Will, translated into speech. He is associated with the arts of magic (dealing with Angels and Demons) and a system of writing, as well as the development of science. He became associated with the judgment of the dead.

"Enoch, like other Messengers, is often shown in the company of a lamb or ram. He is a Healer with Stone Age roots and His head in space. According to Mohammad and Baha'u'llah, another name for the Shepherd of men was Idris."

The first person who devoted himself to philosophy was Idris. Some called him also Hermes. In every tongue he hath a special name. He it is who hath set forth in every branch of philosophy thorough and convincing statements. After him, Balínús derived his knowledge and sciences from the Hermetic Tablets, and most of the philosophers who followed him made their philosophical and scientific discoveries from his words and statements.

— TABLETS OF BAHA'U'LLAH, PAGE 148.

"Although there have been subsequent inventions and improvements in writing, and communication systems coincidental with the arrival of other Manifestations, Hermes/Thoth is credited with filling several Egyptian halls with collected spiritual wisdom, science, and magic."

The historian who had spoken up earlier in the day hollered from his seat, "That's a lot of writing!"

After the chuckles subsided, a smiling Destiny continued, "The Egyptians attributed forty-two books on esoteric science to Hermes. The *Doctrine of the Fire-Principle* and *Words of Light* contained in the *Vision of Hermes* became the climax of initiation into the Egyptian priesthood.

"In summary, He was a Prophet, a philosopher, and author of esoteric work that is the source of the occult philosophies and rituals, as well as a host of fraternities, and benevolent and charitable orders, and all the Greek secret societies."

Sage rose and picked up a book. He removed the bookmark to eager clapping from the front row. "Thank you, Dr. Hawkins. Here is a selection from the *Vision of Hermes,* which tells us about death and salvation. And even the possible destruction of a soul as described by Osiris, the Lord of Light, as recorded in Edouard Schure's book *The Great Initiates.*"

One day Hermes fell asleep after having reflected upon the origin of things. A heavy torpor took hold of his body, but as the latter became numb, his spirit ascended into space. Then it seemed to him that an immense being, without definite form, called him by name.

'Who are you?' asked Hemes, startled.

'I am Osiris, Sovereign Intelligence, and I can unveil every-thing. What do you wish?'

'To look at the source of beings, O divine Osiris, to know God!'

'You will be satisfied.'

Immediately, Hermes was flooded with a blissful light. Upon its diaphanous waves, the captivating forms of all beings passed. But suddenly, the terrifying shadows of sinuous shapes descended upon him. Hermes was plunged into a humid chaos filled with smoke and dismal moaning. Then a voice arose from the abyss. It was the cry of light. Suddenly, a faint fire burst forth from the humid depths and reached the ethereal heights. Hermes arose with it and found himself once again in space. In the abyss, the chaos became ordered; the choirs of the stars stretched out over his head and the voice of the light-filled infinity.

'Did you understand what you saw?' Osiris asked Hermes in his dream, suspended between earth and heaven.

'No, replied Hermes.'

'Well, then you will know. You have just seen what is for all time. The light you first saw is divine intelligence, which contains everything, including the archetypes of all beings. The gloom into which you were plunged is the material world where men of earth live. But the fire which you saw flame forth from the depths is the Divine Word, God is the Father, the Word is the Son, their union is Life.'

'What wondrous sense has opened within me? asked Hermes, I no longer see with the eyes of the body, but those of the spirit. How is this?'

'Child of dust,' said Osiris, 'it is because the Word is within you! What in you hears, sees, acts — is the Word itself, the sacred fire, the Creative Word.'

'Since that is so,' said Hermes, 'let me see the life of the worlds, the way of the souls, whence man comes and whither he returns.'

'Let it be as you desire.'

Hermes again became heavier than a stone and fell through space like an aerolite. Finally, he saw himself at the top of a mountain. It was night; earth was dark and bare; his limbs seemed heavy as iron.

'Lift up your eyes and behold!' said Osiris' voice.

Then Hermes saw an amazing sight. Infinite space and the starry heaven enveloped him in seven luminous spheres. In a single glance, Hermes saw the seven heavens above him like seven transparent, concentric globes, whose sidereal center he occupied. The last had the Milky Way as an enclosure. In each sphere, a planet with a Genius of different form, sign, and light revolved. While the awestruck Hermes viewed their scattered efflorescence and their majestic movements, the voice said to him:

'Look, listen, and understand. You see the seven spheres of all life. Through them, the fall of souls takes place, and also their ascension. The seven Genii are the seven rays of Word-Light. Each of them governs a sphere of the Spirit, a sphere of the life

*of souls. The one nearest you is the Genius of the Moon with a
disquieting smile and wearing a silver sickle. He presides at
births and deaths. He disengages souls from bodies and draws
them into his ray. Over him, pale Mercury shows descending or
ascending souls the way with his staff, which contains knowledge. Higher still, bright Venus holds the mirror of Love where
souls alternately forget and recognize each other. Above her,
the Genius of the Sun raises the Triumphal torch of everlasting
Beauty. Yet higher, Mars brandishes the sword of Justice.
Sitting on his throne over the azure sphere, Jupiter holds the
scepter of supreme power, which is Divine Intelligence. At the
boundary of the world, under the signs of the zodiac, Saturn
bears the globe of Universal Wisdom.'*

"The vision of Hermes gives us mesmerizing details regarding
death and salvation. This sort of thing has been used as a basis for all
religious imageries, and I think you can see threads of it used in
Dante's Inferno.

"Next, Osiris speaks of the journey of the soul guided by the
various Revealers of God's Word through the realms of the visible and
invisible worlds—the seven heavens so often referred to in other texts
and the outcome of irremediably base and wicked souls. As you listen,
remember this talk of the planets took place near the end of the Stone
Age—before the Great Flood and way before telescopes. Schure goes
on to say...

*'I see,' exclaimed Hermes, 'the seven regions which make up
the visible and invisible world. I see the seven rays of the Word-
Light, of the only God, who penetrates and governs them by
these rays. Can souls die?' asked Hermes.
'Yes,' answered the voice of Osiris. 'Many perish in the fatal
descent. The soul is the daughter of heaven and its journey is a
test. If in its wild love of matter, it loses the memory of its
origin, the divine spark which was in it and which would have
become brighter than a star, returns to the ethereal region, a*

lifeless atom, and the soul disintegrates in the whirlpool of crude elements.'

At these words of Osiris, Hermes trembled, for a roaring storm enveloped him in a black cloud. The seven spheres disappeared beneath thick vapors. He saw human specters uttering strange cries, carried away and torn to pieces by phantoms of monsters and animals, amidst groans and endless blasphemies.

'This,' said Osiris, 'is the fate of irremediably base and wicked souls. Their torture ends only with their destruction, which is the loss of all consciousness. But see, the vapors disperse; the seven spheres reappear beneath the firmament! Look this way! Do you see that host of souls trying to climb back into the lunar region? Some are pushed down to earth like flocks of birds in the blast of the storm. With a great stirring of wings, others reach the higher sphere which draws them into its revolving. Once they have arrived, they recover the vision of divine things. But now they are not content with reflecting the latter in a dream of powerless bliss. They become infused with the lucidity of conscience lighted by grief and with the strength of will acquired in battle. They become luminous, for they possess the divine in themselves and reflect it in their acts.

'Therefore, strengthen your soul, O Hermes, and quiet your clouded mind by watching these distant flights of souls' mount to the seven spheres and scatter like hosts of sparks! For you too can follow them; it is sufficient to will it, in order to lift oneself. See how they gather into divine choirs, each under its chosen Genius! The most beautiful live in the Solar region, while the most powerful rise as far as Saturn. Some even rise to the Father, themselves becoming powers among Power. For there where everything ends, everything eternally begins, and the seven spheres intone in unison, "Wisdom! Love! Justice! Beauty! Splendor! Knowledge! Immortality!"

Sage closed the book and Destiny came forward. "Think back to the Old Testament. Isn't this amazing? Let's finish the evening with a couple of quotes from the Stone-age Prophet known as Enoch, Hermes, Khonoukh, Thoth, or Idris."

A projector flashed quotes onto the screen. Destiny asked Jamal if he would read them.

'From one Soul of the Universe, are all Souls derived. Of these Souls there are many changes, some move into a more fortunate estate, and some quite contrary... Not all human souls, but only the pious ones are divine. Once separated from the body and after the struggle to acquire piety, which consists in knowing God and injuring none, such a soul becomes all intelligence. None of our thoughts can conceive of God nor can any language define Him. The incorporeal, invisible, and formless cannot be comprehended by our senses...God is ineffable. ...the First Cause remains hidden.'

"Thank you, friends. Feel free to have a postprandial snack and tea before you go home or to your rooms."

The crowd rose and immediately began to discuss their thoughts as they slowly trickled out of the auditorium. Sage met up with Jane, Iris, and Destiny, no doubt to thank them for their magnificent efforts.

Secora yawned. "Glad we don't have to leave for home until dawn, I'm frazzled."

Gideon put his arm around her. "Me, too. Busy day tomorrow, let's get some sleep." They wandered upstairs to their room without the luxury of a snack.

2 2

EVERYTHING CHANGES

A few days later, Secora woke up to notice her beloved husband staring at her. She couldn't believe how blessed her life was. She pushed back his dark hair and kissed him.

Gideon smiled, saying, "Tarkio called. He wants to finish his paperwork and grading this morning. I think he is hoping you will join him for a look at the article."

She stretched, rolled over, and pushed herself out of bed. "Mmmph." When she returned from the bathroom combing her hair, she asked, "Have you had breakfast?"

"Not yet."

"If you make the coffee and toast for yourself, I'll half-scramble the eggs. Want green pepper, tomato, and cottage cheese?"

He bounced out of bed. "Sure."

Soon they were munching, laughing, and joking as they discussed the fun and excitement of last weekend at Hasan's Resort. Secora's phone rang. It was Tarkio.

"Hey, how are you managing after last week?"

"Don't want to think about it yet. Just wanted to let you guys know that Bill's family has left Idaho behind and is headed for California. They think the fires will keep away the scary forests and the cryptids."

"He's probably right. Did Dan sell the cows?"

"He found a buyer who will load them out today."

"I guess that is the end of that."

"If Bill decides to join them, he will send us a forwarding address for his grades. Will you be in the office today? I have questions about things that happened in the forest."

"When will you be there?"

Tarkio explained, "I'm already at the office."

"Great. I should arrive in half an hour."

Gideon walked her to the door, teasing, "Why don't we go with Seamus to assess the water project in Afghanistan and leave the craziness here behind for a few days? We could walk the path of Zoroaster."

Secora froze in her tracks for a moment, then grabbing her jacket, answered distractedly, "I suppose we could. But it would also be tempting to go to a place similar to Armenia because of Gayomart, and there, we could honor the earliest Aryans."

Gideon cleared their dishes, saying, "I took today off. While you're at work. I'll look into the possibility."

She kissed him and left.

It was nearly mid-day when Gideon invited Seamus over to discuss joining them in Armenia after he evaluated the water project in Afghanistan.

While Gideon poured the Irishman another cup of tea, Secora arrived and hung up her jacket.

Seamus acted in a cheerful mood. "Hey Secora, Gideon and I are looking at the possibility of seeing both Afghanistan and Armenia."

"Alright, what have I missed?"

"Nothing yet." Gideon had gotten her a mug of hot water and a bag of Constant Comment tea while Seamus absently pulled a brochure from his pocket.

He unfolded it. "Hey guys, check this out. It says Armenia is in the Ararat Plain flanked by Turkey, Iraq, Albania, and Georgia. Smack dab between Asia and Europe. It is bordered on the South and East by

Iran, and Nachjavan, an enclave of Azerbaijan. And there's a pilgrimage site near Mount Ararat that used to be in Armenia before Turkey swiped it."

Gideon added eagerly, "So, it's just underneath the great Caucasus Mountain Range."

Secora asked, "Wasn't it formerly part of the Soviet Republic?"

"Yes. Both Turkey and Russia have taken away land, and Armenia is now a fraction of the original size. At one time, it was home to one of the world's oldest civilizations spread over an area almost as big as mainland China. Although its size has diminished, Armenia is proud to be the earliest of the Christian nations, and it's defined by spectacular religious sites, including the Greco-Roman Temple of Garni, and other fourth-century castles, churches, and monasteries. Its capital is Yerevan, where the Mahendran Library dominates the main avenue and houses thousands of ancient Greek and Armenian manuscripts."

Secora smiled. "Manuscripts, okay. Seamus, now you have my full attention."

Gideon announced, "What a goldmine of religion and history *that* must be."

Seamus nodded, continuing, "Republic Square lies at the city's core, offering musical water fountains and colonnaded government buildings. And the 1920s History Museum of Armenia contains archaeological objects like a 5,500-year-old leather shoe recently found in the Cave of the Birds. I think we could have some crazy fun there."

Gideon agreed and said he would look into travel plans. Seamus was grinning when he left to drive to the ranch, and Secora took advantage of the free time to go on a grocery run. He was already plotting on the computer when she left.

At one point, Jane called Gideon with a message from Kyah, who was on the archaeological crew in Peru and visiting friends.

Through mutual acquaintances, Kyah had received word that Guillermo Santiago, the great Kallawaya healer, had passed. Alai was having a difficult time coping, and he thought Gideon and Secora might want to offer her an open-ended invitation to stay with them in Montana.

Gideon told Jane it would be wonderful if Alai chose to come. Then Jane confided her son had already made the offer on behalf of Secora and himself.

"That was several days ago, and he hasn't heard anything from her yet. But Kyah sounded hopeful."

Gideon reminisced, "I remember this crazy story Jimmy told us. After the initial shock and sorrow of Diego's death, Guillermo started bouncing up and down on his hotel bed because he and Alai knew their son had crossed safely into the next realm, and they would be together forever."

Jane laughed. "I can imagine him bouncing on that bed. Secora will probably want to go after Alai immediately. She and Guillermo had been like parents to her while she recovered from the bullet wound in her shoulder at their home on the isla. They nurtured both Secora *and* baby Monta when they were struggling. She remembered the other day how Guillermo pushed the little boat off the shore so she could go into Lake Titicaca and offer flowers as a tribute to Diego, who had been her beloved fiancé."

Jane shared, "I remember the Great Thunderbird observed the offering from high above and validated the moment with a piercing cry. There are times she simply could not have managed without Guillermo's healing guidance. Beautiful memories. Tell Secora to be patient. I already sent money for Alai's ticket to Kyah, but I'm sure it will take a little time to close things out in Challa before she comes."

"If she comes. That is really kind, sis. Thanks."

"Ask Secora to call me so we can say the Baha'i Prayer for the departed over the phone or maybe at our apartment."

"I will. Give Kyah my love when you speak to him."

"Of course."

"Oh, and Jane, Secora, and I are planning a trip to Afghanistan and Armenia for a few days. I don't know how all of this will fit together. Guess we'll wing it."

"You always do," Jane chuckled.

THAT EVENING, Secora and Gideon met the rest of the family at Jane and Aparu's apartment. They sat on a couch along with L.W. and Sage. Jimmy and Destiny occupied a love seat. Tarkio and Anida sat on the floor flanked by Aparu and Jane, Iris and Kantun, plus a myriad of children whose parents were attempting to calm them in anticipation of the prayer for the Departed.

They waited for Secora to stand and read the main prayer. After it was completed, everyone in the room offered prayers from their hearts, and several of the guests cried.

L. W. wiped her eyes. "What a kind and gentle soul."

Jimmy observed, "The quintessential definition of Kallawaya."

Gideon added, "Every drop of his life was spent in service to God and the creatures around him."

Secora grinned. "Maybe we should bounce on beds in his honor."

Secora's thoughts turned to young Monta. The precious girl baby she had adopted but had to return when the father came home unexpectedly from a slave labor camp. She would be a little over eight now. *Eight years old. Such a precious age.* Secora thought, *I love you and miss you, dear child.*

She knew one day they would be reunited. But time had to pass for the little girl to bond with her people and move forward in her life. Secora swallowed hard, thinking she should move forward herself. Then she remembered she needed to finish preparations for an extra credit osteology lab in the morning.

Suddenly, she froze, listening inside herself. *I will come to see you con mi abuela, Alai.*

TWO NIGHTS LATER, it was nearly midnight when she heard Gideon issue a groggy hello into his phone. Alai called from the airport, apologizing for the late notice, and for the inconvenient time of night. He and Secora rapidly dressed, then called or left messages with other family members before leaving to greet the matriarch and last living soul of her tribe.

Her eyes shone brightly as Secora and Gideon approached. They embraced with tears of joy and laughter at the reunion. Secora thought she couldn't have been happier until she opened her eyes and noticed Kyah was headed their way with a baggage cart. A little girl was riding like a figurehead on that cart with arms upraised and open, wearing a grin to match.

Secora's heart stopped beating for a moment, and she felt like she might collapse. Gideon had already gathered the little girl into his arms and was headed her way.

She said through tears of joy, "Welcome home, precious ones!"

2 3

THE "STANS"

At first, Monta and Alai settled in with Sage and L.W. so they would have continuity when Gideon and Secora left for a week and a half on their trip to Central Asia.

Anida and Tarkio came by daily to let their son, Frederick, play with Monta, and get to know one other. Country girl and city boy, they couldn't be more different, but they were learning to appreciate those differences.

Secora and Gideon visited Alai and Monta each morning before work and in the evening, they pored over maps of northeastern Afghanistan. It was pure joy watching one child playing digital games, while one created colorful paintings and sculptures, both of them loved science experiments.

Alai told them Monta's father had succumbed from injuries and the poor nutrition he endured in the slave labor camp.

ONE EVENING while home sipping tea, Gideon asked, "I feel inspired by Sage's talks about the cave Prophet, Gayomart. Do you think we could fit in an excursion to a mountain cave—either in Afghanistan or in Armenia?"

165

"I sure hope so. Love you so much, Mr. Yellow Thunder. Both places would be excellent representations of the sacred cradle of Eurasian faith but with different modern perspectives, Christian and Moslem."

Prior to Seamus mentioning his friend's water project, Secora had known very little about Afghanistan except what she gleaned from the news.

She and Gideon would visit Seamus and the crew as they worked on a water collection experiment in the Karakum Desert. If things went well, perhaps they could visit some of the dry, stony cave sites in that region.

Gideon said, "It's more likely we'll have free time in Armenia. Wait, where is Armenia on this map?"

Secora squinted and said, "Over there, to the left of Azerbaijan. It's the little area below Georgia where it says Yerevan in small print."

Gideon grinned. "It would be exciting to poke into a few of those caves which look to be splattered across the hills above those wild rivers."

"You and I think so much alike. Remember those pictures we saw online?"

He said, "Yeah, they looked like real-life Hobbitons. Can you imagine looking out of those entrances like Gayomart?"

She stopped to think. "Gideon, I draw the line at wearing skins, but those caves might hold a range of artifacts from the Paleolithic, Mesolithic, or the Neolithic, and the possibilities don't stop there. Elsewhere, there might be artifacts from Bronze or Iron Age trading networks. The entire geographical region was connected by culture and commerce. It's amazing."

"Down girl! With you, *anything* is *way* too possible."

"Okay, okay. Let's fix sandwiches for dinner and make concrete plans." She got up and headed toward the kitchen, then stopped in mid-step, turning back to look at him. "Did you ever think that perhaps some Central Asian tribes were ancestors or at least cousins of our own American tribes?"

"I thought everyone knew that." After a moment, Gideon continued, "Wouldn't Hitler be surprised to find out that I was Aryan?'"

"Yes, he would, my love—but he wouldn't pay attention to you or the billions of other Aryans past and present who have red, black, or brown hair—only the relative few among them who have blond hair or blue eyes."

Christian Mission Map of Central Asia - used with permission

"What about Zoroaster? Didn't your dad say He had reddish or golden hair, and He lived in what is now called Afghanistan between 3800 to 3500 years ago?"

"Yes, Thor Heyerdahl also said that about Viracocha/Quetzalcoatl. Golden red hair and blue eyes and possibly spooled ears that were reserved for dignitaries in Afghanistan."

Gideon was excited. "Wow, look at this. It says the ancient religion survived in Kafiristan until the 1800s when it was pressured by its neighbors to become Moslem."

"Kafiristan?"

"Yes, it was located in the upper east side of Afghanistan, near the 'tail' or would that be called an 'arm'? Either way, that general region where we will be going. The name came from its Nuristani Kafir inhabitants, who surprisingly, had followed a form of Hinduism. Remember, Sage said one of the Aryan threads ran through the teachings of Rama and Krishna. Huh, the area that extended from modern Nuristan to Kashmir was once known as *Peristan*."

She laid out the bread. "That's a whole lot of 'stans.' Kafiristan, Nuristan, and Peristan. Never heard of them."

"Me neither. But it sounds like Peristan is part of the area where Manzoor and his crew are working. Until recently, it was a vast region containing a host of cultures that spoke Indo-European languages. Eventually, they were all pressured into following Islam. To this day, the Moslems equate the name *Kafir* with *disbeliever* or *infidel*."

She laid turkey slices on top of the lettuce and tomato, saying, "That's rude. I wonder if that affected the people we are going to visit?"

"I guess we'll find out. Didn't you say Mohammad would honor people of another faith as long as they practiced it reverently and to the best of their abilities?"

"Yes, if only the fanatics among His followers had listened with hearing ears." She paused, then said, "Greater is God than every great one."

After a moment, he looked back at the page and continued, "This is even more interesting. That exact region earlier had been surrounded by several Buddhist territories that brought literacy and state rule to the mountains. As Buddhism declined by the sixteenth century, the region became empty and isolated—completely surrounded by Islamic states. The remaining Kafirs were closely related to the Kalash, a fiercely independent people who persist with their distinctive culture, language, and religion to this day."

"And goats."

"Goats?" He stopped reading and looked up. She put the plates with the sandwiches on the table and couldn't help reaching out lovingly to run her hand along the side of his face.

"Are you hinting that I'm an old goat?"

She burst into laughter and couldn't help but kiss him. Then she brought him a cup of Constant Comment tea and said, "I had many breeds of goats when I was younger. The first cross between Angora and milk goats were not yet cashmere goats. I called them 'Kalash' because I saw similar animals in a National Geographic magazine that belonged to Kalash people. They had a beautiful pearlescent undercoat of silky white, reddish, or brownish hair. I found it was highly sought after by spinners, and besides, they had fancy horns."

"I've never heard you talk about having goats before."

"It was a long time ago. I raised sheep and goats. Must be the Navajo in me."

"You aren't Navajo, are you?"

"No, but I was strongly influenced by Dine' women who lived with my family and looked after us girls when our parents went out of town."

"Oh yeah?" He thoughtfully considered his knees. "I never had a goat or anything useful, but I had a cat when I was a kid."

"I like cats. Was it pretty?"

"Pretty cranky. I called her Dracula. She wouldn't let me pet her with my hands, so I had to take off my shoes and socks and pet her with my feet. She was okay with that. But if I forgot and reached down with my hand, I needed alcohol and bandages."

"Ouch. Doesn't sound like she was very tame."

"Guess not. She was attacked by something and crawled into our trailer one day."

"Maybe not an animal—perhaps someone's hand."

"I suppose that's possible. Anyway, I got good with the feet. I could even put one foot on either side and cuddle her with the soles. She never jumped up near me on the couch or the bed but she trusted my toes."

"What happened to her?"

"Not sure, she went outside one day but never came back. I don't think my grandmother or my mom liked her very much. She wasn't cuddly. I guess I don't blame them. They probably expected cats to be lap quilts."

"I've had my share of cats—no two of them were the same. Very individual and a delight, most of the time."

He touched her arm. "Guess we're still learning about one another."

"Probably will be to the end of our days."

"That's cheery."

Without transition, she said, "Well then, I guess it's decided. We're going to Afghanistan *and* Armenia."

Gideon looked somber.

"What? Did I read your interest wrong?"

"No, it just struck me. I'm a little hesitant to land in Kabul after the insurgent attack last January."

"I remember. Seven victims were killed in a luxury hotel. So, we'll be staying in a cheap hostel?"

Gideon snickered. "Not even. We'll be in the desert near a campfire."

"Not funny Mr. Yellow Thunder."

He kissed her.

"Hmmm, maybe a little funny."

He hugged her, then kissed her forehead.

"Okay, okay—FUNNY." She cleaned off their plates and followed him to bed.

24

COLD DESERT

Secora and Gideon waved goodbye to her parents at the airport and were now on the thirty-six-hour flight. Seamus had left a week earlier to get the feel for the project and the crew. From the air, Secora considered the longevity and sacredness of Afghanistan and the timelessness of its rich cultures. Nearly a million years of human footsteps imprinted the land.

Seemed like forever since they left home, but they were finally on the last leg. She blinked as a flight attendant offered them coffee, which she and Gideon gratefully accepted.

The next time they looked out the window, they were passing over the mountain pinnacles of the Asian ranges and could see how the elevation sloped down across rocky desert toward the Southwest. According to an announcement from the pilot, they were following the snow-tipped Hindu Kush Mountain Range—from its highest point in the Pamir Range near the Chinese border toward the mountain-free lower elevations in neighboring countries to the South and West.

She sat next to the window, but Gideon was the one who said, "We must be getting close. Isn't that the Oxus or the Darya River, or should I say the fabled Daiti?"

She strained to see it. "Yes, it's beginning the long trek toward the Aral Sea. According to the first chapter of the Vendidad, the land drained by the expanse of the good Daiti is to be venerated as the 'first of the best countries created by Ahura Mazda.' Whatever that means," she mused, "since He created the entire planet."

Her family had lived in awe of this land as far back as she could remember. Time couldn't diminish the awesome Amu Darya that flowed beneath them.

Gideon nudged her from her thoughts, asking, "Does this river end up in the Aral or farther west in the Caspian Sea?"

"According to my sister, people built regular settlements along the lower Amu Darya around AD 400 and created a thriving chain of agricultural lands, towns, and cities. At that time, the waters emptied into both the Caspian and the Aral Seas with an assist from a major branch known as the Uzboy River, which split from the main river just south of the gigantic Aral delta. Sometimes, the water flowed through both branches, but most of the water flowed to the West into the Caspian.

"In 1221, Genghis Khan's troops destroyed the massive Gurganj Dam built in 985 AD., diverting all the water back toward the Aral. Later, the river shifted again, distributing its flow between the main stem and the Uzboy. By 1720, a Russian surveyor noticed it didn't flow into the Caspian at all."

"Okay, I'm already sorry I asked." By now, Gideon had stuffed his fingers into his ears and was humming to himself.

"Sorry." She stopped and closed her eyes. Several minutes passed before she spoke out loud. "Da, Dayadvam, Damyata... Give, Sympathize, and Control."

"Isn't that from T. S. Eliot's poem, *The Waste Land*?"

"You know that?"

Gideon grinned. "Yes, I loved that poem. Wrote a three-page paper on it back in high school."

"No kidding. Me, too. I don't remember how many pages, but those words seem appropriate for such a venerable river."

"I agree and well said."

"Aww, you've just won my heart."

"Again? You're kidding." He grinned. "If I'd known this was the key, I'd have read you the *Waste Land* when I first met you."

"We're lucky you put enough magic into the Johnny Rivers song."

"Oh yeah? Which one?"

"You remember. "Baby I Need Your Lovin," don't you?"

Reflecting, he looked careworn. "Oh yeah, I remember. I was afraid you would never break out of the depression from losing Monta to her rightful father."

"Life seemed impossible at the time. Alai and Monta have also helped me heal the wounds, but it was you who changed the sorrow into joy."

The fasten seatbelts light turned on as they began the descent into Kabul.

SEAMUS'S SKIN was already deeply tanned, and he wore a mauve cloth wrap on his head with a tail that dangled down past his right shoulder onto his chest. He dashed over to hug Gideon, who did a double-take when he saw a guy rushing him. After grabbing Gideon in a bear hug, Seamus hugged Secora, saying, "Gosh, I am so excited to see both of you. You can't believe how magical this place is. I can't wait to show you everything and introduce you to my new friends. The Afghanis are amazing people! I'm thinking of moving here."

When they could breathe again, Secora and Gideon hustled their bags over to the all-terrain vehicle of some sort that Seamus was using. It was late morning, and they ate lunch at a little shop called *Mantu. Me and We* were written on the sign in English for foreign guests.

"Me and We seem appropriate that we eat here among new friends before traveling to the experiment camp."

Gideon clapped him on the shoulder as they took their seats. "It's amazing to see you so excited, brother."

"The people here are wonderful. In some ways, it feels like I have come home — very healing. I've been treated with nothing but kindness, compassion, and respect, both during deployment and now. I'm happy to give something back with our project."

Gideon sighed, "Thank God. So great how this worked out."

They drank tea while they waited for plates of beef and lamb and orders of big dumplings, similar to empanadas and appropriately called *Mantu*.

After savoring a delicious bite, Secora led, "Seamus, have you heard of the Good River Daiti?"

"Don't think so. Is it important?"

"It's the sacred River where Zoroaster was anointed. If it was a physical river, it has been identified by some scholars as the Oxus, otherwise known as the Amu Darya."

"Yeah, the Darya! It's a pretty amazing waterway. Really sticks out in a desert." He laughed. "The guys on the crew tell me it begins as glacial meltwater up in the Tian Shan and Pamir Mountains, but the land it flows through is usually dry as a bone. Life is a struggle, and that's why we're here."

"Let's finish lunch and get out there to see it," encouraged Gideon.

Secora interjected. "Like all ancient rivers, the Amu Darya's course experienced major shifts over the past few thousand years because of climate change and seismic activity."

"I believe it. There were over a dozen big earthquakes out here during the twentieth century alone. Lots of high mountains around with seismic activity at the plates."

Seamus sipped his tea and seemed to be thinking. Then he said, "Speaking of rivers, have you heard about the Panj River? Folks here are excited about the new two-lane Darwaz Bridge that was recently completed, the latest of four Tajikistan-Afghanistan bridges."

Gideon became animated. "Hey man, I think I saw it from the plane. Yeah, we flew over it, just past the crater, before landing in Kabul. It looked a lot like a bridge crossing a river in Nevada, for example, sandy, arid land all around except where there was irrigation."

Seamus grinned. "I know, right? They say that sucker cost

$40,000,000 financed by the US Army Corps of Engineers if you can believe that. An Italian company designed and built it. It opened last August. They say the US Secretary of Commerce was at the opening ceremony along with the Tajik and Afghan Presidents. I remember it was the 26th of August because that's my son's birthday."

A slow smile covered Secora's face. "Congrats, Seamus, I didn't know you had a son."

"Yeah, lives with his mom. I miss him, but I'll see him in a few days, God willing, and can hug him then. Meanwhile, I have collected a few Afghani toys and do-dads here. Anyway, in a backward answer to Secora's question, the Panj River is a tributary of the Amu Darya. Panji Poyon, a Tajik town, is right on the corner near our camp. Sherkhan Bandar is on this side.

"Central Asia split into the many smaller countries that lie within the Amu Darya basin after the fall of the Soviet Union in the 1990s. The resource-sharing system that was set in place by Russians called for Kyrgyzstan and Tajikistan to share the water from the Amu and Syr Darya Rivers with the Kazakhs, Turkmens, and Uzbeks during the growing season. In return, they received coal, gas, and electricity in the wintertime. When the Soviet era ended, the infrastructure collapsed. Now, water management is inadequate and irrigation methods are outdated. Afghanistan is struggling to recover while insurgents are compounding the difficulties."

Seamus pulled out a map and unrolled it on the table. "The Hindu Kush mountain range runs northeast to southwest across the country, dividing Afghanistan into three major regions. The Central Highlands contain roughly two-thirds of the country's area. The Southwestern Plateau accounts for a quarter of the land and the smaller Northern Plains area encompasses the country's most fertile soil. It is there, we are starting the experiments.

"Today we will head for the Northeastern 'cold desert,' East of Kabul. The experimental site is in the Karakum, not far from the bridge. Anything that can produce sustainable water out there would be a welcome gift. There is even low-key talk of replanting trees and shrubs and diversifying crops. Something other than just goats." He laughed.

"During the 1970s war, Soviets invaded through that valley to reach Termez, an old city ruin in southern Uzbekistan bordering Afghanistan. Manzoor, one of the guys working with the project, is from that area."

Gideon said, "Can't wait to get out there. Let's ride."

Secora wanted a nap—not a bumpy ride in the Jeep-like contraption, but she clambered in with a sigh. "I hope this thing is softer than it looks."

As THEY DROVE, she noticed that wavy dunes of yellow sands covered layers of dark shale sand, creating an interplay of light and dark that was stunning. There was almost nothing to see. No people, no plants.

Seamus was saying, "The place we're collecting water is out there in the boonies, barely one person in two and a half square miles. Most of the rainfall passes over that area into Turkmenistan. Our crew is small but dedicated. I really like these guys. Even on the tough days, their jokes keep me rolling."

Gideon observed, "I guess they'd need a sense of humor to succeed out here."

"I can't believe the genuine politeness and respect my new friends share with me, an outsider."

The vehicle climbed a little rise onto a plateau created from the hard-packed black sand. They wandered toward the lush river basin, then diverted to the broad dry valley near the border north of Kondoz. Secora wasn't expecting to see much when they got to the encampment that was located on the plain just West of the cleft of a spectacular, dry mountain canyon carved by a tributary of the Darya.

When they stopped, she said, "It amazes me that there is even a border between these countries at all. They are just an extension of one another."

"And so, it was for most of history. Just one nation, culture, religion, and language." Gideon paused for a moment, then added, "Sure feels like the same ground Zoroaster may have passed three and a half thousand years ago."

It was dusk. The sun had set behind them, and Seamus pulled on the lights. "Almost there."

Secora moaned, "Thank God."

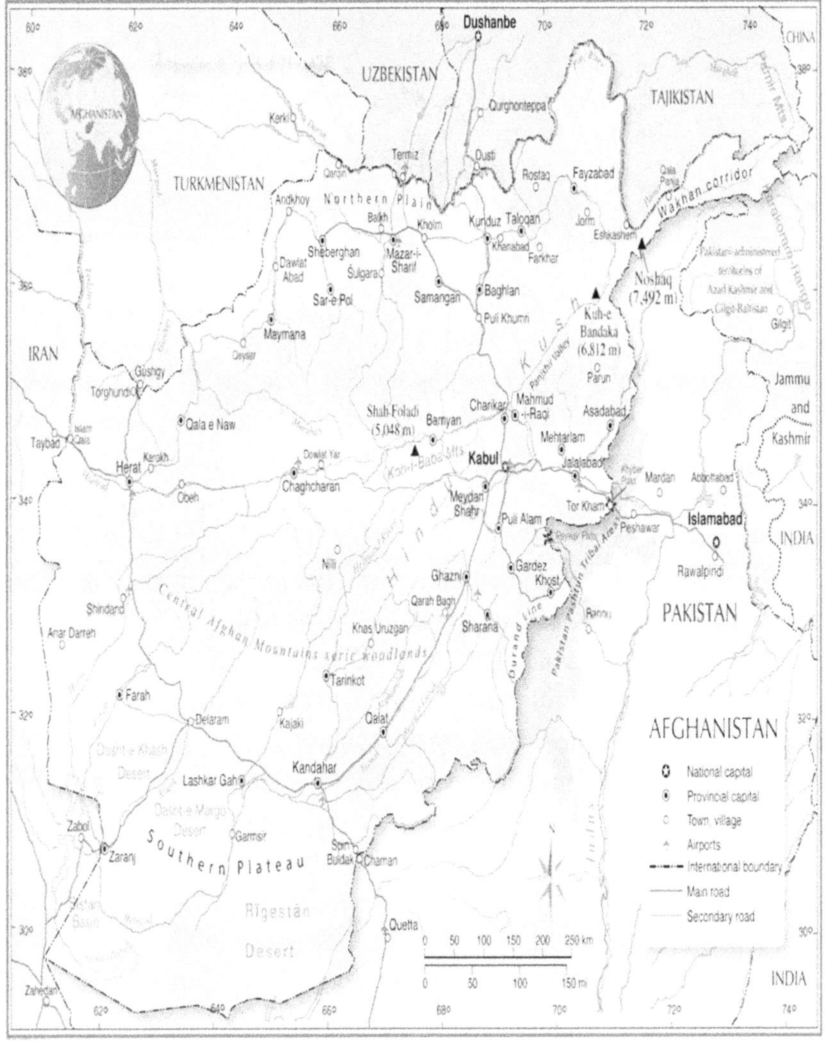

Political map of Afghanistan - source The Nations Online Project. Permission for education.

25

THE CAMP

It was dark by the time they pulled up by a small fire. Four men shaded their eyes from the glare of the headlights. As the new arrivals climbed out and came closer, the four men rose to inspect the newcomers—a custom for labeling them as *friend* or *foe* before humbly greeting each of them.

"I am Raffique," said the first to offer his hand. His small red cap, beautifully covered with designs of white stitched lines and glittering little silver stars, resembled the top of a doorway arch in a mosque. The next man's cap was similar, but it had a dark taupe background with a beige squiggle outline, a gold star design, and little pieces of mirror sewn in. *So elegant,* thought Secora. Sher Rahm grasped her hand next. He wore a thinner, bright, orange wrap tight around his head, reminding Secora of orange sherbet. Finally, Manzoor stood smiling before her. He had a thickly wrapped cream-colored turban. All the men sported thick beards. Manzoor's had silver accents.

They bade their guests sit around the grill and pointed to a meal they had prepared of tender Roti, a circular unleavened bread, and stewed vegetables that included greens, tomato, onion, herbs, potato, and squash in a spicy gravy. A teapot rested to the side of the grate.

Gideon pulled out paper cups from his backpack. Manzoor grinned

178

and filled three of them for their guests.

After a delicious dinner of food akin to flavorful dessert tacos, Secora and Gideon unpacked the ingredients of a decadent dessert which they had brought. Whipped cream, semisweet chocolate *and* butterscotch morsels, two bags of marshmallows, and two boxes of graham crackers.

"Want to try something new?" Secora pressed the nozzle of one of the whipped cream cans and the men's eyes became wide.

Manzoor asked, "Shaving cream?"

Secora giggled and put a finger full into her mouth. In no time at all, they had consumed messy versions of s'mores and were washing the sugary treat down with tea.

Moments later, they wrapped up in thick jackets, for the air had chilled. With flashlights in hand, they walked over to see the fog catcher. Secora and Gideon were new to this desert, and they followed in Gullah's exact footsteps so as not to step on some creature or fall into a divot.

They watched the formation of dew across the netting. Droplets ambled down to the drip tray that resembled the chalk tray of an old blackboard. Then the little stream trickled into the five-gallon bucket. While they waited, they talked.

With a down jacket wrapped securely around him, Scamus said to Secora, "I was at one of those talks given by your father, and I'm pretty sure the history of this area would fascinate him. Manzoor hails from Termez on the northern border. He'll tell you."

Secora hunkered down, reaching for her russet leather backpack, and pulled out a tape recorder, a tablet, and a pen. Turning to Manzoor, she asked, "May I record our conversation?"

He nodded. "First, let's go back and sit on the rocks around the fire if you don't mind."

When she was ready, she looked up at the silver-bearded man's face. The deep, dark eyes were careworn for a person who might have been in his early forties.

"Sir, could you tell me about that place?"

"I come from ancient Termez, one of Central Asia's oldest town ruins. It is located a few kilometers Northwest of here along the Amu Darya, near the border with Uzbekistan. They say its roots are over 5,000 years old and may have been a center to the Achaemenids, a Persian Empire founded 730 BC. The Shahnameh validates its early existence."

"I am familiar with portions of the book." Secora bowed slightly as she looked into his eyes.

"In April 2002, the newer city built nearby celebrated its 2,500th anniversary. I'd say that falls short of 5,000, but hey, any reason for a celebration out here is a good one." They all laughed with Manzoor.

Sher Rahm, a young man of twenty-something, said, "You have no idea. We party at the drop of a hat—so to speak."

Gullah, Raffique, and Manzoor nodded and had another laugh.

Gideon asked as he poured cups of Constant Comment from a large thermos and offered them around. "Weren't there slaves in North and South Carolina that were descended from people known as Gullah in West Africa?"

Seamus, who had a reading of two bars, was scrolling with the aid of a local cell phone. "No link to Arabic from what I can see on the internet."

For a moment, they sat quietly drinking their tea and listening as the occasional drips of water hit the drip tray of the mist catcher. It seemed to Secora that the number of drops was noticeably increasing as the temperature fell. *Makes sense.*

"All that's left of Old Termez these days is part of a wall on a hill. It looks like a longboat, maybe like part of Noah's ark or perhaps a chain of boats on top and off the side of an arid hill. A few scrub bushes and an occasional conifer surround it."

"You know we're not that far from Ararat," Gideon offered. "Maybe some people could mistake it for the Ark."

"True." Manzoor chuckled.

Secora said distractedly, "It is probably already the subject of a program on *YouTube or Ancient Aliens*."

Raffique asked, "What's *ansinliens?* We're not familiar with that."

Seamus answered, "It is a television show that tries to find the causes of mysterious things and places. Often, they suggest it might have been the work of spacemen." He pointed toward the stars. "From the sky, traveling in metal ships."

"Oh, those guys."

"The guys on the television show or in the ships?"

"Seamus, we don't have televisions."

Secora lifted her eyebrows. "You've seen the ships?"

Sher Rahm and Gullah nodded at Secora. Then both said, "Several times, yes."

A few minutes later, they rose to check the water collection depth against the lines painted on the bucket. While doing so, Seamus mentioned to Secora and Gideon that the two men were brothers.

Manzoor continued, "In 329 BC, Alexander the Great of Macedonia conquered Sogdia, as the land in upper Afghanistan was then called. Some say Termez is the site of Alexandria on the Oxus that we call the Amu Darya. Others say Alexandria was a place called Ai-Khanoum, which means "Lady Moon" in Bactrian."

Secora's pen hesitated. "I recognize the word khanoum from a great lady in the Baha'i Faith, named Amatu'l-Baha Ruhiyyih Khanum."

Seamus asked, "Lady Moon? Is that similar to the Goddess Diana?"

Manzoor looked puzzled. "I've never thought of that, but the Greeks were deeply intertwined in our history. The Kushan Empire used Greek as the official language, especially for administrative purposes, before they began using the Bactrian language."

He pointed to Sher Rahm. "My friend Sher is the archaeologist. He says the people in this area spoke Ionian until the end of the Tocharian period when it was replaced with Bactrian by the Kushans. It would be hard to say what was the origin of 'Lady Moon'."

Gideon stirred the dirt around the grill with a stick. "Where did the Bactrian language originate?"

"It is now extinct, but it *was* an Eastern Iranian language spoken by people who lived in southern valleys between the Pamirs and the Hindu Kush. The same valleys that are the womb for the Amu Darya whose waters melt down from the Tian Shan and the Pamirs. Without glaciers, the Amu Darya would not exist. Those mountains, exactly like our mist nests, collect atmospheric moisture that otherwise would escape elsewhere. It rarely rains in the arid lowlands.

"The annual rainfall is twelve inches or less. Thank God. Even though the river's course has shifted in the past few thousand years, it is still powerful enough to flow across the Karakum Desert. We need to learn how to collect water before the glaciers leave, or people who depend on the life-giving waters of the Darya will exist no more."

Gideon said respectfully, "I pray this small beginning can become a lifeline."

"For us, it has to."

Manzoor stood and began to clear the dishes, washing them in the sand.

Secora came alive. "Wait, wait, wait. Manzoor, can you tell me more about the Tocharians? I'm curious about the Takla Makan mummies from the Tarim Basin that I think might have been Tocharian. Some mummies had reddish-blond hair and light skin.

"When Sher gets back, he can tell you."

Gullah and Sher Rahm returned and sat again. Gullah announced, "We are at eight liters already."

Gideon whistled softly, "My God, already eight liters? Sorry for interrupting. Sher, will you please tell Secora about the Tocharians?"

The youth continued the tale. "Tocharian refers to a language and a people. However, the inhabitants probably referred to themselves as *Agni*, as did Manzoor's family or perhaps Kuchi, similar to the words *Agniya* and *Kuchiya* from old Sanskrit texts found on the northern edge of Tarim Basin.

"The earliest mummies date from around 1800 BC nearly four thousand years ago. These may or may not be connected to the Tocharians, a name given to the region's Indo-European languages in the early 1900s by scholars who perhaps mistakenly identified the local Aryans with a people known from ancient Greek sources as the *Tókharoi* who inhabited Bacria 2,200 years ago—just before Christ and a little over a hundred years after the passing of Gautama Buddha."

Secora's eyes widened in astonishment. "Wow, Sher, you really know your anthropological history."

Gullah laughed, "We reduced the sheep and sold three cows so Sher could receive a college education to become an archaeologist."

Sher countered, "Don't let my brother fool you. As an educator, he has taught me more about love and service to others than a university ever could."

Gideon replied, "Gullah, that is the most important kind of education."

Sher Rahm smiled and grasped his brother's shoulder before continuing, "Some of us believe that the Indo-European origin of the Tocharians is associated with bands of light-skinned Yueh-Chih who migrated from northwestern Xinjiang and Gansu China to settle in ancient Bactria around 300 BC between the Tien Shan and Altai Mountains."

"I'm having a hard time picturing that."

"They came from far northwestern China, just beneath Mongolia, bordering on Central Asia. Let me see your phone for a moment."

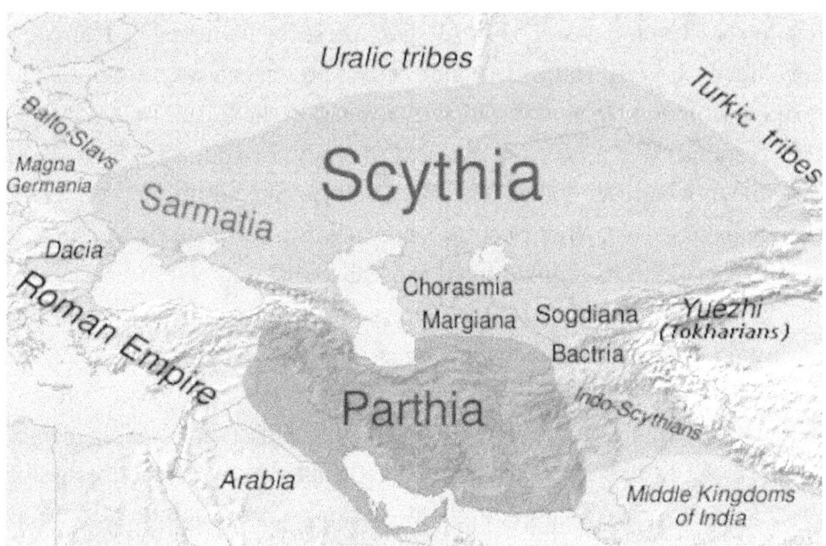

By Dbachmann, CC BY-SA 3.0, https://commons.wikimedia.org/w/index.php?curid=777725

He explained, "Here it is on a map."

Secora looked at what he had found. "I see. Thank you."

"Okay, perfect. Actually, they were all Indo-European cousins. The yellow and orange parts together could be a map of the Achaemenid Empire, and the entire map encompasses holy lands of hundreds of unremembered prophets. I can see that the sacred Tigris and Euphrates Rivers in northwest Parthia and Turkey were accessible to all these tribes.

"Yes, agricultural communities appeared in the oases of the northern Tarim around 2000 BC. Some scholars feel these communities were born from earlier Afanasievo or Scythian tribes that in a broad sense mean early Eurasian nomads. They spoke an Indo-European language known as Iranic from 3500 to 2500 BC in Siberia."

Secora thought for a moment. "That would make sense. It defines a pathway of entry for the earliest Aryans from the arctic into Central Asia."

"Right. Slightly later, Tarim or Oxus settlements flourished in the northern region from 2250 to 1700 BC. That was the Bronze Age civilization of Central Asia. By 100 BC, these settlements had already developed into city-states that later became overshadowed by nomadic peoples from the North and Chinese empires to the East."

"It sounds like this is a major area of study for you, Sher."

Manzoor agreed, "That is true." Then he picked up the conversation by asking, "So, Miss Secora, when was Buddha's time?"

"He is said to have lived from 563 BC to 483BC."

"Well, the reason Buddha is very significant to our people, to my family, and heritage is that the largest of these cities was Kucha, an ancient Buddhist kingdom on the branch of the Silk Road that ran along the northern edge of the Taklamakan Desert in the Tarim, yet south of the Muzat River. Like other cities along the northern edge of the desert, it served as a trading way-station. A more southern route of the Silk Road ran along the Amu Darya, north-westward out of Termez, before turning west toward the Caspian Sea."

Secora was lost. "Wait, I don't know the Muzat River."

Sher assisted, "It flows south and east out of the Tian Shan to Kucha."

"Guess that helps, but I feel a little lost amid such a massive history."

Sher laughed heartily. "Anyone would. I have made it my life's study because I am interested in the Kafirs, Krishna, and of course, Gautama Buddha."

Gideon was enthused. "Your range of knowledge is marvelous. I'm so mesmerized by the flow of religious tradition in this region. Please continue."

"Besides being at the center of trade with Greece and the Han dynasty of China, the Kushans had diplomatic relations with the Roman Empire, the Sasanians of Persia, and the Aksumites."

Gideon said, "Okay, whoa. Never heard of Aksumites."

Sher asked politely, "What is 'whoa'?"

"It's what we used to say to stop our horses."

Laughter flowed. Raffique said, "We sit back and lightly pull the reins."

Now everyone laughed. Gideon reddened and said, "We do that, too."

"Ah, I see. The Aksumite Empire was an Ethiopian kingdom that included Eritrea, upper Ethiopia, much of eastern Sudan, and southern and eastern Yemen at its peak. Northern Ethiopia was the center and its capital was Aksu."

"Ah, I get it. Basically, Kushan was a nexus, a real hub. Were they the ones who *started* the Silk Road?"

"Maybe. Only God knows. Certainly, the Kushan Empire was the center point of trade relations between the Roman Empire and China. And for those people, it was a golden age. Philosophy, art, and science blossomed within its borders. Yet, the only lasting record of its history comes from inscriptions and accounts in other languages, mostly in Chinese. By 200 AD, the Kushan Empire had fragmented into semi-independent kingdoms that fell easily to Sasanian invaders from the West.

"Back to the Buddha. Around 300 AD an Indian dynasty, the

Guptas, pressed in on Kushan from the East. Most of those people supported the Greek religious ideas and icons in the Greco-Bactrian tradition, but their leader also followed Hinduism. He was a devotee of the Hindu god Shiva. Later, Emperor Kanishka also observed elements of Zoroastrianism."

"What a mix-up." When Secora saw the questioning eyes, she corrected, "I mean to say a blend of ideas."

"Indeed, the Kushans were spiritually attuned and became early devotees of the Buddha. Did you know they played an important role in the spread of Buddhism from India into Central Asia?"

Gideon shook his head. "I think I speak for all three of us when I say we had no idea. That gives us a better understanding of the wellspring of religious diversity in this area."

Raffique commented, "Yes, it is rather stunning when one thinks of it."

Manzoor responded sagely, "That's not all. Kanishka sent armies north of the Karakoram Range on a direct road from Pakistan to China for more than a century, encouraging travel and trade across the mountains and diffusing Mahayana Buddhism *into CHINA*. It was during this period that Termez, referred to as Ta-li-mi by Chinese sources, became an important center of Gautama Buddha's teachings, a mere century and a half after His death."

Gideon's jaw dropped. "Are you kidding me? The Kushans taught Buddhism to the Chinese?"

Sher chuckled. "They had to hear it from somebody. Am I right?"

Secora felt awed. "Excuse me. My head is spinning right now. We grew up in America thinking our country was the greatest melting pot of cultures. So, your words are really mind-blowing. You exemplify the phrase 'Unity in Diversity.' Bless all of you."

Gideon agreed. "The history of Afghanistan takes the cake. I mean, it is the crowning example of diversity."

Seamus added, "It's pivotal! The entire world should hear about this."

Manzoor acknowledged their amazement. "Yes, they probably should."

Secora checked her recorder. "Wow, this information is going to boggle my father's mind! Thank you, Sher and Manzoor, and thank you, Seamus, for bringing that to our attention."

Gullah said, "I was going to ask what mind-blowing was, then boggle, and head spinning, and pivotal. But now I think I understand. Amazement?"

Secora said, "Yes, amazement too big for a mind to hold all at once."

Gullah smiled. "I see. I imagine that for you, this is all so new."

Gideon agreed, "It is."

Seamus asked, "Secora and Gideon, can you see why I was immediately impressed by these guys? It's rare to find someone who, like Manzoor, is not Moslem in Afghanistan. Then I was affected by the way Manzoor's friends accepted the totality of this blessed history without the slightest irritation or pressure."

Raffique said, "That is exactly how Mohammad would wish for us to behave."

Gullah added, "Miss, what do you know about His Holiness, Mohammad, blessed be He?"

Secora smiled demurely. "Whatever He allows me to know. He has my utmost respect and loyalty. As do the others, like Buddha and Krishna and Baha'u'llah."

Gullah stretched out his arms and uttered, "Bismillah, In the name of God. My brother Sher Rahm and I come from a small community where we have always herded sheep and worshipped Allah—even though our ancestors were Buddhist."

Loving appreciation blossomed inside Secora. "Bless you for your big, welcoming hearts. I am moved at the way your people continually gravitate to new Prophets by the grace of God." Lost in thought, she yawned and stared into the tiny flames beneath the hearth.

26

JOY, DESERT-STYLE

Secora caught herself nodding off when she heard Raffique change the subject. "One more thing has come to mind that might interest you. We understand from Seamus that you, Dr. James, are also a paleontologist. "

Secora nodded quietly although her gears were turning.

"Have you ever heard of a beast called an Eormanou?"

Secora thought for a moment. "Not that I recall."

"It is a rather large hairy giant who lives in the mountains around Afghanistan and Pakistan."

Seamus chuckled. "Aren't all mountain monsters hairy?"

Raffique also laughed. "Ah, yes. But this hairy one has the form and habits of a human."

Suddenly, Secora was no longer sleepy. "I know the creature you speak of. He also lives near me in Montana, and in Idaho, and well, all of America."

Gideon added, "We used to see a blond one walking past our trailer some mornings in South Dakota. Have you seen them, Raffique?"

"Yes, my family specializes in mining ore. My relatives have worked with melting and shaping metals for the last 5,000 years— since the Bronze Age. We no longer make spear tips and shields, but I

188

enjoy making the little trinkets for use on clothing, jewelry, and head coverings. We also make fun gifts for the Eormanou. Sometimes we spot them in the mountains, and they like it when we leave shiny things for them. Ah, I hear my wife approaching." He grinned. "I live nearby and my family directly benefits from this water project."

Secora took time to send a text to Bill and Tarkio regarding the Eormanou and their interactions with Raffique's family.

The distant headlights of an old Jeep became visible in the wee hours of the morning as the vehicle ground to a halt a few yards away from where they were seated. Four women and three young children alit. In baskets, they brought eggs and roti along with vegetables stewed in beef and gravy.

Manzoor greeted one of the graceful women and introduced her. "This is my dear sister, Noori, who watches out for me since the passing of my beloved wife last year."

Noori extended her arms, heavily weighed down with clothing, to the three westerners. The head coverings she had specifically designed for each of them sparkled with Raffique's glittering trinkets.

Secora donned a beautiful red and cream-colored scarf. She delighted at the tiny clinking of sewn-on minuscule bells when she shook her head.

"What a treasure, Noori. Thank you." The two women embraced. As they did, Secora knew she had a new sister in the world.

Gullah and Sher Rahm returned from the drip line with a fresh gallon of water for tea and ablutions.

Raffique introduced his wife, Katyan, and two of the children, Maryam and Hooshang. Gullah greeted the third woman, Mashya, and her infant, Hamdullah. Secora's tired mind couldn't hold all the names, but she would always remember looking into the glowing eyes of these kind and generous women and such happy and respectful children.

Gullah refilled the teapot and before long it was steaming. "For our people, the significance of this water harvesting is immense."

Gideon was stunned. "I am amazed by your results."

Raffique gushed, "Hard to believe the air is a clean water source. No mud, no boiling, and sifting out the rubbish. Thank you, God!"

Together, they shared a wonderful breakfast of chicken eggs and roti, after which the men laughed and showed the women how to use up the marshmallows and other treats to make s'mores.

When things became comfortably quiet, Gideon cleared his throat. "Thank you for becoming our friends, and for feeding us. And we are honored to receive these lovely head coverings. You have our deepest respect, and I am grateful to all of you for what you have achieved here for the good of people everywhere."

Little Hooshang sprayed Gideon's face with whipped cream "by accident" and everyone laughed as he pretended to shave it off with a razor.

After the squeals subsided, Gideon continued, "Yesterday in Kabul, Seamus took Secora and me around to a bank and several stores. In the vehicle, there are six boxes full of netting and poles, pitons, cable, drip trays, and buckets—enough for perhaps ten or more of these drip lines in other homesites. There is also the equivalent of sixty dollars US for each of your families to thank you for taking the time to do this and for recording your efforts and sending them back to Jimmy Lizardeye and Clive Bull Bear.

"Dear friends, keep up your good work. We will leave after morning prayers, but please keep in touch with us through Seamus."

"We will stop in Armenia on the way home to visit some of the ancient caves. We will offer prayers both there and back home for your communities. Thank you for everything."

Seamus said, "Gideon, after I drop you and Secora off, I think I'll stay for another day or two. I'd like to do a little sightseeing in the Karakum. Maybe visit the Darwaz gas crater."

Gideon asked, "Oh, that's the thing in Turkmenistan that is also called the 'Door to Hell' or the 'Gates of Hell,' right?"

Seamus explained, "The very same. It was created when oil drillers tried to shut down a burning well with an explosion. Didn't work. Natural gas inside the crater has been burning since 1971."

Gullah grinned. "Funny that burning gas has become a major tourist attraction and draws hundreds of visitors each year."

Raffique slowly shook his head. The little stars on his hat glittered in the setting moonlight. "Seamus, my friend, it is with regret I must tell you there are rumors of unrest in the North. It might be safer for you to continue on to Armenia with your friends."

"I will if you think that's best, my friend."

The air became silent as each of them considered what that might mean for all of them. During the stillness, most of the children fell asleep on their parent's laps.

Less than an hour before dawn, they all washed again. Then each soul wandered to a different piece of earth to offer morning prayers in his or her own way, to the One God, Creator of humanity and all that is, has been, or ever would be.

DECISIONS

Three eager faces looked out of the plane at the land beneath them. Armenia was a small country nestled in the Caucasus Mountains and highlands, landlocked between the Black and Caspian Seas. More importantly, it was a Christian nation wedged amidst countries that were unequivocally, Moslem.

As the plane circled before landing, Secora noticed the volcano. A brochure she read before they left mentioned that Mount Ararat was a snow-capped, dormant, compound volcano in the extreme east of Turkey. It had once been a cherished part of Armenia.

Gideon was excited. "Hey look. Mt. Ararat!"

Seamus piped up, "Where?"

The mountain consisted of two major volcanic cones. Greater Ararat was the highest peak in Turkey and the Armenian Highlands at an elevation of 16,854 feet. Its constant sidekick, Little Ararat, was no slouch at 12,782 feet.

Secora wistfully remembered the day she first flew into Lima, Peru in 1999. She had instantly fallen in love with the volcanos surrounding the enigmatic city which hung from the hillsides. Then she was alone with no particular cares in the world. *Seems so long ago,* she thought. Shaken back to the present by the flash of the fasten seatbelts sign, she placed a new brochure from the seatback into her bag to share with Gideon and Seamus after they settled in. Then, dutifully, she prepared for landing, realizing how tired she was. No sleep at the camp and the flight from Kabul had been utterly exhausting. *Too old for this.*

Secora heard Seamus' stomach growl. All three were hungry and thirsty, but they decided to settle into their hotel before eating an afternoon meal. Once they were on the ground, they gathered their luggage and followed other travelers outside to wait for the shuttle from the Tufenkian hotel. The ride, traffic allowing, would be twenty-nine minutes from the Zvartnots International Airport.

Secora had been listening to Armenian conversations on the plane which taught her that the "Ys" were very soft or not even pronounced, as in *Yerevan,* also *Erevan.*

Gideon was the tallest, and he spotted the shuttle not because he could read any of the words but because there was a picture of the hotel's elegant entrance. The young shuttle driver, who introduced himself as Kheridan Kocharyan, was eager to speak—in English which Secora thought was unusual. He shared with them highlights of the town and current events.

Secora focused on the banter to keep her mind off the nerve-wracking top speed drive from the airport. This wasn't going to take any twenty-nine minutes.

Eighteen minutes later, Kheridan parked at the hotel and went inside with them, politely offering them a card advertising his parents' restaurant that was only a half-block away.

Secora thanked him and he handed her another card. She looked at it and shared it with the guys. They deduced he was moonlighting on the weekends as a tour guide. "Not just weekends, if you are interested." He said he would wait for her call.

She checked in at the desk, wondering if she should worry about his super-friendly approach. *Maybe he's just trying really hard to be of service. Lord knows we could use the help after pulling the intense all-nighter on top of two flights.*

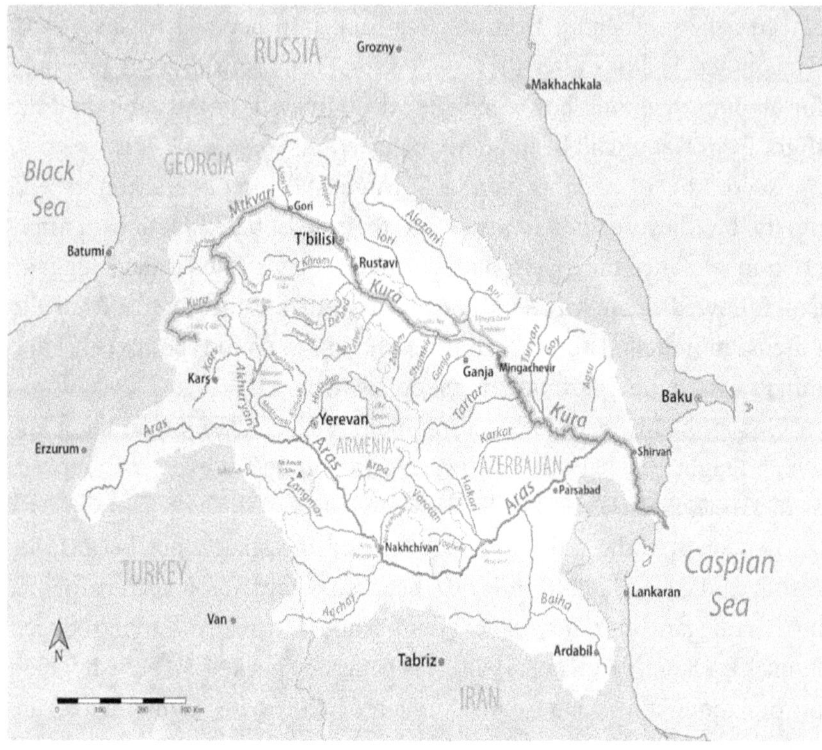

From Wikimedia Commons, the free media repository Author, Shannon 1

He insisted on helping Gideon and Seamus with the luggage as they trekked to their rooms. Oddly, he refused a tip and just asked that they consider the restaurant and the offer of a guided tour.

Gideon said, "Thanks, we'll probably need both."

Secora was thinking about frugality since it had cost them $700 apiece for the plane tickets. She stirred from her foggy distraction when she heard Gideon asking if Kheridan would deliver dinner to their room because they were too exhausted to venture out. Penny-pinching was out the window.

Kheridan was back within the hour with an elegant meal of beef dumplings in a wash of onions and cabbage in a flavorful beefy tomato sauce. He also carried a bag of assorted fresh fruits.

Secora was delighted and said, "This meal is almost like dolmas in a different form."

Seamus asked, "Are these like mantu?"

"Yes, you know this dish?"

Seamus rubbed his stomach. "I love it!"

Gideon paid him generously, and Kheridan left with a dashing smile.

The savory dinner hit the spot, and soon after eating, Seamus passed through the suite door for a nap. The couple settled onto the bed, barely able to keep their eyes open. Secora was reflecting on their amazing time in Afghanistan. So much had happened that it seemed to have taken several days rather than the last thirty hours. She inhaled deeply, grateful for the slightly cooler indoor temperature.

The last thing she felt was an onrushing tenderness for Gideon. It had been a long time, over eight years since she had functioned completely on her own. Now she and Gideon were inseparable, close or within reach in every aspect of their days. "Thank you, God, Allah'u'abha."

LIGHT WAS ALREADY FILTERING through the curtains when Secora opened her eyes and watched Gideon sleeping peacefully. She smiled, then rose quietly to shower and dress. After dawn prayers, she ate a pomegranate leftover from last night's meal, then breaking the seal on bottled water, she took the top brochure off a stack of material Kheridan had provided. This one featured the Khosrov Nature Reserve that boasted one of the oldest protected areas in the world with a history of about 1700 years. It had been founded in the Ararat Province of Armenia by King Khosrov Kotak III, ruler of *Greater Armenia* from AD 330 until 339, that at the time included most of the land between three seas: the Mediterranean, the Black, and the Caspian. In the North, the Caucasus Range was an effective barrier to invasion. It had blocked the Sarmatians, who, at the time, ruled land from Germany all the way across into Russia.

The pamphlet stated the king chose to preserve the forest in order to conserve the animals and plants of the region and improve the natural environment of the city of Artashat, the capital of Greater Armenia, before Ararat Province was overtaken by Turkey.

Secora felt amused as she read, 'As a bonus, it also served as his royal hunting ground.' *They should have probably led with that.* The king had even ordered trees to be planted on the high slopes of the mountains for recreational beauty—*and* use in military exercises. So, for Kotak III, it was a win-win-win situation.

The place also held evidence of a more recent historical past. Remains of secular and spiritual structures from the Middle Ages, such as fortresses, castles, churches, grave-yards, cross-stones, and abandoned villages dotted the Reserve.

After noting the Silk Road also passed through the territory, she became groggy, losing interest in the leaflet. It dropped onto the table, and she faded back into the comfortable chair. It wasn't long before her eyes closed, and she took a couple of catnaps before Gideon was up and moving.

Even after he was dressed, they didn't feel like doing much, both still sleepy from all that happened in the last couple of days, compounded by jet lag. Instead, they perused the literature of the area together, trying to figure out what direction they should move now that they could see more of the terrain surrounding Yerevan.

Secora showed him the pamphlet on the reserve, then put her left hand to her head. "I still don't know how to pick a suitable cave to pray and commune with the ancient Aryans. I'm at a loss."

"Well, the Aras River valleys and gorges seem interesting, and they run onto the Plain of Ararat."

She yawned, "Sorry, I noticed that a tributary of the Aras enters the canyon of Garni, also called the gorge of the Azat River. Those cliffs look like very dramatic, lovely, basalt columns that seem to stretch to the sky."

Gideon noted, "Yes, but they also look like they are nearly impossible to navigate."

"True, not good for hiking, and I think I'm looking for something not as well-traveled as the Garni Gorge."

"Hey look at this. The Azavan Chapel was carved from the rocks high in the Azat River Gorge because it harbored a spring of holy water. Visitors still drink from it and carry its healing waters home. The small cave chapel became a massive complex of ornate structures, praised by Pope Gregory VII around 1075 AD when he tried to extend the reach of the papacy. Its most prominent chapel was carved from the rock in 1215 and blends beautifully into the surrounding stone outcrops. Inside are examples of local stonework—elegant, bare chapels and carved crosses."

"Sorry honey, that sounds intriguing but seems like a popular tourist attraction."

She watched as one leaflet, in particular, drew Gideon's sparkling eyes.

"I like this one with the catchy images of cliff dwellings. He flipped it open. Lots of carved-out caves, featuring generous arched rooms with square columns. It says the Azat River was born on the south-western slopes of the Geghama Mountains before passing through the Khosrov reserve. Sounds like there are tons of historical tour possibilities."

He looked at Secora with the glee of a child, and her heart melted. She couldn't help but smile. "Maybe each of us should pick a favorite place to visit."

He grinned back at her with love in his eyes, then flipped another page. "The Garni area also has a *great* waterfall, and it flows down to a dam which generates hydroelectric power and provides water for drinking and irrigation. After moving through the village of Garni and a few other towns, the river streams into Ararat Valley and finally unites with the Aras River near the ancient capital of Artashat."

Secora nodded but said nothing.

He switched gears. "If you want something more rugged and wild, we could go to the Nameless River area."

"Ooh, Gideon, the Nameless River. That sounds like it has possibilities. The path less traveled?"

"I made it up but thought you might like the sound of it. If it was a real place, it would probably be in the rugged mountains of the north-west corner of Armenia, bordering with Turkey and Georgia."

"Even better. Perhaps we can do a little of each. We'll ask Seamus what he thinks."

A knock at the door saved them from further speculation. Gideon peeked out, then opened the door to admit Seamus and Kheridan who had come bearing breakfast.

Kheridan grinned as he entered. "Hey guys, hope you're enjoying your stay so far."

He set down two bags of pastries while Secora put out paper towels and cups of water, and said, "We certainly are. How are you this bright morning?"

Seamus assured her they were 'peachy keen.'

Soon savory and sweet flavors were tickling their tastebuds. When they finished, Kheridan offered to be their guide for the day and Secora and Gideon were pleased. She thought *maybe I misjudged this boy. He doesn't seem assertive, just excited, and accommodating.*

The young man explained, "Armenia has a rich and unique heritage that is utterly fascinating to explore. I, personally, like the idea of the Khosrov Forest Reserve. Besides its unique plant and animal species, it is rich in prehistoric cultural heritage."

As they finished the pastries, he gave the Cliffs Notes versions of a variety of destinations. Secora and Gideon were amazed at his easy grasp of the English language.

Secora said, "I'm curious. You speak English like an American. I thought only 3½% of Armenians spoke English as a second language."

"Yes. Two years ago, I attended graduate studies at the University of Montana in Missoula. They had a great biology program. My fiancé shared the opportunity with me, so both of us are fluent. She took history courses there."

All three travelers said in unison, "You're kidding!"

Gideon explained, "That's where we are from. Secora works there."

Seamus said, "That's crazy. We could have passed each other on the street."

Kheridan blushed. "We mostly stayed in the dorm and the library when we weren't in class, but it certainly is possible. Perhaps we were destined to meet in the end."

Secora clicked her tongue. "That's amazing. Small world. Anyway, you were about to tell us about the area's prehistoric cultural heritage."

"Oh yes. Did you realize that there are signs of early human culture engraved on the 14,000-year-old Ughtasar Petroglyphs on Camel Mountain? It's quite remote."

Nobody answered. They were still lost in thought about Kheridan's Missoula days.

"Besides those images and caves, we could find other traces of early occupation, like architectural monuments, churches, and castles —sites of great historic value. You've probably heard of Havuts Tar and the Garni Temple in the Garni Gorge?"

Gideon nodded, somewhat uncertainly.

Secora mumbled, "For us, Kheridan, the choice is bewildering."

He laughed. "Jet lag still has you in its claws. Well, a new visitor center in the Garni district will open in a couple of months to present its natural and cultural history. But we don't yet have that luxury. I *can* tell you that there are three hundred and twelve monuments registered in the reserve, including twenty-nine monasteries, churches, chapels, and castle ruins. Although they are mostly tumbled-down now, destroyed in the earthquakes of 1675 and 1679, there are over two hundred cross-stones and gravestones, and forty other medieval monuments that were constructed between the ninth and the fourteenth centuries. One can also find the remains of nineteen settlements. Some were only abandoned because of pressure from the Russians in the 1950s."

Secora was stunned. "Good job narrowing it down, Kheridan."

Everyone laughed but Seamus, who had closed his eyes after eating and was starting to doze.

Gideon paused, then said, "Whoa. Sorry, too much info."

Kheridan looked down. "Right, okay."

"Maybe we could each pick a place and take in a variety of locations that way. I know Gideon would love to see some of those Azat Gorge sites, and I'd like to commune with ancient prehistory farther away from visitor paths. I guess we'll have to wait and see what Seamus wants."

"Certainly. That should work."

Further conversation was blocked by a snore. Turning to her left, Secora noticed Seamus was completely passed out.

Gideon ventured, "We were attracted to the Garni Gorge of the Azat earlier. What do you suggest?"

"Must have stayed up late." Gideon gently shook his friend back from a micro-nap.

Seamus groggily said, "Wait, what about the other forts?"

"Okay, let's say there are many fascinating caves and several major monastery ruins on the Azat. As you know, Armenia is a strong Christian nation even though her neighbors have all become Islamic." He waited for head nods, then continued, "Early Christian relics were brought here from the Holy Land by Crusaders for safekeeping in monasteries, including the Havuts Tar Medieval Monastic complex established back in the eleventh century. It once held relics of antiquity but is a ruin now."

Secora said, "I think I saw a documentary about mountain monks protecting relics years ago."

Gideon interjected, "That's located on a mountain top, east of Garni, on the left bank of Azat, right?"

"Yes, the site can be accessed either by foot or horse."

Seamus snorted, then sat up in his chair, rubbing his eyes as he looked around.

"According to a legend, the name Havuts Tar means 'bird flight.' They say a priest healed an invader who had attacked Armenia. For payment, the priest asked the leader to release as many prisoners as could fit inside the church. As the prisoners entered, the priest converted them into birds to make enough room for them all.

"Anyway, the cathedral had its own diocese, including Yerevan. Besides being an important educational hub, Havuts Tar was a well-known center for manuscript creation. The oldest known manuscript dates to 1214 AD. The complex was also home to a church by the name of St. Rescue because they had a 'rescued' holy crucifixion cross-stone.

"To be honest, I don't know what that means, but they built the walls of the church during the Middle Ages with processed red and black tuff stone bricks upon which texts were carved. An earthquake destroyed the cupola and roof in 1721, and a previous earthquake in 1679 badly damaged two nave chapels. In the early 18th century, the Catholics rebuilt portions of the complex. Currently, the monastery lies in ruins, but there are two monument groups located approximately one hundred meters from one another."

Gideon looked puzzled. "What is actually left after all the destruction?"

"Basically, it is now small hills of rubble surrounded by a partial wall and some brush. There are roads and paths nearby, and it's a great place to find snakes."

Seamus and the couple, surprised by his candor, broke into laughter that sounded similar to chickens cackling.

Seamus asked, "Kheridan, can you please tell us about the tuff stone bricks?"

"Tuff stone is like pumice. It can be carved and cut. Stonemasons mostly carved the caves here. They're not limestone caves, where the minerals dissolve away."

"Thanks." Seamus turned toward his companions. "Maybe it's the Irish lad in me, but I'd like to visit the Gorge of Amaghu. It sounds so cool."

Secora said, "I think you saved us thirty hours of flipping through more literature. Let's start with Seamus' recommendation."

They spent the morning sightseeing the surviving ruins of the ancient fortress and castle, yet still found enough time that afternoon to investigate the Old Saint George's Church ruin northeast of Yerevan, near Ashtarak. Kheridan explained they built it to house the remains of Saint George, the "Slayer of Dragons," which certainly tickled Seamus' fancy.

By late afternoon, they were hungry and tired and barely able to crawl to the vehicle. Kheridan clapped his hands together. "Now, my friends, time for dinner."

They eagerly followed him into his parent's restaurant. A lively clientele, some of whom were singing and dancing to a Georgian beat that sounded like the drumming of galloping horse's hooves, permeated the dining area.

Kheridan told them that only a little over three percent of their culture could be traced to Bronze Age Armenia. The bulk of the population was a mix of Georgians and Azerbaijanis. After they ate, the trio went to the hotel for a shower and a nap.

2 8

MAJA TURANDOKHT

After a leisurely evening, they were back in line for a table at the restaurant, hoping to meet Kheridan and find out more about this enigmatic region. Seamus regaled them with tales of the Afghani desert while they waited in line for a table.

"Here's a little factoid. Did you know the Caspian Tiger once stalked the marshes along the Amu Darya River?"

Gideon's face wrinkled in confusion. "What? Caspian Tiger? No, I never knew that."

Secora said, "I forgot there ever was a Caucasian big cat, or maybe I never knew about it in the first place."

Gideon said, "I can't imagine humans purposefully living near a tiger. Glad we don't have 'em in America."

"We did."

Gideon winced. "That's great, Secora. I don't want to hear anything about them."

Seamus interceded, "Anyway, the wee beasties hung out where people congregated to wash clothes and fetch water for drinking or irrigating crops."

Gideon shivered at the thought.

The waiting line had vanished, and they entered the busy eatery.

Secora chose a fairly large table to leave room for Kheridan's family and friends, who might drop by for introductions or a visit. They were being seated when the young man came rushing in.

His cheerful voice sang, "I found a parking spot."

"Great, Kheridan. Have a seat." Secora offered the chair where she was about to sit. "Seamus was just telling us about the Caspian tiger."

Kheridan's eyes lit up. "Apparently, they are missed by some. The delta was suggested as a potential trial reintroduction site for its closest surviving relative, the Siberian tiger."

Gideon's words were short, "You're joking, right?"

"Of course not, but someone sensible must have decided the entire plan was objectionable, at least at this stage."

Gideon grew impatient, perhaps due to hunger. "There's a time and place for such creatures."

Secora added, "And a size for every age. Perhaps their age has ended."

Kheridan continued, "I imagine the Russians dispatched the last of the big cats."

Seamus asked, "The Russians? How's that?"

"As you know, the Soviets became the ruling power in the early 1920s, and Turkmen, Tajiks, and Uzbeks fled into northern Afghanistan."

Secora said, "I did not know that."

"When Central Asia broke into factions, the tribes became vulnerable to outside incursions and domination. At least that is what my fiancé, who studied Asian history, would say. Anyway, in the 1960s and 1970s, the Soviets started using water from the Amu and the Syr Darya Rivers to irrigate extensive cotton fields on the Central Plains. Before that, water was already being taken for agriculture but not on such a massive scale. Now irrigation became a major factor in the shrinking of the Aral Sea. By the late 1950s, any tigers left would have likely been shot or starved due to the decrease in the water, and consequently, game."

Kheridan clapped his hands together and asked, "Is anyone else hungry?"

In unison, the others responded, "Starving."

They let the young man order dinner for the table. He told his companions that his fiancé would join them after she got off work at the nearby mechanic shop.

Secora smiled. "What a wonderful occasion. Can't wait."

Right off the bat, the gigantic tortilla-style roti bread brought straight to their table after being baked on the sidewalls of a semi-underground oven surprised Gideon.

The owners, who saw how much the Americans enjoyed their food, stopped by to visit with their son's new friends. Secora instantly fell in love with them. They reminded her of an elderly Tongan man and his wife from back home. Rough, tough, and gruff at times, but they had the sweetest of hearts, loving souls, and strong minds.

An argument erupted nearby. Guests from surrounding tables turned their chairs around and joined the heated discussion. Gideon asked Mr. Kocherian what was happening. For his efforts, he was shushed, as Mr. K. grabbed a chair and dragged it over to enter the argument. His wife and son soon followed.

Secora, Seamus, and Gideon could only look on in wonder as they finished their meals alone.

Secora whispered, "I can't understand a single word. They seem angry, but they don't seem to be violent."

"True," said Seamus, "And no one is giving us weird stares. Always a positive sign."

At length, a woman with wide-set doe eyes came to sit at their table. "My name is Maja Turandokht." She took in a ragged breath and asked, "You are Americans, right? I don't know if you are Christians, but I think it's important you understand what we are talking about, and maybe tell others back where you live."

Secora and the others nodded their agreement.

"We are upset because my cousin found an article written by a man calling himself 'Lucifer Sam' who posted a story about the Armenian Genocide. As you may know, we are proud of our heritage from its beginning with Hayk the Progenitor and the ancients who fled idolatry in Babylon, even to now. Repeatedly, idol worshipers and materialists who would love to see the noble Aryans crawl on their knees have crushed us. The worst time in memory was perpetrated by the Moslem Turks on the Christian Armenians in the late 1800s."

She unfolded a printout of the article and gave them a summary in English.

"Sultan Abdul Hamid II of the Ottoman Empire began a disgraceful campaign to eradicate Armenians, much as Russia has since tried to beat the Chechens out of existence. At the beginning of this ethnic hostility, it was simply discrimination against Christians. The Armenians were treated as second-class citizens."

She read from the article.

"'When the Ottoman Empire officially became a constitutional monarchy, they took legal action, marking populations as security threats, and tried to eradicate them. Laws were passed to strip the people of their possessions, which the government then labeled as abandoned... Parliament was then able to take martial action against native Armenians, forcing them out in droves.'"

"During the early deportation and extermination process, our people were driven into the desert to wander across borders. Frequently, militant Turkish factions took Armenians into remote spots to massacre them. The bodies of children, babies, men, and women lay in stacks like sardines. The Turks accused them of aiding the Russian military to justify murdering defenseless people. Very few of our people had, but approximately one to one-and-a-half million, a major part of our population, were slaughtered. Many more were exiled."

Gideon said, "So that is what Kheridan meant about only three percent of the population being Armenian?"

She nodded, then was momentarily interrupted by loud sobs from a woman embroiled in the discussion at a nearby table. After a moment, she picked up the article and read,

"'Since any testimony against Muslims by Christians was

*rendered inadmissible in Turkish courts, the invading armies
could do as they pleased—and they did.'"*

She looked up from the papers to see their reactions. "Armenia was now a small minority in what had become a sea of Islam. As you can see, the repercussions still haunt our people. Only twenty-one countries even recognized the genocide. Not all of the United States agrees with us. Only forty-two states have confirmed it. This is especially difficult for the descendants of the victims, as you can see at the tables over there because the Turkish Government still denies the event happened." Maja became still as tears welled in her eyes.

At length, Secora said, "I remember when my sister and I were little, our dad hushed an Armenia dinner guest, effectively keeping him from sharing a tale. I always felt sorry that the man hadn't been allowed to speak of something that was obviously heavy on his heart. Now, I can also understand why my father didn't think this was a great dinner table conversation for the family."

The woman unrolled the papers again and shared with them a picture of piled sunbaked corpses joined in communal repose.

Gideon muttered, "And yet, here we are."

Secora gently took the page. "We must not forget this atrocity, but we must also remember that our Creator has not abandoned these souls or living Armenians." Secora uttered a Hidden Word for the departed on the spot.

*"O Son of the Supreme! I have made death a messenger of joy
to thee. Wherefore dost thou grieve? I made the light to shed on
thee its splendor. Why dost thou veil thyself therefrom?"*

This moved the young woman to sobs.

Gideon spoke, "Seems like Hitler took a page from Hamid's book, and a similar tragedy happened to my Lakota great grandparents. They were herded into a circle with no horses or rifles to protect themselves and mowed down with a machine gun from a nearby hill."

He then uttered a prayer to remember the souls of the poor Armenians massacred through heartlessness and fear and the grief of their descendants.

At this point, everyone in the room was listening. Maja was translating.

Not to be left out, Seamus sang the 'Our Father' in a dulcet voice and offered a moving story of the potato famine, a time when the dominant culture thought the Irish were lazy and worthless and deprived them of food and amenities during a terrible drought. The English scoffed and told them if they wanted to live, they'd better get busy and farm for themselves. Unfortunately, the climate and conditions of the land precluded most types of farming, so they starved to death with only potatoes to soften the blow. Some outsiders laughed at the gruesome results.

"But not the Cherokee Indian Nation in the southern United States. No, that proud people collected a small amount of money and shipped it to Ireland to help the people. Today there's a statue in Ireland born of gratitude to the Cherokee Nation who stood by them in spirit."

Secora added, "You know, all of these stories involve descendants of Central Asian peoples. We are, in fact, all related. Property seizure, imprisonment, torment, and death are still suffered in Iran, Afghanistan, and other countries to humble Christians, Baha'is, and other non-Muslin groups—a double crime, since the gentle Prophet, Mohammad told His faithful followers to never harm a single hair on the head of a Christian or a Jew, and that they should be left to worship God through Moses or Christ in churches or mosques—and if they were sincere, He would, in turn, call them His own."

Seamus added, "For every tale of sorrow perpetrated by evil criminals, there are extraordinary tales of courage and valor and sacrificial assistance offered to the sufferers. I've heard Mohammad was kind and gentle. His compassion moved me when I heard He forgave the fool who speared and killed his daughter, who was carrying a near-term grandchild. Why can't the ruthless people who claim to be His followers humble themselves in the light of Mohammad's words? Thank God, not all Moslems are hard-hearted. I have heard that many are kind and gentle, willing to risk everything to help the stricken ones."

Gideon was genuinely surprised and turned to Seamus, saying, "Such gentle understanding from a Montana farmer. I never expected to hear this. You are amazing, Mr. McGill."

Secora spoke, "A young Bahai couple from Iran once told me that after their wedding ceremony, the couple had just returned to their home together, and a Moslem woman who lived next door burst in from the backyard and threw a hijab over the new bride. They were shocked when she told them soldiers were coming to the door to take the woman and do what they pleased. Since Baha'is don't wear head coverings, they didn't consider the marriage legal. Bless that neighbor, the Cherokees, and every kind soul who assists us in desperate times. Condolences to everyone in this room, seen or unseen. Our hearts wish to fix the injustices and comfort every sufferer."

With tears streaming, Maja said, "Unfortunately, there are wicked people who devastate others in Mohammad's name. They make up their own rules and shove the words of the Prophet aside when it suits them. They twist the concept of 'jihad,' the internal struggle to quiet the inner self and turn always toward Allah, into war against neighbors who don't think like you. How Mohammad must weep! Curses on the Pasha and his minions."

Secora suggested. "Perhaps we should pray for the forgiveness of those evil-doers in honor of dear Mohammad, Lord Jesus Christ, Baha'u'llah, Black Elk, and all of God's treasured servants. I'm sure souls of the pitiless ones will become repentant for their stupid cruelty at the time of their judgment."

Gideon commented, "Or they will simply be ended—according to Hermes, right?"

The haggard woman thanked them, and as she stood to leave, she said loud enough for everyone in the room to hear, "You three have made us feel heard, loved, and respected. Thank you."

Kheridan returned and stood beside her, putting his arm around her, saying, "This is my beloved, Maja Turandokht."

Secora, Seamus, and Gideon were a little surprised. They smiled as they stood and offered compassionate hugs and supportive words to carry back to their countrymen. As they walked away, Kheridan said over his shoulder, "I'll see you first thing tomorrow morning."

THE TRIO WANDERED BACK to the hotel. On the way, they saw a pair of what looked like eagles soaring in the high currents. Secora joked that it would have been nice to travel around by floating over the land on the high currents, like those eagles or Wakinyan.

Gideon squinted, then said, "Funny you should mention her. I felt as if she was trying to link with me while we were on the plane, to give me a vision."

"Really?"

"Yeah, but it wasn't working just right."

"Did you bring the medicine with you?"

"I did. Alai sent several vials back with Jane that Guillermo had freshly prepared before he died."

Secora rejoiced. "Bless his magnificent soul." *Thank you, Guillermo.*

Back in the room, she dropped onto the bed to rest, and it wasn't long before Secora was sleeping soundly.

WHILE SHE SLEPT, Gideon and Seamus did a bit of reconnoitering. They checked out the Yerevan 'culture hub' that featured the Republic Square fountain shows. Then they went to the library, spending about an hour taking in the art and relics. After that, they visited the Vernissage Market, buying a few wonderful fruits and cheeses, plus pastries and street food to take back with them to the rooms for snacks and breakfast.

29

CAVES AND VILLAGES

The next morning, Kheridan showed up, waving a handful of brochures in front of Secora, Seamus, and Gideon. "My friends, what would you like to do today? Gideon, I believe it is your turn to choose."

Gideon wrinkled his brow, and said, "There are so many caves to choose from."

"Right, but probably the most famous cave is Areni-1, a Boris Gasparyan project called the 'Cave of the Birds' because of the vast accumulation of bird nests. The world's oldest known leather shoe, dating back to 5,500 years ago, was recently uncovered there. They've also found evidence of trade relations across the Middle East with the discovery of four unique types of ceramic. Only one of them was commonly used in local pottery."

Secora nodded. "I understand the cave has at least five or six Neolithic layers occupying a depth of over *four meters* and radiocarbon dates ranging from 6,300-5,500 years ago. Very cool."

"True, and they dug a grid at the entrance where they discovered segments of mud-brick dwelling structures and a paved courtyard. Toward the rear, they excavated an open storage area that still had circular earthen work areas and vessels for storing food. I know this because my parents are great fans of Mr. Gasparyan."

Secora winced. "Sounds like that place would be crowded with visitors."

Gideon asked, "Are there other less famous options nearby?"

Seamus commented, "Wait, is there a place with not just a cave but also a castle or a monastery?"

"Yes, Seamus. That's an excellent suggestion. There are *many* other caves and ruins, my friends, and many with rural communities nearby. Too many for one trip, I'm sure. But Eastern Syunik is considered to be the most ancient in greater Armenia. Little caves pock the hillside, and residents have used them for protection during recent war skirmishes. Today, livestock graze there, and they used some caves for stables."

Gideon commented, "Sounds like a rabbit warren."

"Yeah, like rabbits, maybe," laughed Kheridan. "Once inside the small entrances, you can see rock-cut stairways, niches, halls, and multiple exit routes. Then, there is the Tegh Cave Dwelling Complex."

Gideon replied, "I've been admiring pictures of that."

"Understandable. It is the largest of such villages discovered to date. As one climbs the cut-rock stairs, they become aware of arches and passageways. The loose composition of the volcanic rock allowed internal labyrinths to be carved with interconnecting halls, archways, and living rooms whose walls were flat and polished. There are segregated work and storage areas—even ovens and press rooms for wine-making. Like most cave cities, it is found near water and is one of the largest of all the complexes." He showed them photos.

Secora queried, "So these caves aren't the kind with stalactites and stalagmites?"

"No. They were marvelous housing opportunities carved from rock, like those you see from time to time in photos of Turkey. Like Derinkuyu, right?"

Gideon lit up. "That is too cool! We'll definitely think about those."

Tegh Photo by Reflected Serendipity on Caucasian Challenge website

Khndzoresk Cave - Sean Dunphy on Wikipedia creative commons

"There is also Old Khndzoresk Cave Village. It may have once held as many as 15,000 people in a network of manmade caves which were inhabited right until the 1950s when the Soviets condemned that lifestyle as uncivilized and forced the villagers to evacuate the area."

He passed around a picture from another of the pamphlets he fished out of the stack. The caves and holes vaguely reminded Secora of a hill in Hobbiton, like a strawberry flowerpot with the little pockets cut out around the sides.

"With little flat ground available, the ancients carved communal dwellings into rocky sloping hillsides, blanketed with both natural and man-made caves and niches. They built rooms into and around each other, requiring a system of ladders and ropes to access the more isolated corners. In later centuries, villagers still attended its functional churches and schools."

Secora took the brochure. "Resembles an American cave-dwelling."

Gideon said enthusiastically, "I like it, but what else do you have?"

Kheridan continued, "An old village on the right bank of Khosrov River was inhabited until the 1940s. There are no records of its beginning, only the historical monuments proving it flourished between the twelfth through sixteenth centuries, with a graveyard from the 1200s. But a cupola-centered chapel with a single entrance was likely carved from the rock as early as the eleventh century. The Fort of Birds, at 2000–2100 meters high, rises above the old village. It is the favorite haunt of our diverse predatory birds."

Seamus waved his arm in front of his chest. "What's up with all these ruins and birds?"

"I thought you'd like that one, Seamus. It has caves, a church, and a fort."

"Sorry, everyone. Birds kind of freak me out."

"Well, then, Sakraberd was a fortress constructed on a small mountain plain. At its foot lies a village and large cemetery ruin with many beautiful cross-stones. *Maybe,* no birds there."

Secora brightened. "Hey, I watched a video that showed these carved cross-stones were once beautifully hand-painted with floral and animal designs in cheerful colors of red, blue, green, white, and yellow, like Scandinavian balcony décor. They recorded information about the dead and family events."

Gideon commented, "Sounds a lot like the Northwest Coast tribal totems, carved from cedars instead of stone and then hand-painted. Not too surprising, since I guess we are all relatives."

Seamus grinned. "As long as there are no actual birds, I'm good."

"Mr. McGill, our precious Armenia is literally paved with old fortresses, also parapets and walk-ways reminiscent of the Great Wall, Stonehenge-like standing stones, cathedrals, monasteries, and other stunning ruins. You could spend three lifetimes admiring their staggering aspects, never fully paying tribute to their memories. However, I think I have the right one for you and will make it to the top of Gideon's list—since this is his day."

Gideon friction-rubbed his hands and said eagerly, "I'm ready."

Kheridan took in a long breath. "The Geghard Monastery at the entrance of the Azat Valley contains several churches and tombs. They cut most structures into surrounding rock during the peak of Armenian medieval architecture, dating from the fourth to the thirteenth century. High cliffs surround it on the northern side and a defensive wall encircles the rest like a windowless fortress."

As he pulled out a photo, Kheridan pressed his lips tightly to hold back a grin. "Here's a picture."

"Now THAT looks interesting," said Gideon.

Seamus said, "I am ready to leave anytime. What about you, Secora?"

Mesmerized by the photo, she said, "Let's hear more."

"It began as a small, hillside Monastery called Ayrivank, meaning 'Monastery in the Cave,' because of its rock-cut construction. According to tradition, it was founded by St. Gregory, the Illuminator, and built following the adoption of Christianity as the state religion of Armenia, beginning the fourth century AD. We call it the 'Monastery of Geghard.'"

Geghard Monastery Complex

Seamus drooled. "Oh, I'm in love already. Kheridan, I'll say it again. I might never leave this fantastic area. Gideon, you may be on your own with the water project."

Gideon did a double-take, then said, "Everyone should come here to see this. I can't wait."

"Okay, but I was going to tell you about one more. A castle from the Iron Age Armenian civilization also known as the 'Kingdom of Van,' or 'Urartu' on the Ararat plain that thrived from 800 to 500 BC. Unfortunately, it's under a lake formed by a volcanic crater after the eruption of nearby Mount Nemrut. But it seems you have made your choice."

Gideon responded, "That sounds cool, but I still think Geghard is the one we want."

Kheridan rubbed his hands together, saying, "Okay then, it looks like we have a winner. We need a plan."

Seamus suggested, "Step one, let's dive into the pastries we bagged up last night. The meat and vegetable-filled ones are on the left and the sweet ones are on the right."

Secora added cheerfully, "The teapot is full of Constant Comment tea. I'll grab the cups."

KHERIDAN'S TALE continued as they traveled. "The Geghard Monastery is cross-shaped inside, and it is sometimes called the Monastery of the Spear, named after the spear used against Jesus while He languished on the cross. Legend has it that this spear, dating to well before the Bronze Age, was brought to Armenia after the crucifixion and is now at the Echmiadzin Treasury."

Once they arrived, they found so much to explore. The immaculately constructed buildings filled with special touches like beautiful paintings, Icons, and the spectacular play of light through sunlit domes dazzled their eyes. Earthquakes had destroyed much through the centuries. Still, the location was nothing short of breathtaking.

While wandering through, Secora connected with a painting of Christ and the spear. She reflected, *such complete humility and submission to the will of God, born of the deepest affection for the Beloved. Thank you, Lord Jesus Christ, for that riveting example during your last moments in this realm. Bless you and thank you forever.*

When she looked around, she was alone. She could hear voices, but she wasn't sure from where. Was she imagining the chanting of monks or the chants of wandering Crusaders from centuries past? She could see them vaguely. Their faces raised, bathed in a light that must have been gifted them by their savior.

Gideon shook her arm gently and whispered her name. She looked at him, her eyes adjusting to his face in the chamber's darkness.

"We'd lost you. Are you okay?"

She smiled. "I am. Thanks for finding me."

After finishing the tour inside the complex and cave, she rested on a set of carved stone steps, smiling and absorbing the sun's rays while the men continued their excursions through various structures.

She closed her eyes, listening to a plethora of birdsong and the distant voices of visitors, past or present. She wasn't sure. It didn't matter. The last thing she remembered was a light breeze laden with the fragrance of white blossoms that grew wild among the rocks. By the time Gideon woke her, it was apparent she would soon deal with a sunburn.

Even though they were exhausted after taking in the astonishing views of the mountain, the monastery, and circling raptors above, they felt a deep joy return to their hearts, moving them to offer a round of prayers. For Secora, this was a healing balm, just what the doctor ordered.

Seamus yawned. "Hey buddy, we would very much appreciate a good meal at your parents' place after a glorious day like this. Will you be joining us?"

"I'm off shift in an hour. Barring any surprise fares, I could meet you for a bite, and we could chat for a while."

Gideon groggily said, "Sure, that would be nice."

"Okay, good then."

Secora was grateful Kheridan, in his early twenties, was driving, because his passengers were floating into a nap on the way back to Yerevan. She roused with the bustle of the city traffic and sat up, blinking. Kheridan parked in front of the restaurant. She smiled when the young man opened her door. As she stepped down, she roused and thanked him for his efforts in aiding them to take home a piece of Armenia's heart.

He waved as he drove off. Secora stretched, yawned, and commanded her weary legs to move toward the table, where she joined the men. They smiled, awaiting what promised to be another magnificent meal. While waiting, Gideon called the Afghani crew via the Satfon. He hit the speaker button so Seamus and Secora could listen as Manzoor happily reported no sign of insurgents, and that they had already set up two more rural collection stations. The gentle man of Tellez also shared that the first contraption was producing two full gallons of fresh water daily.

"That's great news! Jeannie is sending you information on an underground enclosed turbine system... oh, you already got it? Good, let me know if you run short of gear."

As he signed off, Gideon told Seamus and Secora that as good as two gallons seemed, the development east of Porcupine Creek would need to generate many times that amount.

After dinner, they decided Kheridan would again be their guide into the hinterlands the next day. Although there were nine major trails for hiking and horseback riding, Secora wanted to check out a remote cave. Kheridan's help would be essential.

"There are some intriguing places in the northwest corner of the country that have been closed off recently because of several reported wild animal attacks."

Gideon smiled, "I guess that would be out in what we are calling the Nameless River area."

"And a good name that is for such a place." The young man felt confident he could give them a final trip they would remember, yet steer them clear of danger.

LATER THAT NIGHT, Secora awoke and turned on a dim table lamp to review the topography and the lay of the land for tomorrow's trip. She also examined the flora and fauna of the region, after which she checked her stash of medical gear, reading a label on one of the vials. *Store at temperatures not exceeding 98°F.* Had she thought of everything? It was the best she could do. Then it was lights out.

30

NAMELESS RIVER

Secora woke the next morning, trying to remember what day it was. She groaned softly so as not to bother Gideon. She checked her calendar. It was Tuesday. They would leave Central Asia on Thursday, and she wasn't ready to go. After seeing the cave towns at Tegh and Khndzoresk Gorge Village on Sunday, then the magnificent Geghard Monastery that everyone agreed was probably the best structure they had ever seen, there was time left for one more tour.

Today they would travel to the sparsely visited Northwestern corner of Afghanistan, nestled between the furthermost reaches of the Kura and the Aras tributaries north of Lake Sevan. Their goal was to find a cave in a dry river system of the rugged mountains at the base of the Black Sea. It would likely be a two-day trip there and back. There was no time to lose. They would leave the following day on Thursday.

She glanced at her watch; it was time for her to wake the others. Kheridan would arrive at their rooms in a half hour. She gently kissed Gideon, who was already rousing. "Time for prayers, dear."

Gideon dressed, and after they communed with their Creator, Secora knocked on the suite door. Seamus was already dressed and set to go.

Kheridan arrived moments later with Maja, who could stay for only fifteen minutes before leaving for work. Together, they enjoyed another savory and sweet breakfast of pastries and tea.

Seamus explained, "So, I guess we've chosen to find a nameless river which drains down from an arid canyon, either in Armenia or Turkey, with Georgia, Chechnya, and Russia just above us. Risky, but at least there is no mention of dreadful birds."

Maja laughed. "I see you've really pinned it down. You know that is Hayk's country?"

No one answered.

Maja looked down her nose, then smiled as she said, "Good. Because I'm going to tell it to you. The Great Progenitor Hayk, son of Togarmah, had been living in the plain of Shinar where he was a prefect, busily directing the construction of the tower of Babel. This hero among men was not merely a saint but also a mighty giant as beautiful as a god. He was a warrior in times of need, and his greatest strength was in the throwing of spears. He was fearless when he fought the giant, Bel, near Lake Van in the land of the white-tailed eagle and in Ararat, the land of golden jackals."

Seamus grimaced. "I knew it. A bird."

Secora asked excitedly, "Maja, from what I've read, there are hints he was part, or a full-blood giant—maybe a type of ancient human, like Gayomart. Perhaps he was Denisovan?"

From the stares she was receiving, Secora could tell she had confused the audience, so she switched gears. Grinning, and glancing at Seamus, she said, "I really liked the last part about the white-tailed eagle and the jackals."

Maja nodded. "I love telling stories about Armenian history."

Gideon grinned. "We noticed, and we love hearing them."

Seamus added. "Such a wonderful gift you have. Where I live in Montana, there don't seem to be many historical storytellers left. More's the pity."

Maja brightened. "Did you know Hayk was descended from Noah through Japheth, and like them, he was always a believer in the ancient faith? Hayk and his people stood firmly against Bel, also called Nimrod. When Bel's devotees became more prevalent, Hayk fled with their sheep and cattle, plus his sons, daughters, and extended family, who numbered about three hundred. They journeyed North until they came to the land of Ararat, where the climate was harsh, but his people stood firm in their faith in one God and maintained their independence from idol worshippers."

Secora said, "I am so glad to hear your story, and I can't wait to share it with my father. I remember an excerpt from *The Legend of Haic*, a book about *Armenian Legends and Festivals,* written by Louis Boettiger in 1920. He spelled the name H-a-i-c."

Maja and Kheridan nodded. "Either way."

"I have a piece of an article I looked up after you mentioned his name last night. As you said, Bel, or Nimrod in other sources, established himself as the patron god of Babylon. But Hayk refused to submit. Bel felt cheated when they left and marched to Mount Ararat to persuade Hayk to come back and worship him."

Secora fished a note from a book on the table and read:

'Thou hast departed and hast settled in a chill and frosty region, urged the Assyrian god. Soften thy hard pride, change thy coldness to geniality; be my subject and come and live a life of ease in my domain.'

Secora looked up. "But Hayk refused the cordial invitation. This so angered Bel that he brought his army to force the hero into submission. In the end, Hayk slew Bel with an arrow from his bow, and they buried the tyrant in a place called Kerezman, meaning grave."

Kheridan nodded. "Hayk knew Bel was a liar."

Maja smiled and continued, "Armenians still sing songs and tell stories about Hayk's great beauty and valor. He died around 2028 BC at the age of four hundred, having stood strong. He kept the Aryan faith intact."

Seamus acknowledged, "Hayk sounds like a true epic hero!"

Eagerness shone in Maja's eyes. "It is true. Many Armenians do not call themselves 'Armenians' nor their country Armenia. They are descendants of Hayk and call their country Haiasdan in his honor. By the way, sdan or stan means 'land of.'"

Everyone sipped the last of their tea, lost in their thoughts.

Then Maja said, "Unfortunately, his descendants have not been a peaceful people. There have been bitter splits in belief and culture over the centuries. Perhaps, in a way, Bel eventually won."

Secora looked up from the carpet into the young woman's eyes. "Maybe not in the end, Maja. Hayk's descendants have rallied again—some around Jesus Christ, others in Turkey, around Mohammad. Both brought them back to worshipping one God. Good for Armenia, I mean Haiasdan."

The young woman's eyes had been brimming with tears, but now her smile returned.

After Haic's story, everyone's desire to go to that region was unanimous. However, it was time for Maja to leave for work.

"I am so tempted to call in sick and go to the place you are going. If I wasn't paying off a medical debt for my mother, I would do it."

Kheridan assured her, "Don't worry, my love. We will take photos and make records of what we see and find to share with you. You can make a collage with the pictures for Hayk's story and set up a night with my parents to tell it again at the restaurant."

"That's a wonderful idea, my love. Stay safe everybody. I will see you tomorrow night when you get back." The two took a moment for personal goodbyes. Kheridan returned as the crew gathered their backpacks, a cooler, and other gear.

SUCH WAS the place they would visit to pray with the souls of the ancient Aryans in a desolate land. They spent a good part of the day traveling up the northernmost tributary of the Aras River toward the craggy mountains in the upper gorge. Along the route, they passed a myriad of ecosystems, beginning with towering badlands of red and white clay.

Seamus remarked, "It's so beautiful. Reminds me of Zion National Park in Utah."

Gideon disagreed. "To me, it's more like the Dakota Badlands. Maybe even more colorful than that."

They crawled onto a side road, a two-track trail, and slogged their way into a gorge along a pristine, wild river.

Kheridan said as he scanned the hills, "I'm hoping to find a spot I saw on a map. It's a valley at the confluence of eight rivers that congregate from side canyons. The rugged mountain range surrounding them forms a dense network of main and branched ridges."

Here and there, they saw high plateaus and deep canyons sheltered by towering peaks covered in dry rocks, volcanic deposits with igneous intrusions. The land seemed to have been freshly created for their visit.

The Jeep road had taken them over lazy lowland dry hills and down into a basin not fifty yards from the rush of what they were calling the "Nameless River." There was no sign of other travelers here—no visible tracks of any kind. They continued up the draw as far as the Jeep path could take them. Eventually, the passage became impassable, blocked by a slide of boulders. After parking, they unloaded the vehicle. A raptor shrieked high above and Gideon said, "My heart raced for a moment thinking of Wakinyan drifting on the high thermals above."

Kheridan pulled out a geo-map of the upper canyons and asked, "Wakinyan?"

"Oh, an ancient bird I knew from where I live. She was a heroine her own right."

"Did I ever tell you I love raptors? We should see plenty of them today if we go up and over into the next canyon, but the hike will be slow and potentially hazardous."

Secora said, "Perfect."

Kheridan warned, "Yeah, perfect for snakes."

"True, but only if there is water nearby. Besides, I have antivenin in the backpack, in case."

Seamus' blinking look of concern made Secora step back. He asked. "Seriously? First raptors, now snakes?"

Secora comforted, "Don't worry, Seamus. Snakes stay close to water because they need to drink every day. They're not likely to travel in this heat."

"The woman just doesn't get it. If it isn't birds, it's snakes. What am I doing here?" Seamus shook his head and walked away.

"Sorry, Seamus, I didn't mean to be insensitive."

Gideon changed the subject. "It already feels like it is ninety degrees Fahrenheit."

Kheridan said, "Good weather to be out on the river."

He opened the back of his vehicle, then turned his rich dark eyes toward Gideon. "Can you help me haul a little rubber raft and some aluminum oars? They should make our passage to the far shore a lot quicker and drier."

Gideon set his gear down. "Happy to be of service and happier not to swim across."

Seamus returned, and he grabbed a handhold and an oar.

Secora was already hauling backpacks and other personal gear to the shoreline. A hopping dance in the long grass within feet of the water's edge surprised her. Shiny round yellow-marbled spadefoot toads and spotted frogs appeared to be snapping up mosquitos. She was mesmerized by their beauty and was surprised to see a garter snake slither into the water to chase one of the smaller hoppers. She was distracted from the little drama by the arrival of the men with the rubber raft.

Kheridan was saying, "We can cross here. Farther up, it would be too wild, lots of whitewater, and waterfalls leaping from the cliffs."

The men set the raft in the grass and glanced up and down the canyon. Kheridan pointed to the remains of two ruined walking bridges. "At some point, people must have lived nearby."

Seamus laughed. "Until werewolves ate them."

Kheridan chuckled. "Yeah, right?"

"Okay. The wee pixies. Not the nice kind."

Secora said, "Right now, I'm more worried about what is in the *water*. I'm not a fan."

Kheridan laughed. "If you decide to look, Secora, you may recognize the brown and brook trout."

Gideon practically drooled. "Brook trout? Sounds like home."

Seamus grinned. "I'm loving this place again."

Secora giggled nervously as she said, "I'm okay with the frogs and toads along the edges."

Kheridan added, "You'll be happy to know that golden grass snakes and dice snakes are not rare in riverbank areas. They don't scare you, right?"

"No, but how deep is the water?"

"Up to a man's chest or shoulders."

Secora's eyes glanced at Seamus. "Okay, I'll admit it. I love snakes —sorry Seamus. But you love fish and stuff in the water. You have that on me. Are we good?"

The Irishman grinned and nodded, then assisted the others as they unfolded the collapsible chairs and a table from the transport before offering Secora a seat at the water's edge.

"Enjoy the view, lass."

"Thanks, buddy."

Gideon set the cooler on the table and passed around water bottles while Secora pulled out baggies of peanut butter and wild plum jelly sandwiches, along with fruit and other snacks. She glanced up, noticing the sun at its zenith, then opened a large Ziplock of celery and carrot slices. They munched in silence for nearly a half-hour while seven ducks and a couple of loons cruised a patch of cattails. Things were utterly peaceful, and the friends found it easy to truly relax.

"Everything here seems so pristine compared to Khosrov, where game species like wild boar, bezoar goats, and hare have been decimated, and many of the trees were cleared."

"For lumber?" Gideon inquired. "I'm curious what sort of trees were taken?"

"Juniper is a very valuable tree. Its resin is used in aviation equipment, its wood for furniture making, and the sap has bactericidal properties. Disease had already significantly damaged the population. Compounded by the illegal tree poaching, half of them disappeared within a decade."

"Are they going extinct?"

"Luckily, no. In recent years, the numbers have increased. Wildlife, in general, has recovered due to improved climate conditions and better conservation measures. A few months ago, rural schoolchildren from the nearby villages were involved in an awareness program that included a conservation campaign for Persian leopards since the reserve is one of the hotspots for sightings."

Seamus seemed resigned. "I suppose that means leopards are also here. Think we'll see one today?"

"It's possible, but more likely, the wildlife will see us first and be gone. Not so sure about those werewolves and pixies."

Even Seamus laughed.

Kheridan took a swig from his water bottle and lazily brushed the ebony curls from his forehead, saying, "I brought along a fishing pole hoping to catch a trout or two for later. We're high enough up the canyon to find some nice-sized brookies."

That was all the stimulus needed to get the guys on their feet. They pumped up the raft and floated it in the water. Then, they packed the gear they could carry while Secora stashed the cooler, chairs, and table in the vehicle.

RUGGED TERRAIN

Gideon grabbed the oars and handed them to Kheridan, who was already aboard to snap into the oarlocks. He was the last to hop in, making Secora's nerves shudder as the boat drifted backward into the current.

"What's wrong, girlie? I thought nothing scared you."

"Seamus, I have a list. My memories of rivers include a shark attack, being flattened into the mud by tapirs, eluding assassins, a giant ground sloth, more assassins, and rhino-like Toxodons that almost trampled Gideon and my father. That was just in the last few years."

"Trampled by what?"

Secora shook her head and gave him a look that said, *you don't want to know.*

Gideon's voice intensified, "The terror birds—you forgot the terror birds by the river."

Her impatient look said, *uh, no, I didn't.*

"Okay then, no more teasing about rivers." Seamus sounded serious for once.

BEFORE LONG, Kheridan pointed out a trio of vultures sitting on a large overhanging branch just downstream from the raft. Black and taupe wings accented their white fluffy crests and their mostly white plumage.

Gideon whispered, "Those are magnificent."

Kheridan stopped the rowing. "We call them Egyptian vultures."

Secora said, "I've also seen them listed in books as cinereous vultures."

The waving oars appeared to make the birds nervous, and as they flapped away. As they did, the contrasting dark and light underwing pattern and distinctive wedge-shaped tails became visible. They rose in flight, then soared up the canyon on midday thermals.

"They feed mainly on carrion but will prey on small mammals and birds. Sometimes they'll take lizards and snakes."

Gideon surmised. "This shoreline would make quite the feast for them."

Kheridan added, "I read an article a few years back that stressed the fact that Egyptian vultures use tools."

Seamus was curious. "Like how?" Immediately, his curiosity was curbed by the five-pound trout pulling his line.

"When they feed on the eggs of other birds, they break the tougher ones by tossing a large pebble onto them, like a hammer."

Seamus netted the brookie and put it on a stringer.

Secora said, "Interesting. The use of tools is rare in birds."

"It is almost unheard of. But apparently, these birds also use twigs to roll up clumps of wool, then use it to bind and soften the nests they build on the tops of juniper trees. Until we saw these three, I thought the reserve was the only nesting area for Egyptian, or as you say, cinereous vultures in all of Armenia."

Seamus said in a subdued voice, "Hey guys, you're missing the point. They were huge! After hearing the kinds of things Secora attracts to rivers, I want no more of it."

Kheridan said, "I don't know about Secora attracting things, but those are one of two Old-World vultures. They weigh up to forty pounds and have a nine-foot wingspan. We also have its cousin, the Lammergeier. Sometimes it is called the ossifrage—bone eater, or bearded vulture, and is the only member of the genus *Gypaetus*. Their numbers continue to decline in Armenia, and it's moving toward a threatened status."

Seamus commented, "What animal isn't these days?"

"Right."

Secora queried, "Lammergeiers don't look like vultures. They have feathered necks."

"They're *cousins*, not closely related to the Old-World vultures. Both the Egyptian and bearded vulture have a wedge-shaped tail—unusual among birds of prey. Together, they form a minor lineage of hawks. Their rusty plumage, with the dark brown wings and face mask, is gorgeous."

"They live and breed mainly on rocky cliff faces high in the Caucasus Range. They also live in Africa, India, Tibet, and in Europe."

Secora said, "Doesn't their diet consist, almost exclusively, of bones?"

"Yes, they crack bones left behind by other predators, dropping them from great heights onto sharp rocks."

Seamus added, "Kheridan, I think I actually watched something like that on a nature channel."

Kheridan continued, "Down in Iran and up northwest Asia, they identify these unique birds as Huma or Homa birds."

Surprised, Secora said, "That's very interesting. Homa was an early Aryan intoxicant. Wonder how the hawks fit in?"

Gideon pulled in a large trout, then recast his line.

"Not sure about the hawks, but people still use homa in rituals in some regions. Besides big predatory birds, we might also see griffon vultures, harriers, peregrines, goshawks, and lanner falcons. I suppose the reason for such a variety of raptors and vultures in this area is the rocky habitats that house tons of small mammals and lizards."

Gideon said, "Kheridan, you seem to know a lot about raptors and vultures."

"To me, they are elegant and beautiful. I've loved seeing them since I was a child. It's almost like some birds have souls."

Lammergeier - Wikipedia

He looked at Gideon and pointedly said, "Wouldn't you agree?"

Gideon's look changed into a questioning expression that said *how do you know?*

Secora's eyes riveted on both of them as the raft drifted into the cattails at the far shore.

They gutted, cleaned, and iced the three trout they caught, leaving the entrails for hungry creatures. They collected and hoisted their gear and hiked up the left side of the river gorge. Secora was thinking about Gayomart and a thousand early Manifestations of God's Word, whose names she would never know. How many of these caves had served as living quarters? How many garments had been washed in this river?

They spent the early afternoon climbing to the ridge top to see the valley on the backside. Ahead and to the North, the canyon walls became steeper and were lined with rugged basalt columns, some of which had sheared off into rubble piles that were covered in thorny brush. They had to be very careful not to twist ankles.

Gideon looked down in time to see a spur-thighed tortoise feeding on succulent herbs. Kheridan smiled at the creature. "They hide and hibernate in small animal dens and also eat snails, mollusks, and other invertebrates such as insects and moths."

As Gideon moved on, he said, "Cute. Bye little guy."

After hiking straight up the ridge, the four sank into a rest break, during which a light breeze dried the sweat in their clothing. Kheridan warned they were aiming for a rugged piece of the canyon that would be only twenty miles away from the closed off area where the recent animal attacks had been reported.

Secora thought out loud, "That should definitely be private enough for us to explore a quiet unnamed cave. If we are lucky enough to find one." A skink rolled over her boot and looked up at her as if daring her to eat him. She thought of Jimmy Lizardeye and smiled back.

Kheridan noticed. "Oh, look. That's a Schneider's skink. They're usually found in broadleaf and mixed forests, so there must be more trees over the ridge."

THEY WERE UP HIGH, trying to find a good place to cross over into the next valley, when Kheridan said, "Use the binocs and look upriver. There are stony slopes of sedimentary limestone and chalky clay which are easily destroyed by wind erosion. We call them 'skeletal mountains.'"

Gideon scanned the area and asked, "What are those animals in the grass patch just before the white slopes?" Everyone strained to see the animals he was talking about.

Kheridan said, "Looks... like a band of ibex, also called bezoar goats. They have been around for thousands of years, munching bushes in sub-Alpine and Alpine meadows. Rock paintings and goat ornaments, found in monuments from the Middle Ages, are evidence of their long history in our territory."

Seamus asked, "Why? Do they puke like owls?"

"Yes, the bezoars form them, much like fur balls in cats. In the past, people used them in folk medicine. The males have long beards and large scimitar-shaped horns. Small herds eat brush in relative peace on the terraced slopes of these deep gorges. They hang out in rock crevices or caves to rest."

Secora looked at her boot and noticed some brush hiding a trickle of water that suggested there would be a spring. She pulled the bushes apart and saw that there was a small crevice in the rocks.

Kheridan warned, "Watch out for snakes in there for sure." As if to prove a point, a viper slithered under a large rock.

Gideon stood, readying his backpack to leave. The variety of flowering bushes awed him. He asked Kheridan if he could tell them about the different varieties.

"Some of them look familiar, but I can't say their names."

"Gideon, those up above us are saltwort, wormwood, and buckthorn." He turned to face the downhill slope and pointed. "Below us, we have flowers. These red or purple blooms are salvia, and that one in the shade is Trifolium. Those tall ones peppered all around the hill are mullein spikes—excellent medicine."

Seamus' eyes shone. "Those salvias are gorgeous."

"And of course, the poppies speak for themselves." Secora touched a delicate bloom.

"Yes, but look over here by my left leg. You probably never saw any of these before. They are Atraphaxis capers. They grow around the dry rocky regions here and all throughout the area—and even across the Mediterranean to Greece. I love to eat them at my parent's restaurant." He bent down. "You should try one. Just bite it a little, you don't have to swallow it." Secora and Gideon gingerly followed suit. Secora realized she was not a fan, but the others seemed to appreciate the tangy taste.

Even though the land was arid, there were several freshwater and mineral springs. Near one of them, Seamus saw larger shrubs in full bloom, and he asked, "Are those white sprays spirea?"

"Yes, they are beautiful. In lower altitudes, you can find cherry and pear, and short, densely branched bushes, often thorny, such as hackberry *and* ephedra—especially this close to the Ararat."

Secora commented, "Kheridan, you are a veritable walking encyclopedia."

"A what?"

"Never mind. You are a great guide, and you know the animals and plants very well."

Kheridan smiled shyly and moved ahead. "We'll drop over the side here and look for our bivouac cave."

As they stood for a moment on the ridge overlooking the valley, they snapped pictures and noticed a pair of birds circling in the blue sky.

"More vultures?" asked Seamus.

Kheridan shaded his eyes. "They look about the size of European honey buzzards, but they might be short-toed snake eagles." Looking through his binoculars cleared it up.

"It's definitely the eagles."

Seamus enquired, "Do they hunt snakes like secretary birds—pouncing on them and ripping them to shreds?"

Kheridan's face cringed in disgust. "I suppose they do, though I've never seen a secretary bird."

Downslope, some small game birds, possibly Chukars, fluttering up into trees, grabbed their attention.

After taking photos of the land up and down the gorge, they left the ridge behind. It was time to find shelter for the night.

3 2

STRUGGLES

Secora planned on camping overnight to take in the ambiance of any remote cave they might find. This turned out to be a good thing since it took the rest of the afternoon to carefully descend the steep, rugged uplands through scratchy thickets of dense juniper and thorn brush. They weren't in a hurry and even though they gained a few cuts, scrapes, and prickers, there were no serious wounds or bites.

The hillside leveled into a sparsely treed meadow, and they spotted a large overhang tucked back into a thicket off to the right about a quarter of a mile below. Across from the entrance, Secora could see pockets of oaks across an arid mountain steppe, causing her to guess that the cave was about 6,000 feet above sea level. Walking became much easier, similar to a normal hike.

Around sunset, shards of light slanted back at them from beneath blackening cumulus clouds that were billowing in from the Caucasus to the North. It was then they heard a high piercing sound, and Secora looked immediately toward Gideon. His eyes were already searching the sky above. Did she imagine seeing dark specks against the clouds?

"Thunderstorm. Gideon, do you have your medicine out and ready in case?"

He touched his shirt pocket and nodded. They finished traversing

236

the gentle slope, then dropped down the final few hundred yards before standing at the edge of a creek that flowed through a small, lush meadow only fifteen yards from the cave entrance. Green grass and colorful wildflowers bordered the creek. Yet Secora flinched, knowing she would need to cross it to reach the cavern. She drew in a deep breath and determinedly followed the men.

There was plenty of headroom at the entrance, which felt like it rose nearly ten feet higher than it looked from the brook. Once inside, they rested on carved stone benches to remove their wet socks and boots. After donning fresh socks and slippers from their packs, they stowed their gear near the up-slope wall.

She stood, intending to check the rest of the cavern for four-legged residents, snakes, or scorpions, but everyone froze as they heard the unmistakable sounds of rifle fire. Secora and the others peeked cautiously toward the ridge. Within moments, they spotted a military presence. Troops, apparently coming from the North, formed a considerable line, marching two abreast until they halted and looked in the friends' general direction.

Secora ducked inside while Kheridan and Gideon quickly crawled on their bellies to pull dried brush across the corners of the overhang.

Seamus reasoned, "We left no tracks on the rocks. How could they know we are here?"

Kheridan returned to the bench and placed a reassuring hand on the Irishman's shoulder. "I doubt they do. Probably focused on finding the source of the freshwater creek. If they move to the South a bit, they'll notice a spring outlet ahead of their location—up where the spirea is blooming." He then sat on another bench and rooted around in a drawstring bag.

The soldiers' voices traveled on the occasional blasts of wind. A few appeared to be busy around the upwelling water.

Secora turned to look into the cave behind her, then automatically looked at Gideon, who was gazing at her—anxiously awaiting her thoughts.

"I was hearing things. It sounded as if something or someone was rustling around toward the rear of the cave."

"Ghosts?"

Secora shrugged. "I suppose that's possible. Maybe small animals or birds."

Kheridan passed out power bars from his bag and whispered, "We are only a few miles as the crow flies from Chechnya. It lies beyond us, just north of Georgia and the high mountains. They may be Russian soldiers, but it's unlikely they'll spot this cave from that angle."

Seamus joked, "*They* seem to have passed through werewolf territory unscathed."

Kheridan responded, "Or maybe that is what the rifle shots were all about."

After noticing Seamus' white skin turn paler, he continued, "We have ordinary predators here, Seamus."

The fifty-eight-year-old Irishman looked relieved. "Oh, you have things like bears? I didn't think about that."

"Yes, brown bears are the biggest predators, and although the Caspian Tiger is extinct, we still have a scant few Persian leopards, but they are especially active at night and in the early morning hours. Both animals are rare, and they are on the IUCN Red List. The soldiers may have been startled by any number of creatures like red foxes, weasels, badgers, or even gray wolves."

Gideon asked, "How about pumas or lynx?"

"We do have Eurasian lynx, largest of the species. Bigger males measure forty inches in length, stand thirty inches at the shoulder, weighing up to seventy pounds. Females weigh a third of that. This is the sort of territory lynx and bears love—arid, sparse, broadleaf forests, and alpine meadows."

Surprised, Gideon said, "Wow, that is large—pretty much the size of a puma, but without the long tail."

Seamus asked, "What do they eat up here?"

"Mostly deer and goats, I imagine. Bears also like pears, strawberries—well, any berries, nuts, and small animals, as well as carrion. Oh, and they love honey."

"No doubt," Seamus guffawed.

Secora whispered, "Shhh."

The column of soldiers had stopped again, and Secora thought she could hear laughter carried on a gust of wind. Everyone's attention was drawn again to the ridge.

Kheridan spoke more quietly, even though the wind was blowing away from the ridge. He whispered, "We've experienced unrest in Armenia since Russia released it in the '90s. But poor Chechnya is not yet a sovereign country. It's still part of a Russian Federation and is governed by its rules and regulations."

Seamus looked serious for once. "Wasn't Grozny the site of war crimes and atrocities?"

"Yes, it has yet to find peace. Grozny had been a military outpost for Russia since 1818 and is famous for having been destroyed in two violent conflicts. In late 1999, Russian ground troops surrounded the town. They barely held a foothold after more than two weeks of shelling because they met stiff resistance from rebel units. They pressed forward in a neighborhood-by-neighborhood advance, trying to reach a strategic hill that overlooked the city, but the terrible outcome was that each side accused the other of launching devastating chemical attacks."

Secora sympathized. "I cannot imagine living through that."

"I know. I lost an uncle up there." Kheridan sat down cross-legged on his bench and the others relaxed into better positions. He added, "Recently, Armenia has experienced terrible problems of its own. These soldiers could be part of an insurrection. Hard to tell from this far away."

"By recent, you mean 2008?"

"I do. You see, former president Levon Ter-Petrosyan, who had been elected in 1991, was forced to step down for several shady reasons. Prime Minister Robert Kocharyan succeeded him. No relation." He laughed.

"Kocharyan was re-elected for a second term in 2003 amid allegations of electoral fraud by the pro -Ter-Petrosyan opposition. In early 2004, demonstrations by opposition protestors called for Kocharyan's resignation. Even so, he was able to complete his second term as president, but under the Armenian constitution, no one is eligible for a third term.

"To regain his lost power, Ter-Petrosyan announced his candidacy for re-election last year. He still had an enormous fan base who accused Kocharyan's government of massive corruption involving the theft of over three billion dollars.

"Presidential elections were held on February 19 this year. Prime Minister Serzh Sargsyan won with 53%, over Ter-Petrosyan's 23%. Though Sargsyan was legally elected, the former President strongly disputed the vote, and the opposition requested dozens of recounts. In one precinct, the recount showed a discrepancy of around 300 votes and though it wouldn't have changed the outcome, the opposition claimed the votes had been stolen, and opened a criminal case citing possible fraud. The chairman of the precinct commission was arrested even though the thirty other precincts upheld the original counts. The Deputy Prosecutor, also pro-opposition, condemned the election and urged people to act immediately to 'defend their votes.'"

Seamus exclaimed, "That's wicked."

"The Prosecutor-General asked Kocharyan to dismiss the Deputy Prosecutor because he shouldn't be a member of any party—or be involved in politics in any way.

"Massive protests began the next day. Ter-Petrosyan amassed 25,000 demonstrators, and instigated riots, erroneously promising that the army would not bother their protests since he had the support of two deputy defense ministers. An aide to Ter-Petrosyan, vowed the protests would continue nonstop, demanding a new election by February 22."

"Sounds like an all-out battle."

"We were very close." Kheridan pulled a bag of nuts from his pack, poured them into a thin plastic bowl, and offered them around.

"During the recount, at least eight people were killed in ten days of post-election unrest at Freedom Square in Yerevan, where a tent city was raised. Random looters took advantage of the confusion destroying grocery stores, shops, and police vehicles that were set on fire.

"Sitting President Kocharyan declared a ban on all demonstrations and censored inflammatory political news with the approval of the

Armenian parliament. Opposition leaders argued the looters had nothing to do with their demonstrations and blamed opportunistic activists.

"Police and the military tried to disperse the protestors who had set up barricades using abandoned busses. Thirty protestors were arrested and accused of starting the riot. An additional 400 were taken in for twenty-four-hour holds and asked to give testimony of the events. Information provided by non-governmental sources stated they arrested fifty more people outside of Yerevan. With a state of emergency in effect, Levon Ter-Petrosyan finally asked some of the protesters to go home. In the end, beatings and electric shock killed ten people. Some are still missing, and Levon Ter-Petrosyan has been under *de facto* house arrest since March 1."

Gideon said, "That's crazy!"

"Many countries watched this mess unfold. The Georgian president expressed support for the authorities and people of Armenia. A post-election poll conducted by the British Populus Opinion Polling Center confirmed Sargsyan received 53% of the vote, and he was inaugurated as the third President of Armenia in April."

Dazed, Secora asked, "How did I not know this?"

"A spokesman for the US State Department congratulated us, and the European Union commended Armenia on the conduct of the election. They regarded the result as broadly democratic, noting genuine efforts to address the shortcomings of previous elections. It was an important test of democracy in our country."

The tale spellbound Secora. "Thank God that hasn't happened in America!"

Kheridan shrugged. "It was rough. But for the first time since our independence from the Soviet Union in 1991, we believe we are stepping into a better future."

THE DAY PROGRESSED INTO TWILIGHT. With the soldiers' disappearance, it was time to start a fire in the twilight. Secora and the others collected deadwood and dry brush to pile beside their little fire pit inside the cave mouth. Soon brush crackled and sparks exploded from the dried sap. Secora placed a pot on a tripod into which Gideon had poured two bottles of water, and a hot dinner of fish soup soon became a reality.

Rain sprinkled the land. Not the downpour they'd expected, but enough moisture to cause the grateful earth to surrender its perfumes. Crickets chirped, bringing a feeling of wellbeing and peace.

33

THE CAVE SCOURGE

After a pleasant dinner and brief rest, Seamus helped Kheridan set up the four-man tent he had packed. Secora yawned as she and Gideon unpacked four headlamps and two Maglites. Everyone was tired after the exertion of the day, but Secora insisted, "Before we sleep, let's take a quick look around this place."

While the entrance had been tall enough for everyone to stand and walk with ease, the next chamber was somewhat shorter. Secora peered into several niches, locating a mortar and pestle in one that had likely been used to grind seeds or grain.

Gideon's voice echoed from beyond the wall, and she joined the men in a third chamber.

Gideon said, "I think this could have been a dormitory area with the low walls for privacy."

The floor was smooth underfoot, adding to the perception this could have been a living and sleeping space.

Seamus added, "They left these two stout columns for support."

Secora gravitated over to inspect the columns for decorations or inscriptions, but it was too dark and she was tired. "I can see more in the morning."

Kheridan offered, "There are two cubicles at the end which are pretty much enclosed."

Seamus said, "Over in that far corner, it looks like there was a fourth doorway or exit arch, but it has been closed off by a rockfall. Look, there's a skylight where the rocks from the roof fell in. I can see clouds reflecting moonlight and a couple of stars."

That thought gave Secora a chill. The back wall no longer seemed comfortably enclosed and protected. She wanted to fall back to the fire, but she used her Maglite to check for bird or animal droppings under the hole in the ceiling. "Guys, there are some old wooden poles in the corner. Could you help me stand them up and wedge them into the hole in the ceiling to stop a large critter from entering?"

Afterward, Gideon said, "Guess that's it. We can look around more in the morning after prayers."

They added wood to the blaze. Kheridan suggested, "It would be a good idea to pee around the entrance to ward off prowling creatures."

"Like what," questioned Seamus.

"It doesn't matter," said Gideon, who stood up and walked to the front of the cave. Everyone joined him to mark their territory.

Secora pointed out, "Imagine, this being the 'Holy Land' for many Prophets over the last 900,00 years. The sacred Euphrates and Tigris rivers of Mesopotamia arise not far from here. Like Africa before, this is a holy land of the highest nature."

Gideon said, "All land is sacred."

Seamus agreed, "True. You've got a point."

Secora chuckled, acknowledging the truth.

Kheridan wisely suggested, "Let's get some rest and recharge our batteries."

It reminded Secora of childhood pre-sleep whispers between sisters that had drawn her father into the bedroom to hush his daughters. Smiling at the thought, she fell asleep almost instantly.

SECORA AWOKE, listening so hard she could hear her blood pulse. Was anyone else awake? There was nothing to hear, no sound—no crickets.

Maybe that was it, or maybe it was the cool air that woke her. There was a chilly sweat inside her shirt. She rose quietly and piled brush on the diminished fire until she could feel the warmth.

She took a trip outside to relieve herself, listening in all directions. When the sense of dread had passed, Secora returned to the tent and went to sleep.

At the glow of dawn, she felt her beloved beside her, yawning and stretching. She snuggled against him as the others returned from an early morning trip to mark the arc. Amid yawns, they built up the fire and boiled eggs in the pot.

Secora offered peanut butter and jelly sandwiches and poured coffee crystals into the boiling water after fishing the eggs out with a spoon. Gideon dipped the brew into paper cups, and as soon as their batteries were recharged, they were all active and laughing.

They took a half-hour to re-examine the three rooms and large cavern that made up the cave, after which they offered their gratitude to God for their amazing adventure in a treasured land.

Gideon offered a prayer to Grandfather, the earth, and the four directions. And Secora recited the Blessed is the Spot prayer, and to their joy, Kheridan offered an Our Father and a from the heart-prayer, as well.

"You can feel the Holy Spirit in this place." Seamus' voice crescendoed into Ave Maria, and the ambiance of sacredness pervaded everyone. They carefully photographed everything for Maja and posterity.

As they finished packing, they heard a distant ruckus that sounded like a pack of hunting coyotes, yet not quite the same. They doused the fire, covering any coals with water and dirt, then quickly picked up their gear and left the homey cave. Kheridan walked ahead, doing reconnaissance to see if there were any soldiers in the area. The path seemed clear—no signs of danger.

AN HOUR LATER, they were sitting on a downed tree snag near the ridge top when the clamor rose again, but now it came from the area of the cave entrance, one and a quarter-mile away. It sounded like the animals hesitated at the arc the humans laid down. Whining was heard, but eventually, they must have jumped the barrier and the creek.

Secora ordered, "If they're tracking us, we can't beat them in a race on these rocks. We're better off here. Get on top of the snag."

Large beasts burst through the brush a quarter-mile away. Seamus shouted as the animals became visible, "What the hell are those?"

Gideon said, "They don't look like wolves, are they... hyenas?"

Their wiry, spotted coats and half-length bushy tails ranged in colors from blackish to brindle brown and gray. Secora noted four adults and a cub on the hunt—necks stretched low, sizing them up as they dashed forward.

Kheridan seemed out of breath. "They act like hyenas, but they are too large. They must be the werewolves!"

Although Secora had seen nothing but a dark blur in Idaho, she did a double-take at the suggestion. These animals were very large, black bear-sized—three hundred pounds at least. Overall, not so different in appearance from the Amphicyon, but about half their size. These were not solitary hunters. The approaching beasts displayed powerful predatory physiques—thicker, muscled shoulders and chests, with hind legs shorter than the front. The powerful back sloped down to the rear. Their triangular heads featured thick rocker-shaped lower jaws and rounded ears that sat high on the head. The clincher was an upright, black mane originating at the neck and running down the ridge of the back. A few hundred yards away, they slowed the charge, crept forward, then stopped.

Secora couldn't look away from the eight-inch glistening ivory fangs. One bite would remove her arm.

Seamus' voice quivered, "They look like sabretooths."

Secora carefully slid two cans from her top shirt pockets, handing one to Gideon. She popped the cap off of the can she held in front of her as the creatures began circling, dodging in to find the weakest point. Closer each time, testing them.

She whispered, "Either way, we're in trouble. Or so they assume." She froze as if listening. Monta's voice was in her head, *Become much taller. Bark, grab bark chunks. Don't worry, Momma, it will be okay.*

Secora relayed the message verbatim. Kheridan and Seamus, who stood on the outside edges of the foursome, grabbed chunks of loose bark which remained on the downed tree and held them aloft.

At that moment, lightning shattered over the ridge. Thunder crackled in immediate response. Gideon screamed, "I'm getting a headache!"

His legs crumbled as piercing shrieks from the sky made them all cover their ears and momentarily stopped the advance of the attackers.

Secora gave her pepper spray to Kheridan and grabbed a bottle from Gideon's shirt pocket. "Gideon, open your mouth. Time for the medicine."

The animals dashed towards Secora, believing she had turned away in weakness. Secora poured the liquid inside, then appropriated Gideon's can of spray. Wheeling around, she screamed as loud as she could.

"Breathe in and hold it. I'm using bear spray." She ran towards the two closest beasts and sprayed their faces from inches away.

"Don't be crazy, Secora. Get back here," Gideon yelled.

She retreated to the log as the maced animals screamed and pawed at their assaulted eyes and muzzles. The other adults, and the cub needing to prove its pack solidarity, side-glanced at their detained companions, then warily took their places, moving in.

Torpedoes shot down from the clouded heavens. First one, then another struck the advancing adult hyenas behind the shoulders and lifted them off the ridge with talons the size of huge grappling hooks. One beast was snapping and biting at the raptor's legs, fighting for its life. The thunderbirds flapped high into the air before dropping them on a rocky outcrop.

"Like giant, freaking lammergeiers," Seamus observed.

Their flight path carried the winged giants down the other side, where they disappeared.

The spray-damaged animals and the cub wheeled, making their escape back to the cave. The only remaining sound was the panting of panicked humans.

Kheridan's voice quivered. "Do you suppose those were the animals that attacked people in the nearby village?"

Gideon added, "Makes sense to me."

Secora said in a loud voice, "Cave hyenas, I think. But I can't rule out bone-crushing dogs. People need to leave this place and these creatures alone!"

34
DEATH OF AN ICON

Wakinyan Tanka rose aloft with the second bird. A patch of white feathers adorned its chest. Both landed on the ridge top about thirty yards above the humans. Gideon and Secora clambered up to be near them, rushing ahead as lightning and thunder crashed around them, immediately followed by a stunned Kheridan.

Seamus called out, "I think I'm good here."

Finally, they arrived at the divot between rocky outcrops where Wakinyan huddled. Her body, not counting the enormous tail, was as large as Gideon's. One wing was partially outstretched, perhaps for balance, the other was folded beneath her. She looked weak and broken and was breathing through her mouth. Kheridan tentatively approached and squatted near Secora. She turned and saw Seamus had also arrived, despite his fear.

The second bird, perched on a higher boulder, looked anxious. She raised her crest and alternated her weight from one foot to the other, twisting her head in various positions while observing their actions with piercing eyes. Secora again noticed the blaze of white feathers on her chest and white speckles on her wings.

Lightning cracked the sky open. Rain dropped in sheets, soaking everything. Wakinyan Tanka's head drooped, beak nearly to the ground. Secora broke into tears, sobbing openly.

A thought came to Gideon. Oddly, Secora felt it, too.

"The old one wants us to bond with her daughter. Her day of quiet is here."

One last time, Wakinyan raised her glorious crest and her eye turned toward Gideon and Secora. As she lifted her head, they noticed blood oozing from her leg and chest feathers. Without speaking, they removed their coats and spread them over the old bird, hoping to give her the feeling of being a protected nestling. The two other men followed suit. They all shivered beside the noble creature in awe of the event—as well as the powerful storm.

It wasn't long before the downpour moved off to the South and the imminent threat of lightning passed. So, too, had Wakinyan.

Gideon, his head pressed on top of his mentor's, was sobbing openly.

This reminds me of Black Elk's final prayer, thought Secora.

Suddenly, they felt human hands on their shoulders and heard Kheridan saying, "Let's think about this another time. We are a long way from safety, and I'm sure those animals aren't the only dangers in the area."

Seamus captured as much as he could of the epic situation on a digital camera.

The young bird, that would from here on be referred to as "White Feather," spread her wings and rose quietly, circling the currents until she was barely visible. Two piercing shrieks signaled her departure. The rain had moved on, and the fragrance of the grateful earth became redolent and calming.

STILL GRIEVING, the four travelers collected their packs and gear, then crept over to the riverside of the mountain, moving as quickly as they dared through the rough thorny brush and slippery volcanic rocks, down toward the canyon, the raft, and their car.

"Maybe we can beat the flash flood."

"I don't think we will, but I pray we can locate the raft, or we might be in real trouble." Clouds again darkened the sky. Intermittent rain kept the terrain slippery and treacherous. At times, they had to creep down with their knees bent, using their hands to feel from rock to rock.

Secora lost patience. "This is crazy."

Seamus panted. "It's almost as difficult as facing those creatures."

Kheridan warned, "Be careful. No way to carry an injured person from here."

BY LATE THAT AFTERNOON, they were slogging through muddy piles of long grass and reeds near the river. They located the raft flattened against a leaning tree half-mile downstream. Kheridan crept out on a limb to retrieve it, and after a brief rest, they grabbed thick branches and poled their way to the far bank.

For Secora, crossing the torrent was pure torture. The rapid water had carried them quite a distance past the vehicle. By the time they arrived where they parked, early moonlight exaggerated the unfamiliar shapes of rapids, rocks, and brush.

After what seemed like hours, they deflated and dragged the sodden craft up the ravaged shoreline and packed it along with their wet gear in the back of the vehicle, which, fortunately, remained on the hill where they'd left it.

Secora slid in and closed her door, saying, "I'm afraid all the dear frogs and toads have been washed away."

Kheridan, trying to be cheerful, said, "Perhaps some of them made it far enough up the hill to survive." Trying to shake them from their somber mood, he said, "Okay, then. Who knows a rollicking song to get us on our way?"

Gideon started, somberly, "Ninety-nine bottles of beer on the wall..."

The others joined in, though it sounded as if none of them ever drank a beer—or sang that song before.

MANY HAPPY RETURNS

After several days of travel and layovers, they reached Missoula. Secora tried to prepare herself for entering a vastly different world than the one they recently left. Late Friday morning, she left the terminal, dragging way too much luggage. Outside on the sidewalk, Jimmy and Clive greeted them with massive balloon bouquets and huge smiles.

Secora's jet-lagged face metamorphosed into a smile as she first snapped a photo and then ran over to hug them both. "What a sight! You guys and balloon bouquets!"

Jimmy pulled back after the hug to say, "We see you brought some friends."

Seamus introduced the newlyweds. "Yes, this is Kheridan Kocherian, and his wife, Maja Turandokht."

"Welcome to Missoula."

"We came here to meet you all on our honeymoon."

"Bless you two," said Clive.

Gideon grinned as he hugged his buddies. "You look *ridiculous*, but it's so good to see you."

"Really? Such kind words... spoken by a heyoka, no less."

Clive said, "We need a *heyoka* to tease us from the gloom of this reality."

Jimmy said, "We, too, mourn the loss of the Thunder Being."

Tears rushed to Secora's eyes. But after a prolonged silence, the men gave away the balloons and helped load the luggage into a van. A small task, but one that caused Clive's breath to rattle.

After the seven of them crammed in, concerned, Secora asked, "What's wrong, Clive?"

"I inhaled smoke, and the doctor said it 'challenged' my lungs."

Gideon leaned forward to look into his face. "What are you talking about?"

"There is much to discuss."

Jimmy interceded. "But before that, let's stop for lunch. We can catch you up on some of the happenings tomorrow."

Seamus commented, "We are more than ready for a good meal."

DESTINY HAWKINS GREETED them at the restaurant door. They walked in to find the place was nearly empty. Tables had been pushed together, with enough chairs for twenty diners, some already seated—her parents, Iris and Kantun, Jane and Aparu, Jeannie, Josh and Mitch, *and* Alai and Monta.

Secora ran over and hugged Monta and Alai. Monta reached out her arms to be held. Secora obliged her for a moment before putting her back down. "Sorry, little one, I'm still a bit bruised and stiff."

Secora hugged Sage and L.W., then the others. She sat in the chair next to Monta. A sign, evidently colored by the child, featured the name, "Guillermo." It hung by a ribbon around the chair on the other side of Alai.

Gideon introduced Kheridan and his bride, Maja. "People, this brave couple was married yesterday before we got on the plane."

Maja said, "I suppose this would be our what...?"

Secora chuckled. "We would call it honeymoon."

Maja then asked, "Is it possible for us to have some introductions?"

The friends and family gave their names and a bit about themselves. Then, for a suspicious instant, people sat still with silly grins on their faces.

What a sight thought Secora. Before they even ordered, waitstaff carried out trays of German chocolate cake slices, each bearing a sparkler. Before serving, they sang *Happy Birthday* to Gideon.

Gideon's face reddened in astonishment at the attention, and Jimmy chuckled.

Kheridan took pity on his new friend and, as a deflection, joked, "All of this for me?" There was laughter, along with a bit of embarrassment.

As a piece of cake was placed before him, Gideon asked, "Clive, is everything okay? You don't look so good."

"I guess I'm mostly good now. Got smoke in my lungs. I'll tell you more after I have some of this cake!"

"Take a bite. Then tell me. I'm serious."

Clive finished chewing and said, "Well, my trailer burned to the ground. We couldn't salvage much, but the family and dog are safe."

"Whoa, sorry, man. What happened?"

"You may have noticed my wife's cousin, Owings, isn't here today. He's getting a psych eval over at Warm Springs, near Deer Lodge, at the Montana State Hospital. He got hold of some bad medicine from an online pharmacy and started hallucinating. Thought my wife was part of ISIS. He knifed her in the arm, and she fled with the dog when he became distracted by some other vision.

"Luckily, the kids were outside already. Anyway, the family was getting into the car and she was calling 911 when they noticed the trailer burst into flames. When I got there just before the fire crew, I ran inside, found him, and began to drag him out. Some sort of chemical in the fumes got to me, and the firemen had to rescue us both.

"Owings suffered some second-degree burns and a complete mental breakdown. Poor guy. He was trying so hard to make a life here. Not sure what happened, but we'll be there for him during his recovery."

Secora's voice came from down the table. "You know that you and your family will always have our full support."

"Oh, we'll be okay. Sage is helping us build a new place."

Mitch chimed in, "The good news is that he and Josh are going gangbusters on the Porcupine Desert low-income housing project with us. Clive will be our first resident. Already has his water station going."

Concern welled in Gideon's eyes. "In the meantime, where are you going to live? You could stay with us, right, Secora?" He looked over for her approval.

She reassured him with a nod.

Clive looked sheepish. "Funny you should say that. The last few days we've been staying in Missoula, at your house with Alai and Monta."

"Good thing we have extra bedrooms," laughed Gideon.

Clive said, "Oh, you'll be sleeping on the floor with me and my kids. Alai and Monta have your bed, and my wife and her dog have the couch."

Secora sighed. "Okay then, time for more furniture." Then she laughed.

Jeannie swallowed a last bite of cake, then said, "So, they've put a moratorium on the Desert Park property because the testing for radioactive material was inconclusive."

Gideon replied, "I'll gladly take them to court. Jeannie, please call my attorney."

"Yes, boss, I already did. You have an appointment scheduled for Monday at 11 a.m."

Josh added, "I'll be there with you, Gideon, if that's all right. They're being ridiculous. I did an independent study and I'll bring the report clearing the land for development."

Gideon smiled and turned toward Secora.

Josh continued, "I feel confident the second report will be enough."

Suddenly, Secora heard Seamus' voice rise above the others.

"Those giant cave hyenas were coming straight for us. Drool dripping off their eight-inch yellowed fangs, eyes drilling us for weakness. I was so scared my knees were knocking. She told us to hold up bark pieces as per little Monta. Then all hell broke loose. There was a tremendous shriek after a thunderclap. Gideon fell, and torpedoes plummeted from the sky against the jagged lightning. It was on. Suddenly, Secora was like, 'Hold my tea.' Off she runs toward the two closest beasts and maces them straight away."

Secora noticed people's eyes growing wide as their jaws dropped. Then Seamus laughed and everyone seemed relieved—sort of. There was a hesitance, as some of them tried to picture the situation, and others tried not to.

Seamus continued, "It astounded us when two of the biggest flying creatures the planet has ever seen hit the two remaining adult beasts and lifted them high enough to drop them on the crags of a cliff."

After a solemn pause, he said, "That was too much for the old bird. Wakinyan Tanka was spent. She landed on the ridge to be with us when she took her last breath. We covered her with our coats to protect her from the downpour and comforted her as if she was a nestling during those last moments. And me, right there with everyone, as if I wasn't scared speechless by even small birds. We all knew we were in the presence of a sacred being—no doubt."

After a moment Maja said, "So, Montana actually has a storyteller."

Seamus countered, "If you want stories, you should all listen to this lady. She knows her trade."

Secora excused herself for a bathroom break, and Monta hopped out of her chair to join her. "I saw that happening, Mommy."

"Thank you, little one, for telling us about the tree bark and that we would be okay. It helped me be strong!"

After finishing the prolonged meal and vivacious conversation, Gideon suggested, "Let's climb to the top of the mountain, past the 'M' over to Artist's Point. We can offer our prayers there."

Secora turned away to take a call from Tarkio. "Hey, buddy, I've been thinking of you. Heard you're out of town."

"Sorry I missed the lunch, but Bill and I just parked in the lot and went to the office looking for you."

"We are about to leave the restaurant to climb past the 'M.'"

"We'll join you on the mountain. Can't wait. We have something 'blow your socks off' interesting to show you."

"Not wearing any, but I'm excited to hear your news. See you in a few."

IT TOOK a while for the string of climbers to make it up the steep trail. The elderly and children led, and the others doted on them. Once they arrived near Artist's Point and stood around visiting and catching their breath, a sharp, piercing whistle hit their ears, coming from down the Hellgate canyon.

"What the *heck* was that?" winced Mitch, covering his ears.

At that moment, a gigantic bird soared up over the cliff. Gideon froze in mid-step, and Secora reached for his medicine. He took her hand and, looking into her eyes, said, "I don't think I will need it with this girl."

"You knew she was coming, didn't you? Was it telepathy?"

Gideon smiled and nodded. "She is not so battered, and I can connect easier."

Secora said, "I'm thinking telepathy is the language of the future. We already use it in communion with God, the Wakinyan, and other animals, even the plants."

Jimmy said, "Sometimes with spirits and each other..."

Gideon cut in, "Don't forget aliens and the departed."

Everyone around them was silent, staring at the enormous raptor circling the sky.

Seamus muttered, "Reminds me of the eagles saving Frodo from Mount Doom."

Secora whispered in awe, "She seems almost as big as her mother."

Bill and Tarkio nudged her. "We made it."

She hugged each of them. "So good to see you."

Bill, still wearing his camera, slipped her a photo of two snarling beasts. She shook her head and nearly fainted, but they caught her.

Tarkio put the photo away and said, "We'll talk later... gotta watch this."

"Oh my God! I didn't believe thunderbirds were real," Jeannie croaked.

Clinging tightly to Jimmy's arm, Destiny reverted to her Catholic childhood and said, "Saints preserve us."

Josh uttered an Armenian prayer which he ended with, "Lord Jesus, save us from destruction!"

Kheridan and Maja added, "Amen."

Alai's face was lit with joy. "Dios, Mio! Ella es un Milagro."

The bird flew higher and higher above Gideon. Then something black began to fall. A whirling tail feather corkscrewed into the land, burying itself in the sod beside him. The feather of acknowledgment, similar to the one which had been given by Wakinyan Tanka many years ago. It waved listlessly in the almost non-existent breeze.

Everyone was breathless as the bird descended. Finally, she brought her huge wings together in a flapping motion across her breast. Whoosh-whoosh. The air reverberated like the sound of a passing freight train as she landed and folded her huge wings, then wiggled her three-and-a-half-foot tail.

Monta ran towards the rock on which the animal perched with arms wide open. Alai came to stand beside her.

Gideon politely gathered the feather, that from the ground came to his rib cage. He held it above his head like a spear in acknowledgment. "This is White Feather, daughter of Wakinyan Tanka. Our new friend and protector."

Jimmy already had his pipe out of its beaded bag and began to dance and raise a singing voice of joy, appreciation, and gratitude. Everyone else shuffled their feet a little, dancing with him to celebrate the addition of a precious new friend to the family. After a few minutes, their noble guest turned and leaped silently off the cliff and soared back down Hellgate Canyon on other business. The overjoyed humans trickled down the mountainside and off to their homes with love and respect filling their hearts with joyous celebration.

EPILOGUE

On Monday morning, while Gideon prepared for the meeting with his lawyer, Secora headed to her office. Upon arriving, she found an article Destiny Hawkins had left on her desk. Cave hyenas, long thought to be extinct, had attacked humans in the rugged Armenian Mountains. She read on. Luckily, the humans had survived. It wasn't until she finished reading that she noticed the byline. Eliot Stearns, for the BBC. Smiling, she laid it on the desk.

She couldn't help but think about what she had learned in Armenia —Central Asia, in general. For two million years, the ancient homeland had embraced its noble, kind, and generous people. For untold ages they suffered, hidden beneath the cloak of domineering and often cruel empires. She determined it was time for the people of the dozens of stans, like Haiasdan, Tajikistan, and Afghanistan, to step into the light of noble leadership once again. Maybe, like Seamus, she would return one day.

A second sticky note caught her eye. Scrawled in Destiny's hand were the words,

Just to let you know there have been recent reports of large

cave creatures in North Central Africa—in case you become bored again.

Her mind spun, considering the possibilities. However, the spell evaporated when Tarkio and Bill burst through the door. Both were grinning from ear to ear.

"Some picture, huh?"

"Hey, men."

Bill handed her a photo.

"This looks to me like a dead... Amphicyon laid across a fence. Did the weight of its body break through the top two rails?"

Bill grinned. "Maybe, with help from the big guy who placed it there."

Tarkio said, "From the state of decomposition, it looks like it might be the one Bill's dad shot over the sheep a few weeks ago."

"Wow, I never got to see the body in person. Only Bigfoot could pick up a... Oh... I get it. Why would he do that?"

Tarkio continued, "He was making a statement—*you don't need to return to his forest for evidence.* He made sure of that."

"I don't suppose you have a photo of..."

Bill cut her off. "No, out of respect. But we saw him, and we will leave presents once in a while to maintain contact. Here are photos that show our first offering and his acknowledgment with a crystal."

Tarkio added, "Two journals have accepted our article for publication."

"Congratulations. You guys are nothing short of amazing."

Bill placed another photo in front of her. She picked it up respectfully... lost in its content. It was an image of herself, Alai, and Monta standing directly in front of the towering raptor, White Feather.

"We wish we could have gotten a picture of her mom for you."

Secora blinked back the tears, remembering Seamus might actually have done that. She took a deep breath. "You two are a new breed. Spiritual paleontologists and I are proud to work beside you gentlemen."

Bill smiled. "It's our turn to take you out for a cup of coffee."

She hesitated, then Tarkio encouraged, "Come on, Teach, let's go."

"Right. To celebrate our survival—yet again."

She said softly, "Hetchetu Aloh. So be it." The three left the office as equals.

In whatever lamp it may shine

ABOUT THE AUTHOR

 Diane Olsen is the prolific writer and award-winning author of her debut book titled: *Ancient Ways: The Roots of Religion,* a Bronze Medal Winner awarded by Christian Illuminations Book Awards.

Diane's debut release of *Ancient Ways* is thought-provoking and an informative look at the development and evolution of religion throughout time and a well-considered concept—the idea of a connective thread of monotheistic faith throughout history from the birth of human creation.

Born in Colorado Springs, Colorado she now lives in the beautiful Pacific Northwest in Washington state. She was an undergrad at Colorado State University Ft. Collins: Pre-vet med, Anthropology, then attended and received her BA and MA at the University of Montana, Missoula: Anthropology, Archaeology, and Paleontology. She was a Graduate Teaching Assistant for two years.

Diane has raised two sons Andrew and Gavin, has four grandsons Dylan, Brayden, AJ, and Asher. She is an animal lover and enjoys living in Washington State with her two girls, (doggies) "Ladybug and Charlie," along with two ancient "retired" Zebra, finches, and one African Black-footed Cat. She has raised sheep and goats and about forty other species of critter over the decades.

Diane enjoys writing, reading good books, spending time with her grandkids, and cooking. A few of her favorite books are *The Book of Certitude (Kitab-i-Iqan), The Upanishads,* and *The Great Initiates.*

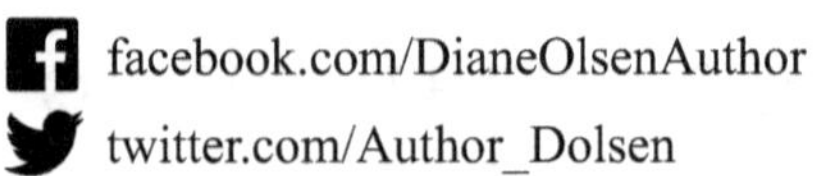

facebook.com/DianeOlsenAuthor

twitter.com/Author_Dolsen